SUICIDE SHOT

DOUG GIACOBBE

Dedication

To Gayle and Katie, with love.
Thanks as always for your patience.

Acknowledgements

I thank everyone who helped me with the writing this book. Thank you, Jay Fisher, for your service, and thank you for telling me how communications work inside of a submarine. Thank you, Keith Dunn for taking time out from your Alaska vacation to find me a connection with the Ninilchik Tribe. And most of all, thank you fellow Professor John Connor for telling me what it's like to be dead and come back to life.

Thank you, David H. Roth, from DHR Headshots Photography for taking some years off me. Dhrheadshots.com.

Chapter 1

Well, Michael Callaway thought, *I don't think we're in Miami anymore.* He strained his eyes while negotiating a very dark part of the coastal waters of the Kenai Peninsula in the Gulf of Alaska. He was trying his best to make port in the town of Homer, about 220 miles from Anchorage but he still had a long way to go. It was a moonless mid-October night, and he was shivering even though he was wearing the warmest clothes he owned. He thought he could make it to Homer, at the mouth of Kechemak Bay, and get a hotel room and some warmer clothes before an impending cold front arrived.

Once again as she had numerous times in the past, Mother Nature dealt him a bad hand. There was no breeze, but the air temperature had just dropped below freezing. His boat, the *Orinoco Flow*, was an old shrimping boat converted from a World War II Patrol-Torpedo boat. That conversion added twenty feet to the boat's hull, stretching it out to ninety feet. The three Packard aircraft engines that had pushed the PT boat to fifty miles per hour while attacking German ships in the English Channel were replaced by one old diesel engine giving the boat a plodding top speed of ten miles per hour on a calm day.

The boat had been converted again by its previous owner from a shrimp boat to a luxury yacht, or at least the

1

interior was converted and equipped with all kinds of comfort items for cruising the waters around Florida. There was one exception, though: there was no heater aboard. "What was I thinking?" Callaway asked out loud, about the journey he had started way back in June. The game plan had been to take a slow, leisurely cruise from Miami, Florida to Alaska to see the one friend he had left in this world, Navy Commander David Eldridge. Eldridge had been summarily shipped out from warm, sunny, Florida, to the extreme darkness and freezing cold of Alaska. This was Eldridge's punishment for the supreme sin of pissing off his boss, a One-Star admiral. Eldridge had put himself between Michael Callaway and a jail cell on two different occasions.

The first time cost him his sea command, but the most recent, where he concealed evidence that would link Callaway to the death of a drug kingpin in the Bahamas, along with the absolute destruction of everything said drug kingpin owned, came back and bit the Commander right in the shorts. Because of this, Eldridge's commanding officer had done what she promised she would do by exiling him to a training station located on the Kenai Peninsula on a remote inlet about one hundred miles south of Anchorage. The aging base, officially designated as *Training Base 359*, originally opened right after World War II ended. The original function of the base, as Eldridge had told Callaway, was to proof-test weapons and equipment in an extreme-cold-weather environment. However, it would later serve another function as a cold-climate training base for Navy SEALS.

Now, since a new and more modern base had been built near the North Pole, the base was scheduled to close within the next year. SEAL training had been slowly transitioning to the new base, nicknamed *Santa's Toy Box*, because of its totally modern equipment, leaving *TB 359* to rot, and those still assigned there to wither on the vine. Callaway told Eldridge that he needed to get out of South Florida for a while to clear his head after the murder of his fiancée, Carrie Marvin. That murder had been ordered by that same drug kingpin that Callaway later killed. Callaway decided to leave when he did in June, expecting to arrive in Alaska by August, but just like the Donner Party, things didn't go very well. Between problems with the route he chose, bad weather, and some major mechanical issues, including having the old diesel self-destruct off the coast of Canada. Now his navigation lights went dead four hours prior on this very dark night, with no lights along the shore to guide him.

My knees are knocking louder than the engine, he thought. He stared hard into the darkness, trying to stay as close to shore as he could without leaving the channel. He looked out toward the open sea, but suddenly he couldn't see the water. Looking up, he saw stars, but all he could see down low was white. "Great," he said. "Now I got friggin' fog on the water." He crept slowly forward as the low fog encircled the hull of the *Orinoco Flow* and crawled toward the shore. *Gotta keep moving. If I try to stop and anchor for the night, I'll freeze to death, for sure*, he thought.

He pushed the throttle forward, giving the boat a little more speed, when he felt the hull bumping into something. Suddenly there was a noise from the stern, and the *Orinoco Flow* stopped completely and then was pulled backward. He tried to give the old diesel more fuel, but nothing happened. The boat was hung up on something. "Son-of a bitch!" he yelled, as he shut the engine off, and walked out the rear cabin door. "What the hell else is gonna happen on this trip? It's been one problem after another since I crossed the Panama Canal!"

He reached the stern and leaned over the transom, trying to see what was holding his boat. Callaway opened a locker near the transom and grabbed a flashlight. He shone it through the fog and into the dark water below. He saw several long, slender objects flowing from under the center of the hull, where the single propeller was located. *Do they have giant squid around here*? he wondered, as he pulled a boat hook on a ten-foot pole from a rack under the gunwale. He grabbed the pole with his gloved, shaking hands and stuck it down into the water, trying to grab one of the objects flowing below. Hooking one of them, he pulled it up to the surface and up over the transom. Shining the flashlight on it, he could now see that it was a thick piece of rope, with smaller ropes attached. "Crap!" he bellowed. "I drove into someone's goddamned fishing nets. Who left this out here in the channel?"

Now he was angry as well as cold. Grabbing the boat hook, he bent over the transom and tried to free the net from the propellor blades. He managed to remove some of it, but he could feel the hook bumping against more of the netting on the prop shaft. He leaned over some more, trying to get a hold of the net. Suddenly, his feet slipped on a patch of ice on the deck. He flipped headfirst over the transom and went straight down into the freezing water. As he struggled to find which way was up in the darkness, his terrified mind recalled the temp reading on his GPS; it was 34 degrees. His previous boat operations training as a Customs Service chase-boat driver kicked in. He remembered to calm down and let himself float instead of swimming farther down into the deep, dark water.

Then he spotted the surface and kicked frantically to get there. He broke the surface, bumping into the hull and gasping for air, as he pulled himself to the ladder on the transom. Callaway attempted to pull himself up the ladder, but the icy cold water had sapped his strength and soaked his clothes, making them heavy. He started to panic. *Get your ass up that ladder, Callaway, or you're gonna die!* he thought. He slowly managed to climb the ladder steps. He rolled over the transom, landing belly down on the deck. He was breathing heavy and wheezing. Putting his hands flat on the deck, he pushed his way up to his knees and grabbed the gunwale. He faced out to sea trying to see through the layers of fog. Callaway remembered what his Coast Guard friends had told him: "Fifty minutes in water under fifty degrees, and you die of hypothermia." They had been stationed in areas north where the water froze, so they knew. "Thirty-four degrees," he mumbled, then he went into a coughing fit. His mind was getting foggy, but he was able to calculate that given the air temperature of around 26 degrees, that ratio would be accelerated quite a bit. *Got to get into the cabin, now!* he thought. *It'll be a little warmer there, and I can peel off these wet clothes.* He was entering full panic mode when he heard a noise out on the water.

He stared out to sea, his vision starting to get blurry when he saw what appeared to be a person that he could only see from the waist up because of the fog. The person appeared to be walking on the water towards him. Transfixed, he stared in disbelief through the low fog. As the person got closer, he could see that it was a woman, with long dark hair, wearing all white. *What the hell? It's an angel!* he thought. Then he passed out and fell to the deck, rolling over on his back.

The "angel" continued towards the *Orinoco Flow* until the bow of the wooden canoe that she was standing in bumped gently into the hull of the larger boat. She grabbed the gunwale and pulled herself up, swinging a leg over the top. Straddling the gunwale, she yelled, "Anyone aboard?" Receiving no answer, she looked around the deck in the darkness until she saw Callaway laid out near the stern.

"We've got a man down here!" she told the two other men seated in the large canoe. She spun around and dropped to her knees on the deck feeling Callaway's throat to check his carotid artery for a pulse. There was hardly anything. "My God, he's soaking wet," she said. "He's in hypothermic shock." Stripping off his wet clothes, she called out, "Give me the blankets and call the other boats over here!" One of the men climbed aboard with two blankets, and helped her spread them over Callaway, while the other used a portable radio to contact the three other canoes in the area. "Call Halibut Cove and tell them to get the rescue boat out here, now!" she yelled, as she felt the pulse go from weak to nothing. "Crap! Starting CPR," she said. She tilted his head back and gave Callaway four strong breaths and then located the place for her hands below his breastbone and began chest compressions, counting off as she did.

Men from the other canoes arrived and covered Callaway with layers of wool blankets to keep what was left of his body heat from escaping. The rescue boat from Halibut Cove arrived moments later. The woman stopped compressions when she heard Callaway cough. Checking his pulse again, she found it weak but steady. "Get him into the incubator. STAT," she told one of the paramedics on board. "Placing Callaway on a backboard, the medics carried him into the rescue boat's large cabin. There, they slid him into what looked like a big glass coffin. Placing an oxygen mask over his nose and mouth, they shut the door and turned-on hot lights to warm the chamber's interior. It looked like a giant version of a newborn-baby incubator. The woman jumped onto the rescue boat, directing the medics to the nearby clinic at her village, instead of the more distant hospital at Halibut Cove. The vessel roared off through the darkness to save Michael Callaway's life.

Chapter 2

The rescue boat arrived at the small Ninilchik Tribal Village south of Halibut Cove in less than ten minutes. The medics carried Callaway gently into the Quonset hut serving as the village's local clinic. They took him to the two-bed emergency room and placed him on a gurney. The dark-haired woman who had breathed life back into Callaway walked in.

The doctor on duty looked startled. "Abby?" he said. "I know you said you were going fishing with your brothers tonight, but this is the funniest looking halibut I've ever seen you bring home."

Donning a gown and gloves, Dr. Abby Tika'a smiled at her friend Dr. Tony Gordon. "Well, I've brought in fish that weighed more than him, but he is a funny looking one," she said. "How's his temperature, Tony?"

"Not good," Gordon replied. "Mr. Whoever is still pretty cold."

Pulling his wallet from one of his pockets, the nurse told them, "His name is Michael Callaway, and he's from… Miami, Florida?"

Doctors Tika'a and Gordon stared at each other briefly.

"Damn, Florida people just can't stay out of the water, can they?" Abby asked, as she began checking Callaway's vitals.

"Abby, you're not working tonight; go out and catch some more fish. I'll take good care of your new friend," Gordon said.

"You've got other patients, Tony," she replied. "Besides, we weren't having any luck with the fish."

Gordon smiled at her and walked down the hall to help another patient.

Dr. Tika'a turned to look at Callaway when the instruments behind his bed started screaming alarms. She looked at the heart monitor and watched the line go flat. "He's coding, get me a crash cart!" she yelled, starting compressions again. A nurse wheeled in the cart containing drugs and a defibrillator.

"Damn, Callaway," the doctor mumbled under her breath, "how many times do I have to save your life tonight?"

At that very moment, Michael Callaway was in a totally different place. He was in darkness but was then blinded by a bright white light at the same time. "Where am I?" he asked out loud, hoping that someone would respond. He heard a voice that made him freeze. It was the voice of his late fiancée, Carrie Marvin. "Do you want this?" the voice said. Callaway was startled by the words. "Carrie? Where are you?" he heard himself say. He was terrified, but anxious to see her. Looking into the bright light, he could see her, but he could also see right through her.

"Where are we?" he asked. There was silence. "Where do you think we are?" she answered. He stared at her with his mouth hanging open. "Am I dead?" he asked. She shook her head. "Well... you're almost there, she replied. "You're kind of in the middle. So, let me ask you again. Do you want this? Are you ready to be here forever?" He stared at her again. "I want to be with you, Carrie, but I've got this feeling I'm gonna be needed for something, alive," he responded.

"Like there's something important I've gotta do." She looked at him and smiled… the smile he missed so much. "No, you're not ready yet," she said. "You obviously have a reason to be alive." He nodded. "But I want to be with you," he whispered. I'll always love you, Carrie." Callaway heard a strange voice in the background yelling, "Charge to 300!" He kept his eyes on Carrie. She seemed to be fading away as she spoke. "You need to finish the job, Callaway," she said.

He tried to step toward her, but his feet wouldn't move. "You're the only woman I want to be with, Carrie," he said, starting to cry. She smiled again. "Oh, don't worry Callaway, you're going to meet a lot of beautiful women along the way," she said. "As a matter of fact, you're about to meet a very important one right, about, now," was the last thing she said before she disappeared from his sight, and from the background he heard a single word: "Clear!"

Something happened. Callaway felt like he'd been shot in the chest with a combination of a cannon and a flame-thrower. Feeling like he was being jolted backward at light speed, he awoke with his eyes wide open, but his vision blurred, trying to take a breath. He looked to his right and saw someone who reminded him of the person that he saw *walking* on the water as he was freezing to death on his boat. *The angel!* he thought for a second before everything went black. Then he passed out and went into a deep coma.

*****

What is that sound?

It had been three months, and Michael Callaway was showing signs of coming out of the long coma. The doctors had seen his first reaction to pain when they gave him a pinch test five days prior. He was coming around to the point where he could hear and understand.

Sounds like someone tearing cardboard, he thought. He slowly opened his eyes and squinted from the light. He realized it was coming through the window of a hospital room. Hearing the tearing sound again, he turned his head to the left and recognized Commander David Eldridge, his big red eyebrows and all, sitting in a chair with his head tilted back against the wall, and his mouth wide open. The *sound* that he couldn't make out before turned out to be the snoring emanating from his good friend.

"David," he said in a raspy voice.

Eldridge opened his eyes, tried to blink the sleep away and stared at his friend.

"Mike! Holy shit, you're awake," he answered. He jumped up from the chair and ran out the door to the hallway. Callaway could hear him yelling. "Nurse, Callaway's awake! Go find a doctor." He ran back into the room smiling and grabbed Callaway's hand. "How ya doing, pal?" he asked.

Callaway tried to clear the dryness from his throat. "I need some water, David. Really bad," he forced himself to say. Callaway still couldn't handle all the light, so he closed his eyes again.

"Mr. Callaway?" He had heard the voice before, but he couldn't place where. "We're getting you some water to get your throat clear."

Then it hit him when she'd said "Clear." He recognized the voice from his near-death experience with Carrie. He opened his eyes and stared at the woman in white with long dark hair. "You're an angel," he said.

She smiled at him and said, "No, I'm a doctor, but thank you for the compliment."

He stared at her, trying to smile. "No, you're the angel. Dammit," he said, "I saw you walking on the water by my boat."

Eldridge frowned at the doctor. "Brain damage?" he mouthed.

The doctor stared at Callaway with a worried look but then smiled. "Oh, okay, you're talking about what happened when we found you," she said. "You must have been delirious before we got to you. You were unconscious when I came aboard your boat. Then you stopped breathing."

"She saved your life, Mike," Eldridge said. "Twice."

Callaway looked at him, and then back at the doctor. "But how did you cross the water?" he asked. "I saw you coming through the fog."

She looked confused and then smiled at him and answered, "Okay, I was standing up on the front of my brother's canoe. He was paddling me towards your boat in the fog, so that's what you must have seen. By the way, I'm Dr. Abby Tika'a. You're in South Peninsula Hospital in Homer, Alaska. Can you repeat that back to me?"

Callaway repeated what she'd said, which indicated that his brain was in good shape. "How long was I out?" Callaway asked.

Giving him a somber look, she answered, "You were in a coma for a couple of days short of three months. It's January 13, 1993."

His eyes widened and he shook his head. "Wow, I guess Carrie was right," he whispered. Gazing at the doctor, he realized how beautiful she was. "About a couple of things," he continued. He smiled at her and grabbed her hand.

"Who is Carrie?" she asked. Eldridge immediately shook his head at her. Changing the subject, she looked at the instruments over his bed and told him, "Your blood pressure is a little elevated."

Avoiding the doctor's question, Callaway asked, "So, when was the second time you saved my life?"

She grinned at him and answered, "Well, you flatlined when we first got you to the clinic in my village, and I had to use the defibrillator to shock you back to life."

Meeting her gaze, Callaway squeezed her hand. She was about five feet tall, he noted, with a thin build and black hair. He couldn't help but notice that she was strikingly beautiful, with her dark eyes and vaguely Asian features. "Thank you," he said softly. "Where is your village, and what tribe are you from?" Callaway asked, watching her adjust the IV drip going into his arm.

"I am of the Ninilchik Tribe. We have villages all over the Kenai Peninsula and across Kechemak Bay. Interesting that you asked about my tribe. Do you have much interaction with Native Americans down in Florida?"

Callaway thought of his *interaction* with Joseph Eagle from the Seminole Tribe of Florida a year ago, when he was trying to track down the person who killed his fiancée. "Yeah," he said. "Mostly in casinos."

Shaking his head and smiling at Callaway, Eldridge repeated something he'd said many times in the three years he'd known him: "You know, Mike, as usual you are a real pain in the ass. But I'm glad you finally made it up here, alive," he said, looking at Dr. Tika'a. "Oh, sorry about my foul mouth, Doc, but Mike brings out the best in me sometimes."

The doctor pursed her lips. "Oh, I agree with you, Commander. He *is* a pain in the ass. You should see what his boat did to our fishing nets. It tore the hell out of them," she said.

"My boat!" Callaway yelled suddenly, "Where is she?"

Dr. Tika'a answered, "Relax, Mr. Callaway, your boat is out of the water and safe at our village, thanks to my brothers. It took them awhile to get what was left of our nets off the propeller, but 'she' should be fine for the spring. And just what were you doing out there at such a cold time of the year?" she asked. Commander Eldridge told me that you left Miami in June. I'm guessing your boat wasn't built for speed, but it shouldn't have taken you that long to get up here."

Jumping into this game of twenty questions, Eldridge asked, "Yeah, Mike. The last time I heard from you, you were laid up in a little town north of Vancouver. What happened?" he asked.

Callaway closed his eyes before he answered, "The diesel in the old girl… my boat," he corrected seeing the not too happy look on the doctor's face, "overheated and cracked the cylinder head and engine block. I got a tow to a dinky little town somewhere in Canada with only one boat mechanic. He couldn't find a replacement head or do anything with the block because the engine was so damn old, so I had to buy a whole new engine.

That took a while to get to where I was docked, and the mechanic was up to his ears in work for the local fishermen, so I ended up at the end of the line. I tried calling you once I got back underway, David, but my radio just didn't have the range to reach you," he answered. "I burned an entire month cruising up the coast. I will say that there's some beautiful coastline along the Yukon and the inside passage. I did stop in a couple of towns to get fuel and food. Found some really friendly bars there, too."

That last sentence seemed to bother Commander Eldridge. It told him that Callaway was still drinking, and that made him dangerous to himself and others.

"So, Doc," Callaway asked, "when can I get out of here so David and I can go fishing?"

Still looking over his vitals, Dr. Tika'a answered, "Don't be in such a rush, Mr. Callaway. You just came out of a three-month coma. I'm sure you're still weak, so, don't expect to go dancing out of here any time soon. Small steps, okay?" The last words sounded a bit stern. "Besides, a lot of the water around here is frozen."

Giving him an equally stern look, Eldridge told him, "I'm not going anywhere soon, Mike, so listen to the good doctor."

Callaway looked at Dr. Tika'a and smiled. "Yes ma'am," he said softly.

*****

It took about two weeks for Callaway's release, finally, after lots of physical therapy, brain scans, and food, lots of food. He was ravenous after months of being fed liquids through a tube. He took to the physical therapy as much as he did the food, like a man starving to get moving again. He noticed that on more than a few occasions Dr. Tika'a was watching him through the window outside the gym. When the day came to leave, Dr. Tika'a surprised him by showing up herself, instead of an orderly, to push his wheelchair out the door.

He was dressed in some of his clothes that David

15

Eldridge brought from the *Orinoco Flow*, along with a snow parka that the Commander brought from his own closet. Callaway put the parka on as the doctor entered the room and he heard her giggle. Eldridge was a much larger man and Callaway so emaciated that he looked like a little kid wearing one of his father's coats. Shaking his head and smirking at the doctor, Callaway asked, "So, I'm getting the royal treatment, huh? Is that going to cost me more?"

She looked at him without showing any emotion. "Nope," she answered. I'm on my way out for the day, and I just figured I'd give you lift to the front door."

He sensed there was more to it. She wheeled him through the hall to the elevator and then down to the first floor. When they reached the front door, he saw David Eldridge, dressed in Navy fatigues, sitting in a government car. It looked remarkably like the one he had traveled in to go to a meeting with the Commander in Miami months before. It was in the same crummy shape.

Dr. Tika'a stopped the chair and flipped the footrests out of the way so Callaway could stand. Before he did, he tilted his head up and smiled. "Thank you, Doctor. I owe you a hell of a lot for saving my life, twice. And I owe you and your brothers a new net, too," he said. "Can I... take you to dinner?" He was shocked that he was asking another woman out. Thinking of Carrie, he almost choked on the words.

Smiling down at him, Dr. Tika'a answered, "This hospital has a strong policy about doctors dating patients, Mr. Callaway."

Callaway stood and started walking towards the car when he suddenly stopped and did an about face. "Okay, I'm no longer in the hospital, and I'm no longer your patient... sooo?" he asked smiling.

She looked at him, biting her lower lip. "Well, okay then," she answered. "But I'm warning you, I may be little, but I can eat a lot." Callaway smiled at her, but then turned his head toward the parking lot at the sound of some kind of commotion. He saw two men carrying an apparently unconscious man from a large truck. His face was badly burned. They were followed by another, larger man, who was yelling at them in Russian. Callaway noticed that all of these men were dressed alike in orange cold-water survival suits, and they all had thick beards. He moved to one side of the covered entrance, while Dr. Tika'a pushed the wheelchair forward for the injured man. The two men carrying him spun the injured man around and dropped him into the wheelchair. One of them began yelling in broken English at Dr. Tika'a. "You get doctor for him, now!" he demanded.

Turning the wheelchair, she shouted back "I am a doctor!"

Grabbing her arm, he shouted back, "I want a man doctor for him. You understand!"

Callaway grabbed the man's wrist and, with the little strength he had, pried his hand off her arm.

Glaring at Callaway, the Russian, who was about a head taller, pulled away easily, given Callaway weakened state.

The doctor pushed the injured man into the hospital and headed towards the emergency room, leaving Callaway alone with three large and very pissed off Russians who seemed intent on sending him back to the emergency room. None of the Russians seemed to notice that Commander Eldridge had climbed out of his car until, standing behind them, he bellowed, "That's enough!" The larger Russian turned, looking at the rank insignia on Eldridge's uniform.

17

"This has nothing to do with you, Commander," the larger man growled, while pointing at Callaway. "And you have no powers here, so why don't you just leave so we can discuss matters with this *Sukin sin*."

Shaking his head and gritting his teeth, Eldridge answered, "That's not going to happen, Pal. You're from the *Put' Stalina*, aren't you? Yeah, I've seen that rusty old tub cruising by our base a few times. And yes, I don't have any power to arrest you or anything, but it would be a real shame if somebody made an anonymous call to the Coast Guard and told them that your ship is leaking oil into Alaska's pristine waters. People around here are *really* touchy about stuff like that since that mess with the *Exxon Valdez*. The Coast Guard just might just have to go onboard and do an inspection of your ship." He noted an instant change in the Russian's attitude.

"Ah... I tell you what, I will not bother this man today, since he looks so sick," he said, smiling and indicating Callaway. "But some day, perhaps we will meet again." He smiled at Eldridge and motioned his men to follow him into the hospital.

Breathing a sigh of relief, Callaway got into the passenger seat of the government car. Still fuming over the encounter, Eldridge joined him and drove them away.

Chapter 3

"So, what was the Russian guy's problem?" Callaway asked as he and Eldridge left the hospital. "And thank you for bailing me out of that mess, by the way."

Eldridge, sighing, answered, "He and his buddies are crew members from a Russian registered freighter that's anchored along the strait and a little south of Anchorage. They're a really interesting bunch. Their captain is a guy named Acardi Frankovich. Well, at least that's the name on his passport. He's the one who was calling you names. Personally, I think the guy is ex-KGB."

Confused, Callaway asked "So, is anyone investigating him or the crew?" I mean those guys at the hospital seemed like a really salty bunch."

Shrugging, Eldridge answered, "The crew has a habit of getting into fights with the locals, but that's about it. Nothing to warrant an inspection by the Coast Guard, or Military Intelligence. And remember, the Russians used to own Alaska, until they made the big mistake of selling it to the U.S. There are a lot of them that never left. Still, I just threw that line about an inspection at the guy to get us out of a fight, 'cause, well, you're not in shape for any battles yet."

Smiling, Callaway answered, "Yep, you're always there to pull my ass out of the fire, David. Thanks. But that was some look on that guy's face when you threatened an inspection."

Eldridge smiled, in turn, and answered, "Yeah, I think the guy you tussled with is the second-in-command of their ship. I don't know his name," Eldridge said. "But Frankovich sure backed down in a hurry when I mentioned an inspection… for some reason. Well anyway, we're supposed to be nice to our new Russian 'friends' since the Cold War ended, so the Coast Guard would need a pretty good reason to do an inspection against the captain's will. And from what I've heard about Frankovich, he's not the type to give the Coasties permission if they asked to come aboard."

Opening his eyes wide and looking sideways at his friend, Callaway joked, "Well, maybe I can get him to invite me aboard."

Glowering, Eldridge answered tersely, "Mike, you came up here to visit me, not get into any crap like you have in the past. Don't get involved, Pal. Please don't get involved. Remember how I ended up here, in the wasteland of the Navy. If I want, I can retire in two years with full medical benefits, and a nice pension. Do **not** fuck this up for me."

Callaway couldn't help but remember that last time he rode in a government-owned vehicle with David Eldridge. It was in Miami, and it was a balmy eighty-five degrees, and they were heading to a meeting with Eldridge's boss, Admiral D. May Slingo. The meeting also included a bunch of other federal big dogs trying to scare Callaway out of going after the drug lord responsible for killing his fiancée.

Up to this point, the atmosphere during this trip was much more comfortable than the past ride. He knew that Slingo had a hand in Eldridge's transfer, or more literally, his sentence to finishing out his career in the navy at the base that was due to be shut down. "Okay, David," he said. I promise to behave myself, and I won't kill anyone, barring any future entanglement with the Ruskies, of course. I wish I knew what he called me back there. I wonder what *Sukin* means."

Grinning, Eldridge answered, "He called you a son-of-a-bitch."

Staring, Callaway asked his friend, "When the hell did you learn to speak Russian, David?"

Keeping his eyes on the road, Eldridge answered, "I spent a lot of years fighting the Cold War, remember. I came out of Annapolis in September of 1962, Mike. One month before the Cuban Missile Crisis began. That was my baptism of fire. I was an Ensign aboard a destroyer assigned to the blockade of Cuba. We were stopping Eastern Block ships, lots of 'em Russian, and boarding them to check for more Sandal nuclear missiles bound for Cuba to be aimed at our country. We boarded those ships armed to the teeth, dressed in our Class-A white uniforms, because we were ambassadors of the United States. My commanding officer was a tough bastard, but he taught me a lot. He handed all of his young officers a Russian dictionary and told us to learn what we could quickly, so we didn't accidently start World War Three. Hell, they didn't need us to do that. The leaders of our respective countries almost did it themselves. We couldn't have any misunderstandings going on when we boarded those ships."

Callaway was amazed at what Eldridge told him. It reminded him of the stories his father, a sonar operator aboard one of those destroyers in the blockade, told him about how close we and the Russians came to destroying the planet.

Continuing, Eldridge, said "There was one really close call. We picked up a Ruskie attack submarine on sonar. One of the five that they sent over to Cuba to mess with the blockade of the island. Unknown to us, each one had a single torpedo armed with a nuclear warhead.

"Oh, my God!" Callaway exclaimed.

Nodding nonchalantly, Eldridge continued, "Yup. The game plan was if they got cornered by our fleet, they would fire the nuke to take out as many of our ships as possible. Of course, this would be a suicide shot since the sub would be destroyed by the blast, too. We had a drill where we dropped hand grenades in the water to let the Reds know that we knew that they were down there.

"And that didn't scare them away?" Callaway asked.

"Apparently not," Eldridge answered, nodding. "Despite the fact that their submarines were old diesel-electric boats, so they could only stay underwater for a maximum of about 24 hours before their air gave out. When they surfaced, we would radio them and tell them to steer a safety course out of the area, with one of our destroyers escorting them. If they didn't want to be sunk. The Russian captain of the attack sub we found surfaced and agreed to run parallel to our ship.

"So that was the end of it?" Callaway asked.

"Not really, Eldridge answered. There must have been some kind of miscommunication aboard our ship though because the gunner in our forward turret spun his five-inch cannons around and pointed them right at the sub's conning tower. The Russian skipper reacted by opening his torpedo tube doors, like he was going to shoot, and for one moment, the fate of the world hung on what happened next at that little spot in the ocean. My captain made it across the control room to the communications phone in about one step. I never heard the old man yell so loud for those guys to turn those guns around. 'Now!' he shouted," which they did. Fortunately, the Russian closed his torpedo doors, and they followed us out of the area with no further problems. I remember standing on the starboard wing of the bridge and seeing one of the Russian junior officers up on the conning tower yelling '*sukin sin!*' over and over at me, so I gave him the bird with both hands. Later on, I got out my dictionary and looked up what the guy at the hospital called you."

Callaway shook his head. "One nuclear torpedo," he said. "A suicide shot. Do you think their skipper would have had the balls to cause the end of the world?"

Eldridge shook his head and answered, "I don't know if the skipper would have, but that fanatic on the bridge, yeah, he'd pull the trigger in a heartbeat."

Okay, David, I'll say it again, I won't antagonize the Russians as long as they don't bother me." Callaway continued, "And again, I won't kill anyone. I promise."

"That's one promise you had better keep," Eldridge answered. I know your penchant for getting involved in really bad situations.... So where do you want to stay, Mike?" Eldridge asked, giving Callaway a doubting look.

Smilng, Callaway answered, "Well I had reservations at the Marriott in Homer, but I never got to check in due to my unexpected swim in that very cold water," he replied, staring out the window at the snow on the ground. "I may as well give them another try. Hopefully they won't be too pissed off because I stiffed them by not showing up."

Eldridge laughed and answered, "You'll find that the people up here are a lot nicer than the ones in South Florida. I think they'll take care of you."

They entered the town, and Callaway checked in with no problem. Then they headed for Eldridge's place of employment, the lonely little training base along the rocky coast, forty miles north of Homer. Callaway was surprised to find just how old the base actually looked. As Eldridge had told him, it was built shortly after the Japanese attack on Pearl Harbor in 1941; its original purpose was to serve as a base and supply depot for submarines and PBY Catalina flying boats trying to stop the Japanese from conquering any more of the Aleutian Islands then they already had. The base was also the stepping- off point for U.S. Army Pathfinders, soldiers trained to operate in the stark, cold conditions on those islands as the war progressed.

Eldridge stopped at the front gate and an older sailor stepped out of the booth where he was, apparently, attempting to keep warm.

"Good morning, Commander. Who's your friend?" he asked. He looked around with a glare implying that there might be ten thousand other places he would rather be.

Eldridge answered, "This is Mr. Michael Callaway. He is a close friend of mine. He will be coming to the base on and off until spring, so get him a long-term clearance. You should have no problem since he's a former federal agent."

The sailor took down the information and let them pass.

Callaway looked at the buildings as they drove through the base, shaking his head at their dilapidated condition. "Damn, David. Did we just time warp or something?" he asked. "This place looks pretty ragged out and deserted."

Eldridge let out a sigh and answered, "Yeah, and this is the newest part of the base."

Callaway's stomach started gurgling loud enough for the Commander to hear. "Is there any place to grab a bite around here, David?" he asked. "I'd like to eat something other than hospital food."

Eldridge turned left and drove about a block. "How about a nice, greasy cheeseburger?" he asked. "If there's one thing we do have here, it's pretty good food." Eldridge parked the car by a large Quonset hut and the two men got out. Callaway was still trying to get used to walking on snow, as he slowly headed toward the building. Once inside, Eldridge directed Callaway to the rear of the building where the tables and chairs were a little newer.

"This is the officer's club," he said waving a hand over the three tables in the rear area. "Everything else in here is the NCO club," he continued, motioning toward the rest of the room.

Looking around, Callaway noted the three-inch-wide masking tape marking the floor between the two sections. Confused, he stared around the nearly empty room and asked, "The officers and the Non-Commissioned Officers share a building?"

Eldridge sat down and stretched his back. "From what I understand," he explained, "there used to be two separate buildings, but the NCO club literally fell down. I mean it was built at the beginning of World War II, for God's sake. So when it crumbled, which from what I was told happened during a very weak earthquake, they just moved the NCO's in with us. D.O.D. was already moving people out of here since they knew they would eventually shut the base down, so they told us to share."

Still confused, Callaway asked, "Officers and Non-Coms together? When my dad was in the navy, the last place he wanted to be was around officers. Are you telling me that everyone just gets along?"

To this, Eldridge just smiled. "Yeah, most of the time," he answered. We have one particular group that can be a little troublesome. They're three guys, one Navy, one Marine Corps, and one Air Force. All were trainers for the SEAL team members."

Getting comfortable in his chair, Callaway asked, "So, what's their problem? And when, by the way, do we get to eat?"

Reaching around to another table, Eldridge grabbed a menu and handed it to his obviously starving friend. "They're in the same boat as me," he explained. "They know the end is coming because when this base close, they'll have no place to go but out of the military. And they're just not ready to go yet. And just like me, there's no place to send them because all of the training bases are being staffed with much younger people, including the young ones that were based here.

Eldridge went up to the counter, since there was no service staff anymore, and ordered Callaway's cheeseburger and some fries. He came back to the table and sat down looking happy. "So, we gonna talk about the other interesting thing that happened today?" he asked, raising his big, red eyebrows a couple of times.

Smiling down at his menu, Callaway pretended to be confused again. He asked, "What other thing was that, David?"

Eldridge sat back and crossed his arms. "I couldn't help but hear you ask the good doctor for a dinner date," he remarked. "Or were my old-man ears deceiving me?"

He looked guiltily at Eldridge and in a voice trembling with fake fear, he asked, "Oh, no Pops, I shouldn't have asked her, right? I mean for our first date?" In this case, though, it would be Callaway's first date since Carrie was murdered a little over a year ago. And the only person alive that he could talk to about this was sitting across the table from him. "Too soon, right?" Callaway asked.

Eldridge looked at him and smiled. "Hell no it's not too soon," he answered. "It's been a year, actually more than that, since Carrie was taken from you," he said, reading the look on Callaway's face. "And by the way you're drooping around, I'm guessing that you haven't been with anyone else since?" Callaway was silent. "Damn, Mike, don't turn into a monk on me, man. I feel old enough just being stationed up here already. You're still young, and your whole life is ahead of you. So, go out with the doctor! Have some fun. You don't have to marry her. You're gonna meet a lot of beautiful women along the way."

Callaway's head snapped up when Eldridge said that, remembering what Carrie had told him in what he thought was a dream when he was frozen half to death. *Maybe it wasn't a dream after all*, he thought. *Maybe I almost went… there.* He finally smiled at Eldridge and answered, "You know what, David, you're right," he said and took a big bite out of the burger to seal the deal.

27

Chapter 4

Callaway had just finished his meal when the door opened and three men wearing uniforms entered. Callaway thought it interesting that one was Navy, one Marine, and one was Air Force. Callaway's father was a Navy Chief Bosun's Mate, and, as a child, he had moved from base to base with his parents but saw very few joint service bases.

So these are the guys David was talking about, he thought. He looked at their uniforms closely, checking out their ranks and insignia. The navy guy, also a Chief Bosun's Mate, and the oldest of the group, was a SEAL as evidenced by the trident emblem on his shirt pocket. Likewise, the Marine Gunnery Sergeant, ironically, showed more wear and tear while looking younger than the Chief. He wore the Marine Recon emblem. The Air Force guy was kind of a question mark. He looked to be in good shape, but not like the other two. He had Sergeant stripes on his sleeve, but no other emblems identifying a specialty.

Heading for the exit, Eldridge and Callaway stopped by their table.

Giving them a hard look, Eldridge said, "Gentlemen, I want you to meet my good friend Mr. Michael Callaway. He's a former federal agent. He'll be coming to the base pretty often because he's recuperating from a little bout of hypothermia. I asked the CO if he could use the gym, and he approved. I know you guys are in there a lot, so please treat him well."

The SEAL looked at Callaway as if trying to size him up. "Federal Agent, huh?" he asked. "What agency?"

Put off by the man's tone, Callaway answered, "United States Customs Enforcement, Miami District."

Smirking, the SEAL asked, "So, what did you do, hang around the seaport looking for people with contraband cigars?" His two friends laughed.

Eldridge looked at the SEAL with fire in his eyes, and asked quietly, "Flanders, could you refrain from being a complete asshole for once?"

Glaring back, the SEAL asked, "What are you gonna do to me if I don't, Commander? You gonna write me up so they can ship me to a base worse than this? Oh wait, there is no base worse than this," he said with a smile.

Eldridge wasn't smiling back. "Look dickhead," he replied, "he's been through some bad shit, so you **will** treat him right. Besides, his father was a CPO like you." Flanders' expression changed from antagonistic to only moderately angry.

Callaway jumped into the conversation. Showing Flanders that he read him perfectly, he told him, "Yeah, and he didn't like officers either.

Tilting his head slightly, Flanders looked into Callaway's eyes. "Okay Mr. Callaway, since your dad was one of "us," he said, glancing at his friends, "You're welcome to our section of this barn and at our table." Pointing at the Marine first, Flanders introduced him as Markham, and the Air Force guy as Cheshire. Callaway shook hands with the three men and then he and Eldridge headed out the door. They crossed the street to Eldridge's office in the administration building.

Seeing Callaway shaking his head and smiling, Eldridge asked, "Okay, Mike, what?"

Callaway crossed his arms. "I've seen people who didn't like their superiors before. A prime example was my old boss Richard Todd from Customs in Miami. You remember him, right? AKA Major Dick? But these guys have a serious hard-on for officers. What gives?"

They stopped short of his building where Eldridge could explain the situation without being overheard. "Mike, just about everyone assigned to this base during the last three years was basically sentenced here by someone higher up who they pissed off," he answered. "I mean look at me. I didn't hand you up to that bitch-on-wheels, Admiral Slingo, and I paid the price. She got me exiled here, and most likely I'll be cashiered out when this base folds. In the meantime, I'm stuck here freezing my ass off and behind a desk instead of commanding a ship.

Callaway instantly felt guilty about what happened to Eldridge, which was what brought Callaway to Alaska from Miami to see him. He was after all; the reason Eldridge had not received another sea command after his boat the *USS Pegasus* was retired to the mothball fleet. And then to make matters worse, he had been assigned as an assistant to the overbearing, and just plain nasty, Admiral D. May Slingo in Miami. And then Eldridge had stepped over the big line with her by not handing Callaway over for prosecution after he'd killed drug kingpin Derrick Drake. This was after Drake had Callaway's fiancée and two of his closest friends killed.

Eldridge put a hand on Callaway's shoulder. "Mike,

yes I'm pissed off about being stuck here, but it was worth it, believe me," he said, in an obvious attempt to quell his friend's obvious guilt. "Anyway, we all got someone mad, and we paid the price. They are a little younger than I am, but they have enough time in their respective services for this to be their last gig. They will be booted out of their respective service branch when this base ends its days.

Callaway couldn't help but ask, "Well, what did they do wrong?

Eldridge leaned against a pole holding up the porch of his office building and zipped his jacket up all the way. "Flanders was leading a SEAL team in Kuwait during Desert Storm when they got hammered because of some bad Intel they received from one of our coalition partners," Eldridge began. "The result was sixty percent casualties on his team. When he threatened to kill the idiot officer who'd provided the bad info, he was sent here to train people. He superiors were real certain that he'd follow through with his murder threat if he remained over there in the Sandbox…"

"Just because of a threat?" Callaway asked.

"You bet," Eldridge answered with a wink and then continued, "So, because he opened his mouth, he was buried here instead, so deep that he couldn't ruffle the feathers of any coalition people. I mean the guy had an exemplary record for all of his team's previous missions. He trained his men well in hand-to-hand combat and knife fighting. They took out a lot of really bad people. But here he is."

"And the others? Callaway asked.

Eldridge went on, "Markham was a Marine Recon. He got in trouble over there, too, because he decked an

Army Ranger captain who ragged on him and said that Marine Recon was a bunch of pussies. I mean Markham is totally immersed in the Corps. And he's one of their top shooters too. And you know how the Marines pride themselves on their marksmanship. He's a friggin ghost in the field, too. He can just appear out of nowhere. Either one of these guys would bare-hand an Alaskan brown bear to win a battle."

Callaway asked, "So how do you know so much about these guys?"

Eldridge tilted his head up, looking at the overcast sky. "Because they report to me, Mike," he answered. "Yeah, that was one of the other ways I got screwed when I came up here. They gave me the three biggest malcontents on the base to deal with, but I treat them with respect."

"So, what about the Air Force guy," Callaway asked. "I mean he looks pretty tough, but he's not a snake-eater like the other two."

Eldridge chuckled in response, and asked, "You mean Technical Sergeant Cheshire? He used to be Master Sergeant Cheshire until he got in a shit-sandwich with a colonel at Ramstein Air Force base in Germany. The guy's a technological genius, but without the college education. The Air Force trained him in mechanical and computer engineering. Name the gadget, and he can take it apart, put it back together, and make it work better at the same time. He was in Germany working in a unit using computers to mess with the Russians right before the end of the Cold War. And he was good at it. Then a secret order came through to his unit from the Pentagon to covertly check out what was on the computers assigned to the top brass at the base to make sure none of them were communicating with the Russians.

He found a bunch of pornography on the computer of the colonel I mentioned, and as he should have, he reported it. Now before you think the pornography was pictures of naked women, take my word for it that it was a lot worse. There were children involved. So, you might be thinking, 'Why did he get demoted and sent to this shit hole for doing his job?' Well, when said Colonel happened to be the son of a high-ranking member of the Senate Military Appropriations Committee, the Air Force wanted this situation to go away instantly, with no press involvement at all. Cheshire was hit with a bullshit charge for looking at material that he was not authorized to see. He was demoted and shipped here within twenty-four hours to teach SEALs how to get into the enemy's computers. He was told not to raise a bitch about it or he would be court martialed and given a dishonorable discharge.

So, you can understand why these guys are a bit pissed off. Now, if I have satisfied your curiosity, Mike, can we go inside to my office, please? Before my balls freeze off."

They entered the building and walked to Eldridge's office. It was small, and just like everything else on the base, old and cheap, except for Eldridge's chair, which, while not being exactly new, was a decent piece of furniture seemingly covered with nice leather. Callaway plopped down in the other chair, made of solid wood with a cushion on the seat. "Well, it looks like they at least gave you a pretty good chair, David," he said.

Eldridge looked at him, shaking his head. "I got this from an estate sale in Homer," he replied. "The dead guy had a great matching couch, too, but it wouldn't fit in here. You're sitting in the chair the Navy originally gave me."

The two men talked for a while and then Eldridge drove Callaway to Homer so he could rent a car. On the way, Eldridge pulled the car off the road and pointed at one of the shipping channels in Kechemak Bay. "There's the ship your new Russian friends you met at the hospital came from," he said, pointing at the vessel cruising north in the channel.

Callaway could only make out the basic shape of the freight ship. "She's a big one," he said. "Didn't you say her name when we were at the hospital?"

"Yep," Eldridge answered. "*Put' Stalina*—Stalin's Way. Not too obvious about how her skipper feels about the demise of Communism in Russia, I'm guessing."

Callaway laughed. "Yeah, some people just can't let go," he said. "What kind of stuff do they haul over to Russia?"

Eldridge got back on the road heading toward Homer. "From what I've heard, a lot of used farm equipment," he answered. "Tractors, pumps, and a lot of real powerful welding equipment. Nothing that's gonna raise any questions. And yet that idiot at the hospital shut up really quick when I talked about an inspection."

Callaway watched the ship as they moved away. *Something ain't right,* started bouncing around in his head.

Chapter 5

Callaway spent almost every day for a month using the gymnasium at the base. The workouts were extremely painful at first, but after a while he felt like he couldn't go a day without them. He was getting strong on the equipment, which was old but still in great shape. Eldridge told him that the mechanics servicing all of the equipment on the base paid particular attention to the gym machines, since the majority of the people stationed there used the machines to keep in shape and to alleviate boredom. Use of the machines and free weights and a daily run inside the base and around his hotel were giving him the strength and endurance he hadn't had in years. He was also surprised how quickly a guy who grew up in hot, humid South Florida could acclimate to the cold and sometimes freezing weather of Alaska.

Running on base along the shore of Kachemak Bay one day, he heard an outboard motor running hard, coming from behind him. He had slowed to a walk to get his breath when he saw a fifteen-foot inflatable boat moving parallel to the shore. The outboard on the boat sounded like it was working a lot harder than it should, since it wasn't moving the boat very fast, and it was putting out a plume of gray smoke. He stared at the lone pilot wearing an orange survival suit as protection from hypothermia in case he fell into the water. "You see that dumbass?" he mumbled to himself. "If you were wearing one of those when you fell off your boat, you wouldn't have died a couple of times." Callaway watched the boat while taking a couple of more steps when he heard a voice to his left.

"You want to get out of my field of view, Mr. Callaway?" Technical Sergeant Cheshire asked, motioning with his hand for Callaway to back up. "And I would appreciate it if you'd stop the self-commentary, too."

Callaway saw that Cheshire was videotaping the boat as it went by. He joined the sergeant and turned to watch what he was trying to capture with the camera.

"The microphone is directional, so you can whisper back here," Cheshire said, pointing at the camera on the tripod in front of them.

Callaway looked at the boat, which didn't appear to be doing anything other than cruising parallel to the shore about one hundred feet out. He shrugged. "Uh, Sergeant, what exactly are we looking at?" he asked, looking harder at the boat. Callaway stared at the driver who was also wearing a hat and goggles, and realized it was Chief Petty Officer Flanders. "So, you're out here in the cold, videotaping your pal the Navy SEAL driving a rubber boat slowly through the bay?" he asked. "Damn, you guys **are** bored. Where's your Marine buddy? I thought you three went everywhere together."

Cheshire smiled, looking through the viewfinder. "Wait for it," he whispered. At that moment Callaway saw something break the surface of the water behind the boat. Watching intently, he saw two oval-shaped boards pushing against the water. Suddenly, he saw something poke out of the water behind the boards. The object slowly emerged until Callaway realized it was the head

36

and upper body of a person wearing a dry suit. On his feet were oval shaped objects like water skies.

"There's Gunny Markham right now," Cheshire said. As Callaway watched, the man's upper body emerged completely. He saw that the man was breathing from a small scuba tank strapped across his chest. Markham pulled a cord on the front of the vest and deployed a paraglider chute from a pack on his back. From the frequency shift, Callaway could tell that Flanders had run the throttle on the outboard up to full, which didn't change the boat's speed much. However, as soon as the chute fully opened, it caught enough air to lift the Marine like a shark breaching. Markham continued to ascend, pulling on the static lines of the chute to move himself toward the shore. He rose up above the second level of a three-story cargo dock, and then Flanders slowed the boat down, allowing him to land on the dock running. Markham punched something on his chest, apparently a quick-release button, and the chute fluttered down onto the dock. He slowed to a stop and thrust both of his fists in the air triumphantly, letting out an extremely loud "Oorah!"

Cheshire switched off the video camera and said, "Cut! Well, I guess we can call that test a success." Flanders ran the boat up to the dock and secured it. He met Markham, who came down the stairs from the upper dock and the men high-fived each other, the two of them were talking and laughing about their successful experiment, until they saw Callaway. "What's the matter Callaway, you get locked out of the gym?" Flanders asked, frowning as he had when they'd first met.

Callaway cocked his head to one side and smiled. "Nope, just finished in the gym," he answered. "I was out for my daily run when I saw you cruising around in your little boat, and I got curious." Then he pointed at Markham. "And then I see this guy rising out of the water like a Polaris missile, and damn, you really stuck that landing!" The three servicemen looked at him as if not sure if he was being sincere or sarcastic or a little of both.

Closing his eyes, Cheshire told him, "Dude, these are the last two people on the planet you want to be an asshole to."

Callaway squinted at the three of them. "Look, I don't want to have a problem with you, but I've been respectful to you and all you've done is bust my balls," he said. "Sorry, but I don't take that crap from anyone. I had a boss who was a total shit to me and all of the other agents I worked with. Besides which, he basically lost me my job, so I understand how you feel about your situation, but you need to get off my ass. And if you can't do that, then let's settle this right here!"

The three men looked at each other and then looked at Callaway and burst out laughing.

"What's so fucking funny?" Callaway asked tensely.

Smiling, Markham told him, "Relax Callaway. We just wanted to see how you would react. You passed the test. We don't accept people as our friends unless we know they have the cajones to fight.

Callaway looked at each of them and smiled. "Well, I really was impressed with the landing," he said. When did the military develop that maneuver?"

Cheshire cleared his throat and answered, "Actually, they haven't. We did. And we'd appreciate it if you didn't mention it to anyone."

Why would men on their way out bother? Callaway wondered.

Markham walked down to the water's edge to

collect his parachute, while Cheshire went to get the camera, leaving him with Flanders.

"We're going to chow as soon as I put the boat away," he said. "Join us?"

Still trying to process the change of attitude in the previously antagonistic Navy SEAL, he answered, "Okay, Chief, lunch sounds good. Do they serve snake in the mess hall here?" He was jokingly referring to the nickname "snake eaters" given to members of military special forces units.

Flanders grinned at Callaway as he turned around and headed for his boat. "There **are** no snakes in Alaska, Mr. Callaway," he replied.

Callaway met up with his new friends in the mess hall for lunch and coffee. He found the conversation about where each of them came from interesting. They were intrigued with Callaway's former occupation as a pursuit boat driver for the U.S. Customs Service since they hadn't been involved in any military action since they had been exiled to Alaska. Flanders and Markham rambled on about battles they had been in, and Cheshire talked about the future of what he called computer warfare, but Callaway was keeping most of his past to himself. He didn't talk about Carrie, who he constantly thought of, and he didn't elaborate on why he'd left the Customs Service, or how he'd won $82 million dollars from a very lucky Lotto ticket. In the back of his mind, he was still wondering why he hadn't called to ask Dr. Tika'a out to dinner, which also had to do with him constantly thinking of his murdered fiancée. After more than a year, he still couldn't reconcile himself to what had happened to her.

Deciding it was time to change the conversation

from his thoughts of the past, Callaway said, "So, I'm not trying to be a jerk, but Eldridge told me that you're in the same situation he's in. I mean you guys are just floating up here until they shut the doors on this base, and you'll probably be retired from the military, so…"

Cheshire interrupted to say, "There's not probably about it, Callaway. When the doors close, we're gone."

Stirring his coffee, Callaway asked, "So why were you out there working on new tactics with the boat and parachute, today? I mean it's dammed freaking cold out there, and you were playing in the frigid water."

Flanders leaned back in his chair. "We're not dead yet, Mr. Callaway," he said. "We didn't develop the parachute thing just to kill time. We did it so that future SEAL teams will have another tactic to use in battle. We need to get to where we can land someone on the deck of a freighter or a cruise ship, if one gets hijacked like the *Achille Lauro* was six years ago. The only problem is the outboard on our boat is so old that it can't pull Markham, skinny as he is, fast enough to get him high enough to do it."

Callaway remembered the *Achille Lauro* hijacking in 1985, when members of the Palestinian Liberation Front had boarded the ship with submachine guns hidden in their luggage. They took control of the cruise ship off the coast of Egypt and shot and killed an elderly, disabled American.

"We're in the process of writing it up to present to the higher ups." Cheshire again cleared his throat. "I'm the one writing it up," he interjected.

Shaking his head, Flanders said, "Yeah, the 'gadget master' is writing it up. It's all about staying vital and not giving up."

Callaway looked at Flanders and smiled. "You

know, I spent many of my younger years rebuilding old outboards when I lived in the Florida Keys," he said. "You want me to see if I can squeeze a few more horsepower out of that old motor?"

The three men looked at each other, and Flanders answered, "Sure!"

Callaway told them, "I am curious about one thing. Have you let Eldridge in on your little experiment?"

Markham answered first. "Oh, yeah. We told him what we wanted to do, and he authorized the equipment and the time without any questions," he said. He looked around to make sure nobody could hear the conversation. "Eldridge didn't bother asking the base Commander for authorization, since he knew that the CO would say no."

Callaway gave the SEAL a questioning look. "Why would your CO keep you from developing a new tactic?" he asked.

Markham smiled and then took a sip of his coffee. "Because he's old, and when this base is done, he's done, too, but he doesn't care about that" he answered. "He doesn't want to rock the boat with anything that might mess up his pension. The difference is that unlike us, he wants to retire. So, he doesn't want anyone doing anything crazy or dangerous, since that would require paperwork to be filled out. In other words, he doesn't want to make any waves. That's why Eldridge has us working out on the backside of the base, on the opposite side from the CO's office. He even told the base cops that the work was authorized, and to leave us alone." Cheshire picked up his cup, getting ready to leave. "We rag on Eldridge because he's an officer, and frankly, we've all been screwed by officers," he continued. "But he's a good guy. He won't tell us why he was sent up here, but for some reason I'm guessing it had something to do with you? Care to let us in on the joke?"

Callaway looked at the man, smiled, and said "Nope," as he got up, too. "But you're right," he continued. "He saved my ass more than once, and yeah, he will go to the wall for you if he thinks you're good people. So obviously he thinks you guys are worth a shit. And as I said, you're all in the same boat, so to speak. Who knows, maybe something will go on and you'll get to see some action before they kick you out."

The three of them laughed as they left the cafeteria with Callaway.

The next day, his new friends showed him the shed where they had hidden the boat. They had even managed to appropriate a pretty good mix of tools for Callaway to work with, including one that Callaway had specified, a compression tester. He did a compression test and found that there was a lot of air escaping as the outboard's twin pistons moved. Callaway tore the ancient Evinrude motor down and wasn't pleased with what he found. There was black and brown crud all over the internals. "Okay," he said. "I don't suppose you have access to another motor, right?"

The three answered "No" at the same time. Callaway looked up and blew out a breath of air. "Well, the rings are pretty much shot to hell, and I'll bet you serious money that the cylinders are scratched up bad. The reed valves are a mess, too. Is there a machine shop around here with an owner who knows what he's doing? Those cylinders need to be bored out, and we'll need new pistons, rings, and reed valves. I think I can rebuild the carburetor if I can find a kit for this old thing. He looked at the three men.

42

They all looked like their pet dog just died. "We don't have the cash to cover all of that," Markham explained.

Looking at each of them in turn, Callaway asked, "Well, can you get me a truck to get it to a machine shop, if we can find a good one?"

Cheshire answered, "I've got an old Ford Bronco that we can load it into."

Flanders chimed in next. "There are two Ninilchik guys that run a small machining company down the coast near their village. They're supposed to do good work, but we still don't have that kind of money to get it done."

Callaway smiled and told them, "You help me clean these parts up and load them onto Cheshire's truck, and I'll take care of the rest."

They looked at each other. "Look Callaway, we appreciate you wanting to do that, but how are you going to pay for this? Are you rich or something?" Cheshire asked.

Callaway picked up a spray can of parts cleaner and handed it to him. "Let's just say I inherited some money from a rich uncle. Now let's clean her up, boys."

They picked up some shop rags and began cleaning nasty stuff off the motor parts. Callaway went down to the mess hall to get another cup of coffee.

The next day, the three instructors loaded all the parts into Cheshire's truck. "Try to keep it under one hundred," Cheshire said.

Callaway headed south, following a map that Cheshire had printed from his computer. He found the shop and parked near the door. Two men were polishing some metal pieces. They stopped what they were doing and walked to the rear of the Bronco where Callaway had opened the tailgate. Both were from the tribe. One of them was large, and kind of tough looking, the other was small and thin.

"What's up?" the large one asked. Callaway dragged the engine block out. "I need this bored out ten thousandths of an inch," he said. "You know anyone around here who carries engine parts for an old motor like this?"

The smaller of the two looked over the cylinders in the block. "Yeah, we can clean that up for you. You up here on vacation?" he asked, while writing a name and address on a piece of paper and then handing it to Callaway.

"Yeah, kinda," Callaway replied, seeing information for an outboard motor supply place written on the paper. The larger man squinted down at Callaway and asked, "What kind of boat do you have? This isn't the best time of the year to go fishing, unless you're using a net."

Callaway smiled and answered, "Yeah, well the boat belongs to a friend of mine, and I'm just helping him rebuild the motor. We're probably gonna do some sightseeing when the river ice starts to clear."

The larger man grunted. "Come back in a week and it'll be ready," he said, scowling.

Callaway nodded and shut the rear door of the Bronco. He walked around to the driver's side shaking his head at the large man's attitude. He followed the directions to the parts store, where he ordered oversized pistons and rings, and new, slightly larger reed valves, along with a kit to rebuild the carburetor. *At least I'll have some fun getting the old motor running,* he thought.

A week later he returned to the machine shop and picked up the engine block. He was amazed at the quality of the work. Not only were the cylinders bored out and polished, the rest of the engine was also cleaned and polished, too. He brought the motor back to the shed at the base and put it all back together after borrowing a piston ring compressor and some other tools from the base machine shop. He was bolting on the carburetor he'd rebuilt, when Flanders, Markham and Cheshire walked in.

"Holy shit, that motor looks brand new!" Flanders said, actually smiling. Callaway hooked up a hose from a six-gallon gas tank, looked at the three men, and gave the starter cord a yank. The motor coughed one time and began running, albeit a little roughly. Callaway adjusted the reed valves, and the little beast began running smoothly.

Two weeks later, after some cruising around to break the motor in, Flanders came down the channel with Markham in tow. After surfacing, he opened the paraglider chute, while Flanders opened the throttle to full speed, causing Markham to shoot almost straight up and to a much higher altitude than before. When they got to the three-story cargo dock, Flanders cut the throttle, and Markham floated down and made a perfect landing on the third story of the dock. Flanders, Cheshire, and Callaway clapped their hands and started yelling at the success. Markham put his arms out to his sides and took a bow.

A large quantity of beer was consumed by the four of them that afternoon.

Chapter 6

Callaway returned to the hospital in Homer for a checkup late the next afternoon on the last day in April. The doctor giving him his physical was amazed at how he had bounced back from a frozen death. "Whatever you've been doing Mr. Callaway, keep it up," he said, filling out paperwork stating that his patient was good to go and wouldn't need another checkup unless he had a setback.

Callaway had purposely scheduled his session with that doctor on a Tuesday afternoon because he knew Dr. Tika'a would be at the hospital checking on her patients. He sat in the hospital cafeteria with a clear view of the lobby, drinking coffee and waiting for her to leave. He had not called her since the day he was released from the hospital and had asked her out to dinner. He was still wondering if he was ready to go out with a woman since his brain couldn't unwrap itself from his love for Carrie. He thought about it over and over, lying in bed at night, sometimes breaking down and crying in the process.

He thought it only right to at least let Doctor Tika'a know that he hadn't just forgotten about her. He looked at his watch, and when he looked up, she was standing in front of him looking perplexed. He stared at her for a couple of seconds with his mouth hanging open and then tried to smile.

"Mr. Callaway," she said. "Are you okay?"

Callaway stood up. "I'm sorry," he blurted out. "Can you sit down for a minute?"

She sat down in the chair next to his. "Is there something wrong Mr. Callaway," she asked. "Is something in your medical check-up worrying you?"

"No... no, not at all," he replied. "I just had a physical, and the doctor said I'm fine."

Her expression changed from concerned to a little pissed. Clearly, illness wasn't why he hadn't called her to arrange the date that he had asked her to go on. "Oh," she said. "Well, I'm glad you're well. I'd hoped I would see you again soon." She started to get up.

"My fiancée died," Callaway blurted out. Feeling like an idiot, he sank back into his chair.

She stared at him. "I'm sorry," Doctor Tika'a responded. "Did this just happen? And you asked me out anyway?"

Callaway looked down at the tabletop and closed his eyes. "It was a little over a year ago," he answered. "Down in Miami."

Her tone changing again from angry to sympathetic, she asked, "What... What happened to her? Was she killed in an accident? Was she sick?"

Struggling to get the words out, Callaway whispered, "She was murdered." Looking up with tears in his eyes, he saw that she had started to tear up, as well.

"What happened?" she said softly.

"A drug smuggler ordered her death," he responded. "She was a DEA agent, and we both got involved in taking the smuggler's father down, and in the process, killing him."

Doctor Tika'a sucked in a big gulp of air as Callaway continued. "His son ordered her death."

Hesitantly, she asked, "How... Did she die?"

Callaway looked back down, sobbing. "They drowned her," was all he could get out.

The doctor shook her head. "My God," she gasped. "What kind of people would do this? What happened to the person that ordered her death?"

Now Callaway was in a quandary. Doctor Tika'a was the first person he had spoken to about Carrie's death, and it felt comforting to do so since, after all, she had saved his life, twice. However, there was no way that he could tell her, or anyone else, that he was the one who ended Derick Drake's life. Especially the horrific way that it happened. "He was killed," he answered simply. He didn't take it any farther than that, even though he felt it would take a lot of stress off him if he did.

Reaching under the table, Dr. Tika'a took his hand, squeezed it and then held it gently. She looked into his eyes and gave him a slight smile. "You've been through a lot, Michael," she said quietly. "It's getting late…"

"Mike," he said, interrupting her. My mother was the only person that called me Michael, and that was only when I did something stupid."

She smiled. "It's getting late, Mike, and I know a place where they make the best halibut in town," she said. And I'm very hungry. So, if you're up to it…"

"I'm starved," he interrupted to say and smiled at her. They got up and walked out of the hospital still holding hands. It was a short two blocks to reach the restaurant. Callaway looked at the neon sign proclaiming the name of the very old place.

"'Halibut Heaven'… Really?" he asked.

Dr. Tika'a shrugged and smiled. "Yeah, I know." she answered. "It's goofy, but the food's very good. I think you'll like it."

Just inside the front door, Callaway stopped in his tracks and scanned the room. He looked at her and shook his head. "This place is amazing. I swear it looks just like an old barbeque place my dad used to take me to in Miami back in the 60's," he said. "It's got the same red vinyl, button-tufted chairs, the same hokey looking drapes. Wow, this brings back memories. How old is this place?"

Dr. Tika'a pursed her lips while giving him a hard look. "It opened eight months ago," was all she said.

"Okay," he replied as the hostess guided them to a table. "I think we both need a drink." When the server arrived, he told her, "I'll have a Crown Royal and Coke."

Dr. Tika'a told the server, "I'll have my usual, Ellen, oh, and can we have two halibut specials, too, please," she said, looking back at Callaway.

The server smiled and said, "One Wild Turkey straight up and two butts," then headed for the bar.

"So… Abby likes her drinks strong?" he asked her, saying her first name for the first time.

Smiling, she answered, "Yes, Abby likes her drinks strong. When you live in a land that's perpetually dark and freezing for many months of the year, alcohol helps. It's kind of a requirement, like always carrying a large gun unless you're in one of the bigger cities."

His eyes widened at that. "What… Do you have a big crime problem here?" he asked.

"Oh, we have our share of crime, for sure," she replied. "Pretty high rate, too, but we have a much bigger problem with bears."

Callaway tilted his head back. "Well, I know you have lots of them, and they're pretty big, but don't they stay in the woods?" he asked.

Grinning, she told him, "Mike, there are only 360,000

people living in Alaska full time. There are over 100,000 bears living here, too. It's not a case of will you have a bear encounter; it's a case of when you'll have a bear encounter. Plus, there are many of them that migrate through areas where there are small towns. They love humans, and the humans' garbage. Either works well as food for them."

"So," he asked, cringing, "attacks are frequent? Like every day?"

"I have stitched up some of the few lucky people who've survived an attack. It's usually not very pretty. I'll tell you what. Why don't you come camping with me?

"Seriously?" he asked, wondering, *is that the price I'll have to pay for her company?*

"We'll go up into the middle of the state near Fairbanks. There's an area there that is totally wild and isolated. I mean, its winter, so you won't see as many animals as you would during the spring and summer, but there are other things we can do."

Callaway sat there considering what she'd said. *So, she wants me to go camping with her. Just me and her, alone, in the middle of the frozen nowhere.* He thought again about how he had not been with another woman since he lost Carrie. Then he remembered what Carrie had told him in his dream—encounter, whatever it was when he was dead—about a woman he would meet. "Okay," he said, finally. "Camping sounds great. When do you want to do this?"

She rummaged through her purse for a small calendar and checked her schedule. "How is next Tuesday for you?" she asked. "I'm off Tuesday and Wednesday, and our other doctor owes me some time, so that will give me four days to play with."

Callaway stared at her without speaking.

"Mike, you okay," she asked?"

"Um… Yeah, I'm fine," he finally answered. "What do I need for the trip? He already had a few bottles of champagne and some condoms on the list in his mind.

Smiling, she answered, "Well you'll need some twenty-below gear. It shouldn't get that cold, but it can. A good, insulated parka and pants, some heavy-duty long underwear, a wool cap, several pairs of thermal socks in case your feet get wet, soap, deodorant, and a good pair of thermal boots."

Again, he was thinking about being alone in the wild with her. "Yes… thermal boots," he said smiling. "Oh, do you have a rifle that I can borrow? In case we run up on a bear. The biggest rifle I've got in my boat is a .308. That will drop a Florida black bear, but I don't think it will stop the ones that you have up here."

She put her calendar back in her purse as Ellen the server arrived with their drinks. "Umm, no I don't," she replied. "And I won't even ask my brothers to let you borrow one of theirs, because they'll just say 'No.' People around here usually have one go-to rifle that they use for bear encounters, and they aren't too keen on letting anyone borrow it." Grinning, she promised, "Don't worry, Mike. I'll protect you."

Callaway sat back in his chair. "So, what do you carry out in bear country," he asked.

Placing her glass carefully down on the table, she answered, "I have a very old .35 Whelen bolt action that belonged to my father. It can put down most of the bears around here, as long as I load it with heavyweight rounds and do my part," she said.

"So, did your dad pass away?" he asked.

She laughed and answered, "Oh, no. He's still alive and as spry as can be. He just bought a bigger rifle.

Smiling, Callaway asked, "Does anyone around here sell guns, so I can buy one that will be up to the task. I mean I'm a little concerned about being unarmed out there, from what you told me."

Arriving just then with a complementary appetizer, Ellen laughed and asked, "You bringing him camping, Doc?"

"Yep, next week, El," Abby answered.

Ellen turned and looked at Callaway. "Lucky boy," she said and then smiled and walked away.

Callaway's mind went into overdrive, mainly because he hadn't had sex in over a year. *Yes, indeed,* he thought, *Champagne and condoms.*

She took a long sip of Wild Turkey and put the glass down, looking at Callaway. "Oh, you wanted to know where you can buy a rifle," she said. "There's a gun shop outside of Anchor Point, about 30 miles from here. Most everyone in our tribe deals with the guy that owns it because he's fair. His name is Sam. Just be aware that Sam can be a little weird sometimes. I think he had a little too much Vietnam. Just tell him I sent you, and that we're going camping."

Callaway was smiling at Abby when he looked across the room behind her and saw someone that made his smile instantly vanish. He shifted his chair to put Abby between him and the problem. He didn't want anything to spoil what was so far a great time.

Picking up on Callaway's reaction, Abby asked, "What's wrong, Mike? Is someone here? Like a drug dealer you knew in Florida? All the way up here in Alaska?"

He smiled at her and asked, "You remember the asshole that gave us grief when I was checking out of the hospital?"

Frowning, she asked, "You mean the Russian asshole that grabbed my arm and came really close to getting a kick in the nuts?"

"No, the boss of the one that grabbed your arm," Callaway answered. "He just came in and is sitting at a table against the wall on the other side of the room."

She put her hand in her purse and came up with a small makeup case. She opened it and patted some makeup on her right cheek while looking over her shoulder at the man. "Yep, that's him," she said. "Do you want me to call my brothers and have them come over here and kick his ass?"

Callaway considered it for several seconds before he shook his head. "Na... I'm having too good a time with you, and I don't want it interrupted," he said, smiling. His smile died quickly again. "Oh crap, he's walking over here!" he whispered.

When the man got close, Callaway immediately shoved his chair backwards and stood up. He stared the man down and the room got quiet as all eyes turned to them. *Let's see you get shitty with me now that I'm back on my feet, jerkoff,* he thought, turning his body to a forty-five-degree fighting stance.

The man froze. "What are you doing?" he asked in his heavy Russian accent.

At a loss, Callaway asked, "Do you want to continue the conversation we had at the hospital?"

The Russian smiled. "I am Captain Acardi Frankovich, of the motor vessel *Put' Stalina.* Yes, I am the man you met at the hospital when one of my men was injured." He turned and looked at Abby. "Ah, and you are the doctor who took care of him," he continued, before looking back at Callaway. "I came over to apologize to you both for my rudeness that day. My crewman that was injured is a very close friend, and I just wanted to get him the best care." He looked back at Abby. "And from what he told me, he did, so thank you, Doctor."

Callaway wasn't buying the whole, "I wanna be your buddy now" thing, but he decided to play along to see where this conversation would go. "Okay, Captain," he said. "Why don't you have a seat?"

Ellen brought them a very expensive bottle of Russian vodka and three shot glasses.

"Thank you," the Russian said to Ellen. "I like to drink with new-found friends, and please, both of you, call me Acardi." He opened the bottle and filled the shot glasses. "*Nostrovia!*" he saluted in Russian. Callaway and Abby raised their glasses, saluting back. "So, Michael," he continued, "I heard that you were in the hospital because you took a swim in the cold water up here. You look like you are feeling better," Frankovich said.

Leaning forward and smiling, he answered, "You can just call me Callaway. And I'm very curious to know how you know my name."

Frankovich leaned forward in turn and smiled as he poured more vodka. "I have friends, you have friends. . .. We learn things from our friends, yes?" he responded.

Callaway sat back in his chair again. "So, what have you learned about me, Acardi, my new friend?" he asked.

Then Frankovich sat back in his chair. "I know you are from Florida, where the weather and the water are warm, and you were a Federal Agent. DEA, no?" he asked.

"No, United States Customs Enforcement," Callaway answered.

"Yes, of course. You chased drug smugglers in a

boat," Frankovich answered. "And you were very good at it from what I understand."

Abby turned from speaker to speaker and seemed to be enjoying learning many new things about her new boyfriend. Her eyes widened at what Frankovich said next.

"Then you got into, what do you Americans call it, a "pissing match" with your boss and quit your job. And you won $82 million dollars in a lottery."

She turned toward Callaway at this and demanded, "What!?" rather loudly.

Returning her gaze, Callaway smiled and shrugged. "I'll tell you about it later," he said.

"Bet your ass, you will," she answered, and took another sip of her vodka.

Callaway turned to stare at his adversarial "friend." "Okay, my turn, Acardi," he said. "You're former KGB."

Frankovich glowered at him, slammed his glass onto the table, and cleared his throat. "Who told you that?" he asked.

Smiling, Callaway answered, "Nobody. I just guessed."

Smiling back, Frankovich remarked, "Very good guess, but that was a long while ago. Now I am just a humble freighter captain."

Callaway picked up the bottle and re-filled all three glasses. "So, I'm guessing that this meeting isn't a coincidence, right?" he asked.

Frankovich smiled again. "You are correct, Callaway," he responded. "I actually have a request for you. A favor, if you would. I would like you to come aboard the *Put' Stalina* and look around."

Callaway snapped his head back, very confused by

the former spy's request. "What do you mean, look around?" he asked. "Look around for what?"

Frankovich laughed. "When we previously met at the hospital, your friend, the Navy Commander, threatened to call the American Coast Guard to suggest that they board my vessel to inspect it," he responded. "Understand that I have no concerns about passing one of your country's inspections, but such an inspection would take much time, and that would ruin my schedule, and of course, cost me money. A forced inspection could also ruin my reputation as a carrier to some of my clients, and I just don't want that. So, I would like you, a former U.S. Customs agent, to inspect my ship. Then you can go back to Commander Eldridge and tell him that all is well. Once he knows that the *Put' Salina* is clean, he won't turn the Coast Guard loose on me. So, can you help me out?"

Callaway sat and thought for a bit. *What bullshit this guy is shovelin'*, then he smiled. "Sure Acardi, I'll inspect your ship," he replied, preparing to shovel some bullshit back at the man. But you need to understand that if I find anything wrong, I will tell the Commander about it. You know I am certified to do vessel inspections?"

Laughing again, Frankovich stuck out his hand. "Yes, Callaway," he answered. "I knew that already, too."

Callaway smiled and shook his hand. "You gonna feed me lunch while I'm onboard?"

"Perhaps," Frankovich, answered with a grin, "but now I must go back to my ship." He looked at Abby. "Good evening, Doctor," he said and then grabbed the bottle of vodka and walked out of the restaurant.

Abby sat there with her mouth slightly open staring at Callaway. "So, you're going aboard a ship owned by an ex-Russian spy, who, by the way, threatened to kick your ass at the hospital, and now he wants to be your pal. Did I get that all correct?" she asked, grinning.

Callaway smiled back. "Something is really hinky about this guy. He's up to something, and I want to know what it is." he replied.

Abby rolled her eyes. "You don't have to do this, Mike. You're not a secret agent, or whatever you were, anymore," she said, slightly raising her voice.

"So," he said, smirking at her, "you're worried about me, huh?"

She looked down at the table for a couple of seconds and then back up at him. "Well, yeah," she replied. "I like you, Callaway."

Tilting his head, Callaway answered, "I like you, too, Abby." He was happy about the fact that she didn't inquire about the money that he'd won. But he had said he would tell her about it. "About the lottery money…"

"No," she interrupted to say. "That's okay. You don't have to talk about it if you don't want to."

Callaway took her hand. "No, I want you to know," he said. "I was a day away from being fired from my job at the Customs Service when I hit the lotto for $82 million dollars. I mean, I'd never won anything in my life before that. So, I quit my job, bought my boat, and have been a boat bum ever since."

Just then Ellen returned with the food. Callaway dug in and was amazed at how good it was.

Seeing the look in his face as he gobbled it down, Abby said, "I told you, didn't I?"

They finished quickly and headed out the door. Callaway walked Abby to her car and that's when things started feeling awkward, at least for him. Abby wrote down her pager number for him, and he gave her his cell phone number, and then he stood there just like a kid on his first date with his first girlfriend.

Seeming to sense his confusion, she took his hand. Then she smiled, pulled him close and kissed him. A long kiss that told him "It's alright." She got into her car and rolled down the window. "I'm going to show you things that you've never seen when we camp, Michael Callaway," she said with a sultry smile. She started the car and drove away slowly, glancing back when she reached the parking lot exit.

Standing there in the freezing cold watching her leave, Callaway realized he was happy—happier than he'd been in a long time. He walked to his rental car whispering a checklist to himself, "Heavy clothing, boots, a big badass gun, champagne, and **lots** of condoms. Yes sir."

Chapter 7

Two days after his interesting dinner with Abby, Callaway borrowed Cheshire's old Ford Bronco again and headed to the little town of Anchor Point to go gun shopping. He was still not acclimated to driving in the heavy, falling snow, so he'd borrowed the Bronco hoping it would help him stay on the road. Cheshire told him he was always happy to loan the truck to him since he, himself, hardly ever drove the rusty old clunker, and Callaway always filled up the tank when he was done using the truck.

Callaway was happy to be going shopping for a new gun. When he reached the boundaries of the town, he followed the turnoff on the map he'd found to the 5-store building with the gun shop in the middle. He could barely tell that he was in the right place since the painted word "Firearms" on the front of the shop had almost faded out of existence. He got out of the truck and stopped short at the entrance, remembering that the owner was a bit "weird," as Abby had put it. The door was stiff and triggered an alarm as soon as he opened it. Callaway shut the door thinking it would shut off the alarm; it didn't. A short, thin man entered from the back of the room, stopped short of the counter and shut off the alarm. Callaway smelled the strong odor of Hoppes Number 9

Gun Solvent—a scent that every cop and everyone who shoots a lot would know.

The man now standing at the counter looked as worn as the painted sign outside. His hair was grayer than brown, and he wore it in a ponytail down to the middle of his back. His long beard was the same gray as the ponytail. His blue plaid shirt and jeans were unremarkable but the most startling thing about him was the small green and red parrot sitting on his right shoulder. Callaway couldn't help but notice that he had a Colt 1911 pistol holstered on his belt.

"What can I do for you?" the man asked with what sounded like a Texas drawl.

Smiling, Callaway answered, "I'm going camping in the middle of the state, and I need something that will stop a brown bear if one comes around to bother me."

"Bullshit!" the man replied instantly. "You're a Fed, aren't you?"

Taken aback, "What?" was all Callaway could get out.

"Alcohol Tobacco and Firearms, right?" The man asked. "I can smell you ATF guys a mile away. Well, you ain't gonna find no violations here, pal. I run a clean business and I go by the law," he continued, shaking his head. "Come on, admit it," the man continued. "I told you I can smell you guys. You're a Fed, right?"

Trying to calm the man down, Callaway answered quietly, "I'm guessing that you're Sam, right?"

The man just stood there, silently staring at him.

"Okay," Callaway said, placing both hands on the counter. "You got me. I am a former federal agent. But not ATF. I was U.S. Customs Enforcement. I used to chase drug smugglers around the Caribbean. I'm not here to check your store for violations. Actually, you were recommended to me by Abby Tika'a. She's taking me camping next week and suggested that I buy a gun for bear defense."

Sam's eyes opened wide. He turned to get a plastic cup from a shelf under the gun rack on the wall. Callaway swore he heard him whisper "Lucky bastard," as he turned. Callaway also noticed that Sam had parrot crap all down the back of his shirt. Sam turned back around holding the cup. "Got any more coffee?" Callaway asked, in a neutral, calming tone. "I could really use some."

Sam tilted his head slightly and spit tobacco juice into the cup. "This aint coffee," was all he said.

I can't win with this guy, Callaway thought. Then he saw a poster on the wall that he recognized from a long time ago. It hung next to the almost empty rifle rack. It was a cartoon drawing of a rat wearing an Army uniform holding a Colt .45—like the one Sam was wearing on his hip—in one hand, and a flashlight in the other. Underneath the rat was a slogan written in Latin that read, *Non Gratum Anus Rodentum.*

Callaway smiled. "So, you were a Tunnel Rat in Vietnam?" he asked. He was referring to the soldiers tasked with going down into tunnels just wide enough for the soldier to fit through, for the sole purpose of looking for North Vietnamese Army troops, or Vietcong insurgents hiding in rooms dug underground. It was a harrowing assignment, since you'd have to crawl alone through a tunnel that could cave in and bury you, or you could drag yourself across a mine and be blown to bits, or even worse, you could crawl into an underground room seething with thirty or so very angry enemy soldiers armed with AK 47's. The physical and psychological toll of that assignment was enough to make anyone weird.

Sam's eyes widened again as he glanced at the picture, and then back at Callaway. "How do you know about that?" he asked, his voice nowhere near as rough as it had been.

"My dad was a sailor aboard a destroyer during the war," Callaway replied. "His ship provided a lot of close-in cover fire for you Army guys. One of his Army friends was a Tunnel Rat. He gave my dad the same poster."

Sam nodded slightly. "You know what the inscription means?" he asked.

Laughing, Callaway answered, "Not worth a rat's ass."

Smiling at him at last, Sam asked, "What's your name, boy?"

"Mike Callaway, but my friends just call me by my last name."

Sam stuck out his right hand, causing the parrot to walk around Sam's neck to his left shoulder. "It's a pleasure to meet you Callaway," he said. "So, you want something that will do in a big bear?" He sighed, looking at the few rifles he had on the rifle rack. "Ya see I mostly deal with the locals," he said. "And that's why I don't have much of anything that is good bear medicine right now. I don't buy or trade much until spring and summer. I stay open in winter just to do repairs and custom work."

Callaway let out a breath, wondering if he would be going into the great wilds of Alaska with his girlfriend, unarmed. He placed his hands back on the glass counter. He was looking down at the pistols on display when he saw what appeared to be a larger version of an old friend. It looked like the Thompson Contender pistol that he'd "borrowed" from the hit man who'd killed two of his close friends—the hit man who Callaway subsequently killed—the same hit man hired by the drug kingpin who had ordered his fiancée killed. This pistol was a single shot like the Contender, only bigger; it had a much longer, heavier-looking barrel, and a muzzle brake on the front of the barrel, too. Callaway looked up at Sam and asked, "Is that a Contender?"

Sam pulled out the massive pistol. "Nope, this is the Encore, the bigger, nastier brother of the Contender."

Interested, Callaway took the gun from Sam's hands "Holy crap," he said, "this thing weighs a ton!" He bent forward to give it a closer look. "What caliber is it?"

Sam laughed. "It has a custom barrel in a .458 Winchester Magnum."

Looking up at Sam, Callaway asked, "Don't they use those for…"

Sam interrupted, to say, "Yes, for Cape buffalo in Africa. Cape buffalo are some of the most dangerous, hard-to-kill animals in the world, so if you want to shoot one you need a round like this."

Callaway felt like a kid in a toy store at this point. "So, this should put down any bear on earth, right?" he asked.

Sam closed his eyes and turned his head a bit. "Everyone except Big Ivan," he replied. Callaway looked at Sam thinking, *I know I'm going to regret asking this.* "Who is Big Ivan?" he asked.

Sam turned around and opened one of the drawers under the gun rack. He took two photos from the drawer and laid them on the counter. One was of a charging bear by a snowmobile, and the other was of a gigantic blood stain in the snow.

Callaway's eyes narrowed. "Ooo… What happened here?" he asked.

Sam pulled a stool over to the counter and sat down. "We had some damn hippie animal nut from San Francisco come up here about five years ago. He said he was goin' up near where Abby and her family have their camp to take pictures of bears. If Abby's people, or any other tribe people see where Big Ivan goes to hibernate in the winter, they put up warning signs, and email each other telling the Native people to avoid the area, or at least be quiet around where Ivan is hibernating. I mean the damn bear finds a different cave every year it appears, 'cuz male bears tend to travel a lot during mating season. So anyway, Mr. Hippie Bear Guy knew the danger. But he rented a big, long-track snowmobile up near Fort Wainwright, anyway. He was also told by the rental man to stay away from that cave. He was even given a map. He and his girlfriend went out camping and went blasting around on the snowmobile even though they were told that the bears would be there."

"So, they woke Big Ivan out of a deep sleep, right?" Callaway interrupted.

"Well, kinda," Sam replied. "They don't stay asleep during the whole winter. They sleep on and off. They don't pee or poop much cause their system slows way down. Well, Bozo the Bear Photographer woke old Big Ivan up. When Ivan came out of the cave, he was quite upset, and he was quite hungry, too. So, Mr. Wildlife Photographer got off one shot with his camera before he realized he was in trouble. He tried to make it to a tree, but he didn't realize that a huge bear like that can out sprint a thoroughbred racehorse inside of fifty yards.

The bear caught him, and according to his girlfriend, crushed his neck with one bite, and then dragged him off into the woods to eat. The girlfriend jumped on the snowmobile and got the hell out of there. When she reached a road, she lucked out 'cuz a state trooper came by, and she flagged him down. The trooper is an old friend of mine, and he sent me these pictures. He took the second picture of the blood all over the snow."

Callaway looked at the photo of the big bear again. 'So why do they call him Big Ivan," he asked. "I mean he looks like any old brown bear."

"Look closely," Sam replied. "Do you see the size of the bear compared to the snowmobile?"

Callaway looked at the picture again. "Yeah, so what. The snowmobile is way behind the bear, making it look small" he answered.

"Look again," Sam said. "That snowmobile is actually right next to him."

Callaway looked again at Big Ivan compared to the snowmobile, and blurted out, "Jesus, he's huge! I didn't think brown bears got **that** big."

Sam smiled. "That's 'cuz he's not a regular brown bear; he's a Kodiak. Grizzly bears and Kodiak bears are subspecies of brown bear. But where a grizzly might grow to ten or eleven hundred pounds, a Kodiak can hit fifteen hundred pounds. Big Ivan is probably close to eleven feet tall, as well."

Shaking his head and looking at the photo again, Callaway said, "I thought these bears were only found on Kodiak Island."

"Well, that's been the belief for a long time. But bears are great swimmers," Sam replied. "You get a big boy like Ivan, with a lot of fat on him that will give him buoyancy and energy during the summer months, and he might make it across the Shelikof Strait to the mainland. I mean it's only twenty-five or thirty miles of swimming. If he's hungry enough or horny enough it could happen."

Callaway slid the pictures across the glass showcase to Sam. "So how come the state troopers didn't put him down," Callaway asked.

Sam shook his head. "There's no good reason to," he said. "The bear wasn't going into towns and killing people, he was doing what he was supposed to be doing, sleeping. That idiot woke him up. If I was having a good night's sleep and that damn fool woke me up, I'd kill him, too."

Callaway looked at him for a second before realizing that Sam probably wasn't kidding. He picked up the pistol and looked at Sam. "You know, I like this but is there any place around here where I can try it out before I buy it?" he asked.

Sam turned around, opened a cabinet, and dug around until he pulled out a large plastic box. He opened it and took out three very long, very thick cartridges. "I'm not gonna open a new box of these for you to shoot up, 'cuz they're too damn expensive, but you can shoot these three. Grab the pistol and come on."

Callaway followed him to the back room where Sam had his gunsmithing bench. He watched as he lifted the parrot off his shoulder and put him in his cage.

"He don't like the cold, or things that go bang," he said. Sam handed Callaway a pair of shooters earmuffs to keep him from going def, opened the back door and walked outside. "You see the hill?" Sam said, pointing to a snow-covered pile of dirt and rocks about one hundred feet away.

Callaway instead looked around at the backs of the other stores. "Hey, Sam, aren't the people in the other stores going to be a little upset when I fire this thing out here?" he asked.

Sam smiled and told him, "This is Alaska, boy. Gunshots are a pretty normal thing out here. Besides, you got a massage parlor that specializes in happy endings, a homeopathic remedy store that sells pot, and a bar that runs whores." He said pointing his way across the building. "They ain't gonna call the cops. Go for it!"

Callaway opened the breach of the giant pistol and loaded one of the cartridges. He snapped the fifteen-inch barrel closed and pointed the gun towards the mound. Looking through the iron sights he saw three dark shapes about the size of bowling balls in the snow. "Sam, what are those things in the snow," he asked.

Sam sat down on a rusty fifty-gallon drum. "Granite," he answered.

Callaway looked at him. "Aren't you worried about a ricochet," he asked.

Sam's response came quickly. "Just shoot the damn gun! And hold on tight."

Callaway aimed at one of the "rocks," sighted in, and squeezed the trigger. The blast was so powerful that it made him jump, almost knocking the earmuffs off his head. The recoil left his arms sticking almost straight up. When his senses returned, he heard Sam laughing. Callaway looked for the rock he was aiming at, but it was gone. All he could see was a hole, about eight inches wide, going deep into the hill. He smiled and looked over at Sam. "I'll take it!" was all he said.

Chapter 8

The giggles were noticeable at the checkout. Callaway was shopping for his upcoming camping trip with Dr. Abby Tika'a and decided to go to the one drug store in her town for necessities. At the checkout, he placed on the counter a first-aid kit, aspirin, toilet paper, some Kaopectate, because of a situation in Mexico once, and last, but not least, the condoms. That's when the giggling began, from three young Ninilchik tribe girls behind him, and from the woman on the other side of the counter ringing him up. *What's so funny?* he wondered. *Don't these people believe in birth control?*

He paid for the items and left the store red-faced. Abby had told him to beware of the small-town mentality where everyone knew your business. One good thing he learned from her was to go to a store where the locals go for his "twenty-below clothes," as she called them, instead of going to a big-buck outfitter. He bought a pair of boots, a heavy-duty parka, double-thick pants, several pairs of knee-length wool socks, and the latest in high-tech long underwear. He also bought a military surplus duffle bag to carry all his stuff.

On the way to Abby's house, he stopped at a liquor store and bought three bottles of champagne, one for every night of the trip. Abby told him to come to her house so they could have dinner before they left for the long ride to their campsite. Callaway arrived at Abby's place late, at 4 pm, because he got lost trying to find her house. It was already dark because of the time of the year. He parked by the curb and got out dragging his duffle bag with him. He took a deep breath before he started walking toward the meager house.

He knocked on the front door and heard Abby yell, "Come on in—I'm in the kitchen." He took another deep breath, and charged into the kitchen, grabbing her around the waist, ready to give her a long, sloppy kiss, when she gave him a frightened look and pushed him away. Callaway froze, totally confused. She pointed behind him. Callaway turned his head and was shocked to see two Native American men sitting at a wooden table in a small room off the kitchen. One of them was about the same small size and build as Abby. The other was just plain large, both in height and weight. Callaway recognized them as the two men who'd done the machine work on his military friend's outboard motor.

"Um... Mike Callaway, these are two of my three brothers, Mathew and Mark," Abby said. "My other brother John couldn't come camping because he's busy at work, so it will just be the four of us." Callaway suddenly understood his tremendous error in judgment. There was not going to be the consumption of much champagne, nor would there be continuous, or any, for that matter, wild sex with Abby on this camping trip. Both brothers were giving Callaway an evil look.

"Uh... Hello," he said, forcing the words out. "I've been wanting to meet you both, so I could thank you for saving my life, and for pulling my boat out of the water. But I guess I have already met you at your machine shop.

You did a great job of cleaning the motor up. It ran great after I put it back together. I'm sorry about what I did to your fishing nets. I told Abby that I will pay for new nets as soon as you get them."

Silence. Sounding confused, Abby asked, "You were at Matthew and Mark's shop?"

Callaway looked at her. "Yes… I got some work done on a friend's outboard motor that I rebuilt."

Abby tried to lighten things up and cut the palpable tension between her brothers and Callaway. "Uhh… Why don't you boys sit down," she said. "Dinner is almost ready." Matthew and Mark sat down on one side of the dining room table and Callaway on the other.

There was too much quiet and staring going on for Callaway's taste, so he tried to break the ice. "So, I guess your family is very religious?" he asked. "Matthew Mark and John? Makes me feel like I'm in church." Again silence. The large one, Matthew, leaned ominously forward against the table. Callaway could feel the table moving toward him, pushed by the man's body.

"So, Callaway," he said in a low voice. "What's the deal with your boat?"

"What do you mean?" Callaway asked. "What's wrong with my boat?"

Matthew put his arms on the table and clasped his hands. "I mean it looks like a beat-up piece of crap from the outside, but it looks like the parlor in my great grandmother's house inside."

Callaway had heard this from just about all his friends who usually compared interior to something a bit more lurid. The boat's previous owner, who was in his late 70's, went all 1970's on the interior when he tried to turn an old shrimp boat into a yacht. He spent so much on burgundy velour furnishings and wooden paneling that he ran out of money and had to sell it. "Most of my friends call it a floating whore house," Callaway said, trying desperately to get a laugh. It didn't work. All he heard was the wind blowing outside.

The quiet was broken by Abby coming out of the kitchen with a big stew pot. "I hope you don't have a problem with eating wild game, Mike," she said.

Callaway could smell the savory stew. "No, no problem at all," he replied. My dad and I used to go up to Lake Okeechobee and shoot a couple of wild hogs every year. They provided us with a lot of free pork."

"Do the hogs taste good, being wild and all?" she asked. She filled his bowl with meat and vegetables steeped in a red sauce.

Looking up at her, Callaway answered, "Oh yeah. We just marinated the hell out of the meat for a day, and they tasted great. What kind of meat is this?"

"It's caribou," she replied. "Mark shot this one about a month ago."

Callaway asked Matthew and Mark, "Those are the ones with the big set of antlers, right?" More silence. Abby went to fill Matthew and Mark's bowls, but Matthew raised his right hand.

"Just a little for both of us, sis," he said. "We had a late lunch at work."

Abby put the pot down on the table, and poured wine into Callaway's and Matthew's glass, but then the bottle ran out. "Oh, I'll go out to the garage and get another bottle," she said. "Go ahead and start eating before the food gets cold." She walked toward the back door of the house. "I think you'll like it," she said as she walked out the door. "It's our mother's recipe."

Callaway smiled, as he stuck his fork into a hunk of meat and put it in his mouth. He chewed twice and stopped. Matthew and Mark looked at each other and laughed.

Matthew leaned forward again. "You know what else, Callaway," he said in a low voice. We both love our little sister a lot, but she can't cook worth shit. But the three of us will sit here tonight and pretend this is gourmet food," He squinted at Callaway. "Right?"

Callaway looked at them both as he quickly swallowed the contents of his wine glass to kill the awful taste in his mouth. "Of course," he replied.

"We don't come here to eat very much, unless we bring the food," Mark said. "I mean she's a brilliant person, and a great doctor, but she can't cook worth a damn. There's a trick to cooking caribou that our mother knows. And if you don't get it exactly right, it stinks. Abby doesn't know the trick. We bring our own food when we go camping, mostly snacks, so we don't have to eat her cooking out there. That's what we did for this camping trip."

"I don't suppose you brought any extra that I could buy from you?" Callaway asked.

Matthew smirked. "Nope!" he replied. "You probably should have bought your own snacks at the drugstore when you were buying toiletries and condoms."

Callaway stopped breathing. *Oh shit! Damn small town,* he thought. Fortunately, at that very moment, Abby returned with another bottle of wine. "There's more of this in the garage if we need it," she said.

Callaway gave her a weak smile. "Great," was all he could say.

"So, how do you like the caribou?" she asked. Again, he smiled. "It's wonderful," he said. "As a matter of fact, it's the best wild game I've ever had."

She smiled and gave him a kiss on the cheek. Callaway painfully ate everything in the bowl, while his tormentors on the other side of the table smirked at him.

After a while it was time to head north. Everyone brought their luggage to Matthew's two-and-a-half-ton, dually pick-up truck and loaded it into the bed. The truck's paint was faded and covered with rust from the harsh Alaskan winters, but the engine sounded strong. Callaway was glad to see that everyone else had packed small and light like him. There were only two rifle bags in the bed, until Abby brought hers out and then climbed up into the back seat of the truck.

Matthew looked at Callaway's duffle bag. "I thought you were bringing a gun to use if a bear came around. At least that's what Abby told me," he said.

Callaway pointed into the truck bed. "It's in the bag," he replied as he walked to the cab. He headed toward the back door on the passenger side to jump in next to Abby but found Mark already sitting there. He was expecting to have some time with Abby on what he thought would be a nine-hour drive, but Mark smiled at him and pointed toward the front seat.

"You are up front with me, Callaway," Matthew said.

Callaway rolled his eyes and climbed into the truck. *I guess I can just sleep up here since this will be a long boring drive,* he thought. Matthew started the truck's engine and made a U-turn. He headed out and turned northeast on a dark, two-lane road. They drove for about fifteen minutes without much conversation. Callaway looked around at Abby twice. Both times, she just shrugged and smiled. He turned around and rested his head against the headrest and closed his eyes for about five seconds. He felt the truck making a left turn. He turned and looked at Abby again.

"I thought you said the campsite was all the way up near Fairbanks. Why are we heading toward Cook Inlet?" he asked.

Matthew laughed. "If you think I'm driving you all the way up by Fairbanks, you're nuts." he said. He drove the truck through an open gate and past some buildings.

Abby touched Callaway's shoulder. "Why drive when you can fly?" she asked, smiling. Matthew drove around the buildings to a hanger. He stopped next to a single-engine de Havilland Otter, high-winged aircraft. He could see the single gravel runway lined on both sides by tall trees running out into the darkness. "Okay," Matthew said. "Everybody out and grab your gear."

Callaway saw a man walk out of the old, dark hanger. When he came into the light from the distant main airfield building and the full moon that was peeking through the clouds, Callaway could see that he was Native American. Abby walked up to him and gave him a hug. She turned around and smiled at Callaway. "Mike, this is my cousin Paul," she said.

Callaway smiled and shook the man's hand. *Matthew, Mark, John, and Paul*, he thought. *I'm starting to feel real religious now.* "So, what's the deal, guys?" Callaway asked. "Are we flying to your camp, or driving?" The four looked at him like he had two heads.

Matthew shook his head slowly and asked, "Why do you think we're at an airport, Callaway? I'm not driving 500 miles to Nenana tonight."

Abby walked over and took Callaway's hand and asked, "You aren't afraid of flying, are you Mike?" He looked at the airplane and noted to himself that it looked very old.

"Relax, Callaway, this is a de Havilland Otter, one of the strongest bush planes ever made. She'll get us there in one piece," Paul said. Callaway couldn't help but notice that Abby didn't give her cousin grief for calling his plane "she."

"How long have you had the plane?" Callaway asked.

"I bought it from the Royal Canadian Air Force about five years ago," Paul replied. "She's a Cold War veteran and tough as hell."

This time Callaway looked at Abby and squinted and she smiled back at him. "Okay, then," he said. "Let's go do some flying." They loaded their bags and their guns into the cargo hold and then Paul told them where to sit so the aircraft would be balanced.

Smiling at Callaway, Paul told him, "You can sit right seat with me." Callaway just responded with a nod. Once everyone was strapped in, Paul started the engine and taxied out to the end of the runway. The airfield had no control tower, so Paul announced that he was about to take off over the radio. When he didn't hear a response from any aircraft in the vicinity, he lowered the flaps and pushed the throttle forward. He revved the old radial engine, and the plane lurched forward. The aircraft gained speed as it moved down the runway.

Watching the tall trees passing in a blur on both sides of the runway, Callaway muttered, "This is like flying out of a ditch." Paul bumped the throttle forward a little more and pulled back on the yoke. The old de Havilland lifted off with no problem, almost appearing to be flying toward the moon. Callaway felt a little more comfortable as he could see that Paul was a competent pilot. When they reached cruising altitude, Callaway turned around to say something to Abby and saw that she and her brothers were sound asleep.

"They do that every time they fly with me," Paul said. "It's like a baby in the back seat of a car."

Callaway laughed. Looking over the instrument panel of the airplane, he said, "It looks like you've updated things a bit."

Paul tapped on the altimeter. "Yeah, I upgrade when I have some extra money," he replied. "You know much about airplanes? Abby told me that you worked for U.S. Customs, but she said you were a chase-boat driver."

Callaway was still looking at the instruments. "Yes, I was," he replied. "Once in a while I would fly right seat with some of our pilots. Sometimes when we were transiting to the Bahamas, they would let me take the wheel for a little while."

Paul tilted his head back a bit. "Have at it," he said, tapping his hand on the right-seat yoke. "Just keep her steady at this heading and altitude."

Callaway smiled at that like a kid with a new bicycle. He grasped the yoke and took control, checking the compass first and then the altimeter. He was enjoying the ride. After about five minutes, he turned to Paul to thank him, and saw that he was sleeping, too. He got a little panicky at first, until he realized that the plane almost flew itself. The sky was clear, and the bright, full moon illuminated the ground below. He could see a well-lit area ahead to his left. He was about to wake Paul up, when, just like clockwork, he sat up in his seat.

"Yeah, that's Anchorage," he said, rubbing his eyes. "I'll take it from here. Wow, Callaway, you kept the old girl straight on the heading. You fly pretty good."

Callaway smiled. "I can keep it straight and level if

the wind isn't too bad," he said. "I just don't know how to take off and land. I mean, I watched the Customs Service pilots like a hawk when they took off and landed, but they would never let me try it."

Paul took the yoke, shaking his head. "And you ain't gonna land my plane tonight either," he said grinning.

"So where exactly is this place where we're going camping?" Callaway asked.

Paul pointed out the right-hand window. "You see the railroad station down there?" he asked. "That's the main station for the Alaska Railroad," Paul continued. "The trains go all the way up to the North Pole. But we're going to a small airport in Nenana that's about thirty-five miles Northeast of Fairbanks. From there you and my cousins will take the snowmobiles west to the camp."

Surprised, Callaway asked, "You're not coming with us?"

"No, you can only get four people and their gear on the snowmobiles, even though they're good, strong, long-tracks," Paul replied. "Besides, I've got a living to make.

"So, who own's the snowmobiles and the land?" he asked.

Paul adjusted the flaps a little. "Actually, we all kick in," he replied. "Sometimes our family, and sometimes the tribe. It's like I fly family members around for free, and they take care of me and my family in return. Abby treats my kids when they're sick. Matthew and Mark own a machine shop, so if I need anything made to keep this thing flying, they build it for me for free. John is a fisherman, so I get a lot of halibut from him. We all take care of each other."

Callaway smiled and looked out the window. *Nice,* he thought. Being an only child kept him from ever having relationships like that. He laid his head back against the headrest and fell asleep. About an hour later, Callaway woke up feeling the airplane bumping around.

"Relax, Callaway, we're getting ready to land," Paul said, reaching for the microphone hanging on the instrument panel. He contacted Fairbanks International Airport to get landing clearance for the airfield at Nenana. After receiving it, he banked the airplane left and switched his landing lights on. Callaway could see the lighted runway down ahead. He watched everything Paul did, pulling the throttle back to reduce speed, adjusting the flaps, and letting the airplane lose some altitude. He banked the plane to the right and lined up for his final approach. The airplane drifted down slowly, with Paul lining up the nose perfectly with the runway. He deftly kept the de Havilland on a smooth glide path until the oversized bush tires touched the tarmac, bouncing ever so slightly once, and then settling down to a smooth roll. Paul taxied through the airport until he pulled up to one of two dilapidated old Quonset huts surrounded by snow-covered ground. When he got near the hut, he shut the engine down.

Callaway opened his door, and stepped out, landing on the slippery concrete. He immediately noticed that it was a lot colder in Nenana then the Kenai Peninsula. Paul got out on the other side of the plane, while Abby and her brothers exited the aircraft through the door farther back in the fuselage. Callaway walked back and helped them unload their gear. He could see Paul unlocking the large door to the Quonset hut that still had government markings from World War II. Paul entered and turned on the interior light.

"Okay, let's load up," Matthew said, and everyone

grabbed their bags and hauled them into the hut. Callaway entered and was surprised to see a bunk bed, a couple of pieces of beat-up furniture, a small kitchen, and two very powerful looking long-track snowmobiles. Paul was filling a percolator to make coffee.

"Hey Callaway," he said with his back turned toward him. "If you need to go to the can, there's an outhouse out behind the hut. If you just gotta pee, you can just go outside and do it in the snow.

Checking the engines on the snowmobiles, Callaway answered, "Yeah, I'll do that in a few. I didn't know they put turbochargers on these things," he said looking at Matthew and Mark.

"Matthew put them on," Mark replied. "You ever driven anything turbocharged before, Callaway?

Looking at the turbochargers, Callaway smiled. "I used to have a Yamaha WaveRunner with a supercharger on it," he replied. "I did a little over 100 miles per hour on flat water." He looked at Mark and saw that the man's eyes were wide open after hearing that. He smiled at Mark, but the smile quickly turned into a frown. His stomach was rumbling something fierce. *Must be the caribou,* he thought. "A... Paul," he said, rubbing his belly. "Where did you say that outhouse is?"

Paul pointed toward the back of the long hut and told him, "Go out that door, and then keep heading straight about a hundred feet out. You'll see it," he said, reaching into a cabinet to get a roll of toilet paper for him. He had to throw it like a quarterback since Callaway was walking quickly toward the door.

"The last time I had to use an outhouse was near the Everglades, and I had to watch out for snakes when I went in there," he said.

All four members of the Tika'a family responded in unison. "There aren't any snakes in Alaska!"

Matthew loaded the last bag on one of the snowmobiles, as he watched Callaway break into a trot as he went out the door. "Hmm," he said quietly to Mark, "must be the caribou."

Callaway slowed down to a fast walk. He could hear another airplane touch down on the runway and turned to see its running lights. As he got to the concrete outhouse and opened the door, he turned to see the airplane taxi toward the other Quonset hut. Then he caught sight of something else—the figure of a man leaning against the rear of the second Quonset hut. His gut told him to forget about him and get to the toilet. He arrived just in the nick of time and was sitting down when he heard the second airplane pull up to the other hut and stop. The engine shut down, and Callaway heard the doors on the aircraft open and close. He finished his business and was standing to pull up his long underwear and pants when he heard something else that made him freeze. A loud, familiar voice, yelling at someone in Russian. It was the voice of Acardi Frankovich.

Callaway pushed the door open a little and could see the figures of three men speaking in Russian. A light came on at the front of the building, and he saw a fourth man exit the second Quonset hut and hand something to Frankovich. He watched as Frankovich motioned to what he assumed were his crewmen from the *Put' Stalina;* one was the big man who had grabbed Abby's arm in the confrontation at the hospital as Callaway was being released. Callaway's eyes widened when Frankovich started walking toward the outhouse.

Callaway buckled his belt, trying to find a way to

keep Frankovich from recognizing him. He pulled his wool cap down right above his eyes and then pulled his scarf up over his nose. He grabbed the roll of toilet paper and threw the door open. Frankovich jumped back, startled by the appearance of another person. Callaway saw him reach under his coat as he rushed past him.

"You scared me, *sukin syn!*" the Russian yelled. Callaway kept walking. *Is that the only curse you know, asshole?* he wondered. Then he heard a commotion at the front of the other Quonset hut. Two men were arguing. He guessed that the pilot was going at it with one of Frankovich's men, given that he was the only one speaking without a Russian accent. The pilot walked to the Cessna, opened the front door on the left side, and climbed in, closing the door behind him.

Then Callaway saw something very peculiar. The strange man he saw on his way to the outhouse walked out of the darkness and up to the back door of the second hut. The door opened and the light from within allowed Callaway to see the man's face. He was tall and wearing round wire-rimmed glasses. The man walked in, and the door closed. Now Callaway was curious about what was going on. He walked around to the side of Paul's Quonset hut and waited for Frankovich to exit the outhouse. About two minutes later, Frankovich came out and walked to the back door of the other hut. He knocked on the door, and it was immediately opened. He could hear Frankovich say "Hello my good friend," and then something in Russian, as he pulled the door shut behind him.

What the hell is going on here? Callaway wondered, as he walked around to the rear of Paul's hut and entered through the back door. "It's about time, Callaway," Matthew said. "We already loaded all your gear on the snowmobiles. Are you finally ready to leave?"

Callaway nodded and looked at Abby, who gave him a strange look in return. He stayed near the back door and motioned for her to join him.

She approached shaking her head. "Why are you bundled up like that, Mike?" she asked. "It's not that cold out tonight."

He leaned his head down close to hers and whispered, "Our favorite Russian and two of his thugs just arrived and he's in the hut next door."

She looked at him, her dark eyes wide. "What is he doing up here?" she asked. "Did he come in on the plane that just landed?" Callaway nodded.

"Uh... if you two don't mind, we'd like to get going before spring is here and these wonderful machines won't have any snow to run on," Matthew yelled.

Callaway whispered to Abby, "Don't say anything to your brothers or Paul. I covered my face so Frankovich couldn't see who I was. Let's get going, I'll tell you what else I saw when we get to the camp. I don't want a confrontation that might put you or your family in danger."

"Hey Callaway, did you say you have your gun in your duffle bag?" Matthew asked. Callaway nodded.

"If we get separated out in the woods, you could end up as bear or wolf bait without it, so you might want to take it out of the bag and load it up."

Callaway patted his duffle bag and then opened it. He removed the holstered Encore from the bag, loaded the pistol and closed the breach. Then he put the shoulder holster on over his coat. "It's a pistol, not a rifle," Callaway said.

Matthew, Mark, and Paul looked at each other. Matthew closed his eyes, shook his head, and walked to the other snowmobile. "Let's get going before it gets any later."

Chapter 9

Callaway wasn't exactly thrilled with the snowmobile trip to the camp. He had hoped he'd would be riding behind Abby, his arms around her tiny little waist. Instead, he found himself riding behind Mark, with his arms around his tiny little waist. Abby was riding behind Matthew, whose large body blocked the freezing wind. Callaway was freezing since Mark's tiny frame blocked nothing. Both snowmobiles were humming along at about sixty miles per hour. Callaway was shaking, his teeth rattling, and he couldn't see much because the goggles he was wearing were all fogged up. He was wondering how much more he could stand when, finally, they slowed to a stop.

He pulled off the goggles and in the pale light of morning all he could see was snow, and some... bumps. There were four roundish structures poking out of the snow. Matthew unstrapped a couple of shovels from his snowmobile. He handed one to Callaway.

"I want you to get the full effect," he said, smiling, as he motioned with his hand for Callaway to follow him. He stopped by one of the white bumps and started digging. "Go on, Callaway, start digging on the other side of that one," he said, pointing at another bump. "That is," he continued, "if you want to have someplace to sleep tonight."

It took a couple of seconds for Callaway to figure it out. "It's an igloo," he said.

Matthew looked at Abby. "Damn, sis," he said laughing, "he *is* pretty smart."

Callaway dug down until he found an opening blocked by a wooden board.

"There's a rope at the top, Mike," Abby said. "Just pull it to get the door open." He pulled the rope and the heavy board fell over. It was totally dark inside. Abby joined him and pulled a flashlight out of her coat pocket. "Check it out," she said, pointing the light down inside the dome-shaped structure.

Callaway looked inside and was happy to see that there was a very thick sleeping bag, a battery powered heater, and a portable toilet inside. He looked again at the walls of the structure, which he thought were made of solid ice. He took off his gloves to touch the wall and was surprised. "This is Styrofoam!" he said.

"Well, yeah," she answered. "You were expecting ice blocks? My people have evolved a bit over the last sixty-five centuries. This is a lot more comfortable, unless you want to sleep in a freezer." Abby pulled off her backpack. "C'mon," she said, dropping to her knees and crawling through the opening. Once inside, she unzipped the backpack and removed a battery-powered lamp. When she turned it on, Callaway could see the interior in detail. He crawled in and sat down next to her. She leaned over and gave him a long kiss.

"Welcome to camping in Alaska," she said, as she reached into the backpack and pulled out batteries for the portable heater. She started the device up, and Callaway felt the warm air flowing through the small confines of the igloo. "So, tell me about the Russian," she said.

Callaway sat back against the wall of the igloo. "When I went to the outhouse, I heard the other plane arrive and pull up to the other Quonset hut," he said. "I heard Frankovich's voice bellowing in Russian. When I peeked out the door, I saw him, and heard him yelling at his men. One of them was the asshole that grabbed you at the hospital. Then Frankovich scared the hell out of me by coming toward the outhouse. That's why I was all bundled up when I came back to the hut. I walked right past him, and I scared him pretty good. He even called me a son-of-a-bitch again in Russian." Callaway put his arm around Abby.

"Here's the weird thing," he continued. "There was another guy there, too, waiting behind the other hut for them when they arrived. He was about six foot three, wearing round-framed glasses, and super short blond hair. He saw me, but I still had my face covered. He went to the back door and just stood there. Then I heard some yelling at the front of that hut, and then I saw the pilot go out the front door and get into his plane and just sit there. The goons in the hut let the tall guy in at that point. Then Frankovich came out of the outhouse and went to the back door. When he walked in, I heard him say 'Hello my good friend,' and something in Russian before he shut the door."

"What do you think is going on with this guy Frankovich?" she asked. "Obviously you think he's up to something bad the way you're acting."

Callaway was happy that she was interested. They both stopped talking when they heard footsteps coming toward the igloo. The next thing they saw was a pair of extremely large boots landing on the ground at the entrance of the igloo. Matthew leaned over and looked in at them.

"You two gonna sit here and play house, or are we going out to look around?" he asked.

Looking at Abby, Callaway answered, "No, we'll come out."

"Oh, and bring your pop gun," Matthew said, smirking at Callaway. "I can't wait to see this." He turned around and left.

"I guess he's gonna rag on me about my bear protection," Callaway told Abby, patting the shoulder holster.

Abby looked at the pistol, then into Callaway's eyes. "Yeah… I'll go get my rifle," she said as she crawled out the door, "And remind me to yell at Sam for taking advantage of you when we get back to town." Abby crawled out of the igloo and Callaway sighed as he followed her out the door.

Matthew and Mark stood by the snowmobiles with their rifles slung over their shoulders. Matthew squinted as if looking at something very small when he saw the pistol Callaway was carrying. "What the hell is that thing you're carrying, Callaway?" he asked. "That holster looks like something a mother would carry a newborn baby in. Let's see this wonder gun."

Scowling at him, Callaway pulled the Encore from the holster. Both men stared at the enormous pistol.

"What caliber does it shoot?" Mark asked.

Callaway pulled one of the large cartridges from a loop on the holster belt and threw it to Mark, who held the round in his hand and stared at it. "That is a lot of bullet," he said, tossing it back to Callaway. "Maybe you'll let me shoot it?"

Callaway nodded. "But only once," he answered. "These rounds are expensive." Callaway handed the loaded pistol to Mark, and told him, "Cock the hammer."

Mark did so and aimed the pistol at a dead tree about fifty feet away. When he fired, the recoil knocked his feet out from under him, landing him in the snow. Callaway did his best not to laugh. They could all clearly see that the dead tree was split right down the middle.

"Any questions?" Callaway asked, as he took the pistol from Mark, reloaded it, and put it in the holster. He heard Matthew quietly say "Nope." Callaway climbed on to the rear seat of the snowmobile and looked at Mark who was still sitting in the snow. He was happily surprised when Abby slung her right leg over the seat in front of him and then pushed the starter button. The long-track's engine fired right up. Callaway leaned forward and spoke into Abby's right ear so she could hear over the din of the engine.

"So how did you get permission to drive me around?" he asked.

She leaned back and kissed him on the cheek. "My brothers **are** over-controlling, but I don't take any crap from them," she answered. She gunned the engine, and the snowmobile jumped forward. Callaway grabbed her around the waist, hanging on as tightly as he could. He looked around, and as he expected, saw that he was getting a nasty look from Matthew. They rode north through the woods for about one hour, running parallel to the Dalton Highway that led to distant Prudhoe Bay. Abby slowed down between some mountains and shut off the engine. Her brothers came up behind them and stopped.

Abby leaned back, and told Callaway, "I don't think we'll be around any bears here, but you may want to keep that hand cannon you brought with you ready, just in case we run into a moose or some wolves. Callaway nodded, while Abby climbed off the machine and pulled her rifle from the scabbard attached to the side of the seat. He stood up and was climbing off the seat when he heard an earth-shattering explosion. At first, he thought one of Abby's brother's shot at something. He jumped from the machine, lost his balance, and fell face first into the snow. He pushed himself up and wiped the snow from his eyes only to see Matthew and Mark laughing.

"What's so damn funny?!" Callaway yelled, getting to his feet.

Matthew turned around. "Follow me," was all he said. The four walked some distance into the woods and stopped short when they saw a large *Snowcat* tracked vehicle parked next to the highway. Callaway saw a big trailer on skis behind it and was amazed to see a large cannon mounted on the trailer and pointing up at a mountain about a mile away. They walked toward the vehicles and watched as a man loaded a round into the cannon's breach. Looking down the road about a half a mile, Callaway could see the red and blue roof lights of an Alaskan State Trooper car blocking traffic.

Looking the other way on the road, he saw the same thing. The man operating the canon looked at Callaway, Abby and her brothers and smiled. Then he poked his index fingers in and out of his ears warning them to plug their ears, which they all did. After checking that the area behind the cannon was clear, he sat down on a steel chair welded to the trailer next to the gun and yelled "Fire in the hole!"

He slammed his right foot down on a steel pedal that served as the cannon's trigger, and the gun blew smoke from its muzzle and large flames out of its breech at the back. Callaway saw that the snow behind the trailer was blackened, melted, and rutted up from that back blast. "A recoilless-rifle," Callaway said out loud. Just then they heard a loud thumping from the tall mountain on the other side of the road. There was smoke, snow and pieces of rock flying through the air where the cannon shell landed about midway up the mountain. About ten seconds later, the ground moved above where the shell struck. The snow started rolling down the mountain, gaining speed as it descended.

"Holy Crap!" Callaway yelled. "He made an avalanche. That's what the cannon's for."

"What did you think they were doing out here with that big gun?" Matthew asked Callaway.

"Hunting?" Callaway replied, grinning at him. "Yeah, I thought maybe *'Big Ivan'* was on the loose," he continued, figuring it was time to trade one smart-ass remark for another with Abby's brothers.

Mark and Matthew looked at each other quizzically. "How do you know about *Big Ivan*, Callaway?" Matthew asked.

Callaway was watching every move the man operating the cannon made as he adjusted his aim a little to the left. "Sam, the gun shop guy told me about him," he answered, absently, as he gazed at the cannon. "Showed me the pictures of what that bear can do, too. So, how come this thing doesn't wake the big bear up?"

Matthew replied, "Because he's in a cave ten miles from here, with some mountains between here and there. We can take you to see where, but all you're gonna see is a big hole in the side of a mountain. It's back down near the army base near Fairbanks."

Just then they heard the gunner shout out, "Fire in the hole," again. Callaway watched him step on the trigger pedal, and the recoilless rifle fired once more. The flaming blast coming from the rear of the weapon again ripped through the snow and the earth behind it, leaving deeper, burned ruts.

Grabbing Callaway's arm, Abby asked, "How come flames come out of the back of that thing?"

Callaway pointed at the rear of the barrel and told her, "They build it with vents in the back, so some of the gasses from the gunpowder come blasting out, and that keeps the barrel from pushing backwards as much as a regular cannon. That allows them to bolt the cannon on to light vehicles without a big heavy frame to keep it attached. That's why they call it a 'Recoilless-Rifle' instead of a cannon. The downside is that it can't shoot anywhere near as far as a regular cannon. You also don't want to be behind it when it's fired because the blast would tear you up pretty bad. Callaway looked at Matthew and Mark. "So, when can we go down to see *Big Ivan's* cave?" he asked.

Mark gave him a funny look. "All you're gonna see is a hole in a rock like Matthew said," he replied.

Matthew smacked his brother in the shoulder. "It's okay, brother," he said. "We can run down there tomorrow. He wants to see a bear cave; we'll show him a bear cave. Then we can go to that Italian place in Fairbanks for dinner."

"Hey," Abby yelled, "I was gonna cook dinner for us tomorrow night. Besides, we always end up going to that same place."

Matthew smiled at her. "Aw c'mon Sis," he said. "Your boyfriend wants to see a bear cave, and he is our guest."

He gave her a hug, and then looked at Callaway and winked. It took Callaway a few seconds before he got it that if they ate at a restaurant, they wouldn't have to withstand Abby's cooking. He smiled and gave Matthew a thumbs up. Callaway saw the gunner on the snowcat jump off the trailer. He watched the man walk to the cab of the snowcat, open the door, and pull a chart and a thermos from the seat. He poured himself a hot cup of coffee while he studied the chart. Callaway was curious about the man's job, that being firing big guns at snow, so he walked over and asked, "So, how often do you have to use this thing," he asked.

The gunner introduced himself as George and shut off the loud generator he had been using to power his equipment, so they could hear each other without yelling. He sipped his coffee and handed the chart to Callaway. "You see all of those red circles?" he asked. "Those are all places near roads and the railroad with the potential of an avalanche. If we have a bad one, it will block the roads and tracks for quite a while. And since this is the road to Prudhoe Bay, and that's where all the oil comes from, I need to make sure nothing shuts this road down.

Callaway nodded, noticing that the other red circles not only covered this busy highway, but also some smaller ones, too. "Well, I thought the pipeline transported all the oil," he said.

George grinned at him and asked, "Do you know how much work it takes to keep that pipeline running, son? The pipeline runs pretty much parallel to the Dalton Highway, so there are always workers riding up and down this road to keep things in shape. Then you also have a lot of equipment for the oil companies up at Prudhoe that gets transported through here, too."

Callaway smiled and told him, "You have a very important job, George. I noticed that you landed those rounds midway up the mountain. How come you didn't land them near the top to clear that snow, too?"

George pointed at the cars that were now allowed to drive on Dalton highway since he was done shooting for the day. "If I hit too high, the volume of snow would bury this road, and every vehicle riding on it for three or four days," he responded. "I'm here to move snow, not kill people. I have to judge the point that will bring down the majority of the snow without stopping traffic for too long."

Callaway looked at George, trying to judge his age. "Did you shoot cannons in Vietnam?" he asked.

George looked at him with an emotionless expression. "Yeah, and that's the last I will say about that."

Callaway knew not to push Vietnam vets about their time in hell, so he changed the subject. "So, do you keep this thing at your house when you're not working?" he asked. "I mean it's got to be a great conversation piece when you have people over."

Smiling, George answered, "No, we keep it locked up in a block house about a mile north of here." Callaway shook hands with George and walked back to Abby and her brothers thinking, *Ya know, if I hadn't won that $82 million dollars, I could have done this for a living and enjoyed it.*

Callaway, Abby, and her brothers arrived back at their camp about an hour later. The sun was still setting early even though they were on the verge of spring. When darkness came, they built a fire, and Abby set up a wire rotisserie to cook a couple of chickens. Callaway looked at the setup. *It's a chicken over an open fire. She can't screw that up, right?* he thought.

When she was finished cooking, she cut up the chickens. "Do you want white or dark, Mike?" she asked.

Callaway answered that he wanted dark as he sat down in a folding chair. She gave him a thigh and drumstick. It was hard to see his food due to the poor lighting from a couple of lanterns. He bit into the drumstick and could hear a loud crunch. The bird was so overcooked that it was almost incinerated and as dry as the surface of the moon.

He looked over at Matthew, who looked back and smiled. He reached into his backpack while Abby had her back turned and pulled out a large can of Spam. He pointed at Callaway with his other hand and shook his head. Callaway understood the *no spam for you,* message. Then he watched Mark drag his left foot in the snow, while watching to see if Abby was looking. He made a rut big enough to drop his chicken breast in and covered it up.

"Want some more, Mike?" Abby asked, standing in front of him. Callaway saw Matthew narrow his eyes.

He turned his head and looked up at her. "Uh… Sure, sure, baby. I'll have a little more," he replied. She put another leg and thigh on his plate. He could still hear it sizzling.

"I guess my brothers aren't very hungry tonight," she said and walked back to the fire. Callaway bit into the chicken figuring it would be the only sustenance he would have for the night. He dreamed about the Italian restaurant they'd be going to the next day. *This camping trip is not going the way I wanted it to,* he thought.

After a while everyone went to their separate igloo. Callaway crawled into his and pulled up the door. In the light of a battery-powered lantern, he stripped down to his long underwear and thermal socks. He laid his holstered pistol next to him, just in case something large with teeth decided to pay him a visit in the middle of the night. He rolled into his sleeping bag and tried to get comfortable. The thought of a bear or wolf coming through the wooden door of the igloo made it tough to sleep.

After an hour of tossing and turning he finally fell asleep. But not for long. He heard something that startled him awake. Something was walking outside the igloo. Then he heard it come down to the door of the igloo, and then he saw the door begin to shake. He pulled the pistol out of the holster and grabbed his flashlight. The door dropped down, and he began to panic.

"Hi Mike," Abby said quietly. She aimed her flashlight at him. He was breathing heavy, and his eyes were wide open, with his pistol in his hand. "You have a funny way of welcoming your girlfriend, Callaway," she said. "I thought you'd like some company," she continued, as she pushed the door back up and crawled over to him and sat down.

Letting out a deep breath, he asked "Is something wrong? What are you doing here?"

She leaned against him and gave him a long kiss. "Well, I figured you might be cold, so I thought I'd come over and warm you up," she said, kissing him again, and running her hand down the front of his body.

"Uh… What about your brothers?" he asked.

Smiling, she answered, "When they go to sleep, they really go to sleep. They've slept through a couple of level 7 earthquakes with no problem," she said, pulling off her shirt.

Callaway was getting onboard with this quickly. "Um… Are we supposed to rub noses or something first?" he asked, trying to be funny.

She snapped her head back and stared at him. "If

that's all you want to rub tonight, then I picked the wrong guy to take camping," she said. Besides, that's an Eskimo thing. Wrong tribe."

He smiled at her and started kissing her. She kissed her way around to his right ear. "You might want to get one of those condoms from the drugstore out of your bag," she whispered. Callaway began pulling her pants off while thinking, *damn small towns!*

Chapter 10

Abby had set the alarm on her watch so she could get back to her igloo before Matthew and Mark woke up. Callaway woke up feeling very relaxed after some wild sex with Abby. He was amazed that he had no remorse even though this was the first woman he had been with since Carrie. He got dressed and crawled out of his little Styrofoam house. He took a couple of steps and stopped because he smelled something heavenly in the air. "Bacon," he whispered. He looked in the direction that the breeze was coming from and saw Abby kneeling in front of a fire with two pans lying on some burning charcoal. He walked over and saw bacon sizzling in one pan, and scrambled eggs in the other. Her brothers were sitting in folding chairs finishing their breakfast.

"Rest well, Sleeping Beauty?" Matthew asked.

Abby turned towards Callaway with a sultry smile.

"Yeah. Yeah, I did, Matthew," he replied. He sat down, and Abby brought him a plate full of eggs, bacon, and warm sourdough bread. He noticed that both Matthew and Mark were staring at him, like they expected him to spit out his first bite of food because of Abby's lack of culinary ability. He gritted his teeth for a few seconds and then took a bite of the eggs and they were excellent. He saw that the brothers were giggling. Callaway wolfed down everything on his plate. Abby brought him a cup of hot coffee. He couldn't help but smile at her. There was just something about her that made him happy.

Matthew and Mark walked over to Callaway. "If you two lovebirds want to see the bear cave, we'd better get moving," Matthew said.

Abby nodded at Callaway and said, "He's right. I'll go clean the dishes and pans and then we can go see where Big Ivan sleeps."

Callaway stood up. "I'll help you with the dishes," he said.

She looked at him and smiled. Then she turned and gave her brothers a nasty look. Then she said something to them in their native language that didn't sound very friendly. Both turned and walked away without reacting. Abby knelt and showed Callaway how to clean the dishes with snow. He knelt down next to her and started working.

"So, what did you just say to your brothers?" he asked.

Keeping her attention on the pan she was cleaning, she answered, "I called them a couple of lazy shits." When they finished cleaning, Abby went to freshen up, and Callaway joined her brothers by the snow mobiles.

"So, I thought you said she couldn't cook." he said. "Breakfast was wonderful."

Matthew grinned at him. "Okay, that's about the only thing she makes that's edible," he replied as he fired up one of the snowmobiles. "If you two ever get serious, you'll have to raise chickens and pigs to stay alive." Mark climbed on the back with Matthew while Abby walked up to Callaway and handed him the keys to the other machine. Callaway looked at her.

"Really?" he asked.

Climbing on the back of the seat, she answered, "It's time. You've seen us ride enough to know what to do. Just remember, if you don't go fast, we'll revoke your driving privilege."

He looked at her as he climbed on and realized that she wasn't kidding. He started the engine. "Hang on," he said squeezing the throttle lever on the right handlebar grip. The machine jumped forward and accelerated quickly to fifty miles per hour. He caught up with Abby's brothers in no time, only to see Matthew accelerate away from him.

Abby yelled over the sound of the engine. "You'd better keep up with him or you'll never hear the end of it."

Callaway yelled back, "Whatever you say, dear." And off they went. Callaway thought the snowmobile ran somewhat like his one hundred mile per hour WaveRunner, and that made him bold. He kept running up behind Matthew and Mark, until it got to the point that Abby's brothers couldn't get any more speed out of their machine.

Callaway turned his head and yelled to Abby, "Which way are we going?"

Abby yelled back, "Straight ahead down through the gorge."

Callaway turned his head and gave Matthew and Mark a sinister smile. When he squeezed the throttle as far as it could go, he and Abby leaped ahead of the brothers. They continued down the gorge at high speed.

Abby was laughing. "I'm really enjoying the ride, Mike!" she yelled. When they got near the end of the gorge, Abby told Callaway to slow down. He brought the machine down to about walking speed.

"Okay, stop here," she said, patting him on the back and pointing at a red sign about one hundred yards away. Callaway shut off the engine, and they waited, hearing

Matthew and Mark approaching. The brothers slowed down and then crawled their snowmobile up next to them.

Matthew shut off the engine and looked at Callaway. "You ride pretty good," he said, as he pulled his rifle from the scabbard on the machine. Mark climbed off first, grabbed his rifle and slung it onto his shoulder. Abby the same. "From now until we get back here, you whisper, Callaway," Mark said. "Big Ivan has been known for waking up at the worst time. Like when there is a human treat nearby. If he's out of the cave and he comes our way, freeze. Stay still. And for God's sake, don't make eye contact with him. He might take that as a challenge and charge."

Concerned about what he'd just heard, Callaway asked, "Well, what do we do if he does charge?"

"We all start firing and hope we can put enough rounds into him to put him down before he kills all of us," Matthew replied. "Including you, with your little popgun pistol."

Squinting, Callaway said, "Let's go see Big Ivan" and began walking towards the red sign. When they got close enough to read the sign, Callaway could see that it was your basic 'Danger: Sleeping Bear. Be Quiet and Do Not Disturb.' The farther they walked into the forest the thicker the woods became. They approached a pile of rocks, Abby put up her left hand, and they all stopped. She pointed at the base of a small mountain.

Callaway saw the opening to the cave where Big Ivan hibernated. Abby looked down and said something in her native tongue that Callaway assumed was a swear word because of the harsh way it came out. Her brothers looked, and then all three unslung their rifles while they looked in every direction. Callaway pulled his pistol from the holster as he looked down and saw gigantic tracks in the snow.

"Oh shit," he whispered. Abby leaned close to him. "These tracks are going away from the cave," she whispered. "If we don't see tracks going back into the cave we are probably screwed." The four of them walked around the clearing in front of the cave, scanning the ground. Callaway spotted tracks going back into the opening. He wanted to yell, but he couldn't. He started to jump up and down until they saw him pointing down. They joined him and followed the tracks with their eyes. Matthew let out a big breath of air.

"Those are fresh tracks, time to go," was all he whispered, as they walked quickly back to the snow mobiles. Mark walked backward behind the others.

"Okay, time to go eat," Matthew continued. "You up for Italian, Callaway?" he asked, mounting the snow-mobile.

Callaway looked at him and shook his head. "So, we almost become bear food, and you just want to go somewhere and eat."

Matthew looked at him and cocked his head to one side. "Do you know how many people there are in Alaska, Callaway?" he asked.

Callaway smiled and answered, "Three hundred and sixty thousand.... Abby told me."

Matthew smiled. "Very good," he said snidely. And the Wildlife Management people guestimate that the bear population is a little over 100,000." Callaway pointed at Abby, indicating that she told him that, too. "So, do you think we fuss much when we have an encounter or an incident with a bear in this state? Our people had to defend themselves from bears with spears when they crossed the Bering Sea from Siberia, 65,000 years ago. Now we have guns. We don't get too excited as long as we walk away in one piece. We're happy if the bear comes out of the encounter alive, too. You need to calm down and learn to relax, man." He started the snow mobile engine as Mark climbed on, and they took off heading for Fairbanks. Callaway and Abby followed. A couple of hours later, nearing Fairbanks, they skirted the perimeter of Fort Wainwright and headed slowly toward the center of town.

"So, what do you know about this base?" Callaway asked.

"Fort Wainwright?" she asked. "I know that it was built during World War II. It was named after some general who was captured in the Philippines or something."

Callaway was surprised that she knew that. He remembered reading his father's books about World War II, particularly about General Jonathan Wainwright, second in command to General Douglas MacArthur in the Philippines in 1941, when the Japanese were invading that nation of many islands.

He told her the story. "MacArthur was ordered to leave by President Franklin Roosevelt so he could plan the defense of Australia. When the Philippines fell, General Wainwright ended up as a POW until the islands were retaken by the United States. Do you know a lot about the base, like what they do there?" he asked.

Looking upset, she answered, "Well I know that they test rockets and missiles there now. Because we've seen a couple of them go up when we've been here camping."

Concerned by her tone, Callaway asked, "What, you don't like watching rockets flying up into the sky? Hell, in Florida we drive for hours to Cape Canaveral so we can watch whatever NASA is launching. I've been out offshore a bunch of times at night, looking for drug smugglers, and boom, out of nowhere there would be a streak of fire flying through the sky."

She still didn't look happy. "It's not the rockets, Mike," she replied. "Over the years, Fort Wainwright has dumped a lot of nasty chemicals into the ground. The base and the area near it are like one big cesspool. We take that kind of thing kind of serious up here. You heard of the Exon Valdes, and what happened here three years ago, right?"

"Everybody around the world heard about the Valdez incident, sweetie," he replied. "That's why we don't allow oil wells off the coast of Florida." Changing the subject, he asked, "So, what is our loud-ass Russian former spy doing up here meeting with some tall, strange guy?" he asked.

"You're the sleuth, you figure it out," she replied in a sharp tone. When they got close to Fairbanks, they parked the snowmobiles and walked through the town. There were lots of soldiers in uniform. It reminded him of his young life living in Key West when the Navy was there in abundance. The only difference were the low, dark clouds shrouding this town instead of Florida's sunshine. They continued until they arrived at the Italian restaurant Matthew had been drooling over.

The place was packed with people, so they had to wait for a table. They were lucky enough to be seated near a window that gave them a view of the street. Callaway ordered drinks for the table and sat back in his chair to relax. His quiet time didn't last very long. He looked through the window and saw a man standing on the sidewalk across the street. The man looked familiar to him.

That's the tall guy from the airfield! he thought. The drinks arrived, and Callaway toasted Abby and her brothers. He was taking his first sip when he saw something else that almost caused him to spit out his Crown Royal.

A taxi stopped in front of the restaurant across the street from where the tall man was standing. The rear door opened and Acardi Frankovich stepped out. Frankovich looked around and then behind him, and then he walked across the street and into an alley between two buildings. The tall man waited a few seconds, looked around, and then entered the alley, as well. Callaway could see a couple of hand gestures between the two. Then he saw Frankovich hand something to the man and then pat the tall man on the shoulder. The tall man then handed something to Frankovich, after which Frankovich walked out of the alley, looked around and walked down the street. The other man walked out of the alley and Callaway could see him shoving something into his coat pocket.

"Hey, Mike, are you in a trance?" Abby asked, startling him. Not wanting to ruin what seemed to be the first comfortable meal he was having with her brothers, he shook it off and answered, "Uh… Yeah. I must have zoned out a little. I didn't get much sleep last night," he said, smiling. Abby gave him a sly smile.

"How could you not sleep?" Matthew asked. "It's so peaceful at the camp."

He returned Abby's smile briefly and then looked out at the sidewalk across the street, but the strange, tall man was already gone. The food arrived, and it was as good as Matthew said it would be. Callaway couldn't finish his meal since the portions were so large. He saw Matthew looking at him and noticed that he had food left on his plate, too.

When Abby wasn't looking, he gave Callaway a wink. "You might want to bag what's left over and bring it back to the camp for dinner," he said. Callaway immediately got the hint, and instantly understood why Matthew liked coming to this restaurant so much, since there were apparently always leftovers. *I guess any way of not having Abby cook is a good thing,* he thought. He paid the bill, and the four of them walked out and took a tour of the town. When they got back to the snow mobiles, Callaway looked up at the sky. "Looks like it's clearing up," he said.

Mark looked up, too. "Yeah, you should be able to see the Lights..." he stopped short, knowing he had given away the surprise that Abby was expecting for Callaway that evening.

She walked over and kicked him in the rear. "Nice move, jackass!" she said to him.

Callaway smiled at her. "It's cool," he said. "Is this a good place to see the Northern Lights?"

Matthew answered, "This is the best place to see them in Alaska."

Climbing onto the snowmobile, Callaway started the engine. He looked at Matthew and Mark. "I'll race you to the camp." Callaway enjoyed the ride back to the igloos since he managed to stay in front of Matthew and Mark the whole way back, thanks to Abby doing the navigating. When they arrived at the camp, they set up chairs to witness what would hopefully happen when it got dark.

Matthew and Mark went to their igloos to eat their leftovers. The Aurora Borealis, or Northern Lights was something Callaway had never seen other than in travel magazine pictures. As they stood staring at the sky, Abby explained how the phenomenon occurred in the magnetosphere and how it was caused by solar wind. She was just getting into charged particles, electrons, and protons, when the glorious glow began. Callaway's mouth dropped open.

Seeing the lights, Abby stopped the science lesson so Callaway could just enjoy the view. They both sat down, and Abby put her arm around him.

"Wow... I'm starting to see why you love it here," he whispered.

She squeezed his shoulder. "Well, it's all about perspective, I guess," she said. "I'm guessing that you never froze your ass off walking to school when you were a kid or got chased by a moose. I, on the other hand, have never lain out in the sun on a sandy beach in Fort Lauderdale."

"You want to go to Fort Lauderdale?" he asked her, hoping she was serious.

"Well yeah, I'd love to see what it's like in the tropics, and swim in water that doesn't make you go numb."

He smiled at her and asked, "Do you have any more time off coming, Dr. Tika'a?"

"Yes, as a matter of fact, I do. About ten days, I believe." she replied, smiling.

Callaway looked at the lights again. "Well then, after I inspect our dear friend Captain Frankovich's ship, you and I are flying south for a week. I have to see a guy about something down there anyway, so it will work out fine," he said referring to his latest encounter with Acardi Frankovich and the strange man.

Looking shocked, she asked, "Are you for real about this?"

"Yes," he replied. "You've helped me experience

Alaskan culture and beauty, so now I want you to experience wild and dangerous South Florida culture, and a five-star hotel, where nobody knows who you are, and nobody cares what's going on in our hotel room."

Smiling, she asked, "What do I need to bring for the trip?"

"A bikini and a pair of sandals is all you'll need," he replied. "You don't have to buy a gun while you're there. I can loan you one."

A day later they rode back to Nenana Airfield, where they cleaned and fueled the snow mobiles so they would be ready for the next family members who wanted to go camping. Paul showed up around an hour later. The four campers loaded their gear into the de Havilland. Paul fired up the engine and taxied toward the runway. Another aircraft arrived at their taxiway's intersection, and Paul gave the other pilot a hand wave to go ahead.

Instead of a thank-you wave, the other pilot just gave Paul a nasty look and taxied on to the runway. Watching, Callaway realized that this was the pilot and airplane, the same beat-up Cessna 208 Caravan, that he saw the night they landed here at Nenana Airfield—the same pilot that had ferried Acardi Frankovich to the field three nights ago. Smiling at Paul, Callaway asked, "Friendly son of a bitch, huh?"

Keeping his eyes on the Cessna as it moved ahead of him, Paul smiled and asked, "Who, old Lapinski in the Cessna? Yeah, he's kind of an asshole most of the time. He flew Huey helicopters in Vietnam. He got himself in a world of crap over there. He was hauling special forces troops and they were chasing a Viet Cong unit that went over the border into Cambodia. He chased them down and his gunners tore the bad guys up really bad. He should have been a hero. Instead, he gets court martialed and given a dishonorable discharge for crossing the border."

"Did he know he'd crossed the border"? Callaway asked.

"Nah, that's what sucks about the whole thing," Paul asked. He told me he had no way of knowing he had crossed the border line. I mean I'm pretty sure there wasn't a sign that said, 'Welcome to Sunny Cambodia,' or anything. When he came back to the states, he moved up here and started flying. He brought his flying skills with him, along with a huge chip on his shoulder for the U.S. Government. We used to be friends, but that went away when I offered to help him get his plane at least looking like it was in good shape. For some reason, he didn't like that."

"I wonder why?" Callaway asked.

"Well, I think he took it as me saying he's too old to take care of his aircraft," Paul answered. We don't speak much anymore. Why do you ask?"

Callaway turned his head and looked out the window. "No reason," he replied. "Just curious." But he was thinking about how he could talk to Lapinski to maybe see what Frankovich was up to.

When they landed, Callaway paid for the airplane fuel used both ways. He tried to pay him for flying them up to the camp and back, but Paul wouldn't take the money.

"Family discount," he said.

Matthew drove them back to Abby's house, and then he and Mark left. Callaway went inside with Abby. They dropped their bags on the living room floor and proceeded to the bathroom where they stripped down and took a shower together since they had been without that

107

pleasure for three days. From there it was right to the bedroom for some more lovemaking. Afterward, they lay in bed, totally exhausted.

Despite his fatigue, Callaway was plotting their trip south. "So, I'm gonna make airline reservations for Ft. Lauderdale for Friday if you can get five days off.

Smiling at him, she asked, "You really want to take me there, don't you? I wasn't sure if you were goofing around before."

He lay there admiring her body. "You are beautiful, Abby, except there's one thing missing" he said.

"And just what would that be?" she asked, sounding perturbed.

Smiling, Callaway answered. "Tan lines, that I will enjoy traveling like a road map."

She hit him in the head with a pillow. They cuddled for a while, and then slept through the night.

Chapter 11

"What kind of craziness are you getting into now, Callaway?" The voice on the other end of the telephone had a familiar contemptuous tone. Callaway had botched the four-hour difference in time zones between Alaska and Florida, angering his former boss Richard Todd with a call at five o'clock in the morning. He'd been the Special Agent in Charge of the Miami office of the U.S. Customs Service when Callaway was employed there. He and Callaway were not friends in any way, shape or form, but they managed to have a somewhat complicated relationship.

When Callaway had "accidently" blown up a boat carrying millions of dollars' worth of cocaine to the coast of Florida, Todd decided to fire Callaway from the Service. Callaway turned that whole situation around when he won the Florida Lottery a day before his termination was to take effect. Instead of waiting to be fired, he had resigned, right after he sent a folder to the Commissioner of the Customs Service. The folder was full of information detailing what a terrible leader Todd was. That move had cost Todd his position and sent him to the dungeon-like job of writing grants for the Service.

But that was not the end of Richard Todd. In fact, he would later bounce back to become the Acting Agent in Charge of the Miami office of the DEA. He had also covertly helped Callaway destroy the drug kingpin who'd ordered the death of Callaway's fiancée. Now he was a changed man working hard to be a good leader to his agents. He did so well that he was given a permanent position running the DEA office in Miami.

"Um... Sorry about the early call, Richard," Callaway answered. "I'm in Alaska, and I lost track of the time change. How are you doing?" Callaway listened to the pause that probably signaled Todd shaking the sleep from mind.

"Actually, I'm doing fine, Callaway," he replied. "Now why are you calling me so early, and what the hell are you doing in Alaska?"

Callaway cleared his throat. "Well, actually I cruised up here in my boat to see David Eldridge," he answered. "But some interesting things have happened since I got here. For one thing, um... I... died, but was brought back to life by a beautiful doctor, and now she's my girlfriend."

Callaway heard a female voice away from Todd's telephone yell, "What!" There was silence for a couple of seconds. "Oh," Callaway said. "I didn't know I was on speaker. Is that who I think it is?"

Now Todd cleared his throat. "Yes, Callaway," he responded. "It's Donna Kendall, my former secretary at Customs. I told you about us having a relationship the last time we umm... saw each other." Todd was referring to the day he rescued Callaway in the middle of the ocean after Callaway had killed Derrick Drake and a bunch of his henchmen. Callaway heard the two of them fighting over the phone.

"Hi Mike," Donna said. So, Kendall had won the battle. "So, tell me about your girlfriend," she said. "Is it serious?"

Callaway considered two factors before answering the question: One was the fact that Donna Kendall had hardly said anything to him during the entire time they worked together at Customs, and the other was that she and Todd had helped him commit the vengeful murder of Derrick Drake a little over a year ago. "Uh… I'm not really sure yet, Donna," he started. "I mean we've only been out to dinner, and then we went camping."

She gasped and asked, "Camping, huh? Did you do any exploring while you were out there?" she asked laughing.

Callaway heard Todd in the background demanding, "Oh, for Christ's sake, give me the phone back," he said, and Callaway tried his best not to laugh.

"Alright Callaway," Todd said. "I know you didn't call me to announce that you're in a relationship with, whatever her name is, so, what's up?"

Callaway tried to get his mind back to business. "Her name is Abby," he said, and no, that's not why I called you. "I've had a couple of encounters with a Russian guy up here. David Eldridge told me he's probably former KGB, and the guy confirmed it in a conversation we had."

"Alright," Todd answered, you do realize that the Cold War is technically over, yes?" Todd asked. "I mean the KGB doesn't exist anymore, and…"

"Yes, I know," Callaway interrupted to say. "Now they're the kinder, gentler Federal Security Bureau, or something. The guy I am curious about is named Acardi Frankovich. He is the captain of a beat-up freighter that he supposedly uses to haul mining equipment from Alaska, where he buys it, to Russia where he sells it."

There was a long silence on the phone before Todd

111

answered, "Uh, as of the last time I checked federal statutes, there is no law against him doing that, Callaway."

Callaway sighed and answered, "Okay, here's the deal. He wants me to do an inspection of his ship, so I can report to David that all is well."

Todd chuckled. "Okay, now you're telling me that you brought Commander Eldridge into whatever little detective story you have going on in your head?" he asked. "And by the way, how is the good Commander? I haven't seen him since the inter-agency intelligence meeting I attended before he was shipped up to Alaska. I recall him telling me you were heading up there to see him, but what does this all have to do with this Russian and his ship?"

Callaway decided to keep trying to make Todd understand his suspicions. "I got in a tussle with one of his men at the hospital where Abby works—she's a doctor by the way," Callaway said. "David was there, and he threatened to have the Coast Guard do a safety check on Frankovich's freighter; he said that to stop the fight, and it worked. I saw real fear on the man's face when he heard the threat. But there's more. Abby and I bumped into him in a restaurant, and he practically begged me to inspect his ship. I mean, what's up with that? He heard Todd moan over the phone.

"Okay," Callaway continued. "When we flew up to a little town near Fairbanks to go camping, we landed at a small airport. Another plane landed, and who gets out but Frankovich, and a couple of his thugs. They ran the pilot that flew them in out of his own building and made him sit in the plane while they met with some spooky looking dude. And two days later, we were eating lunch in Fairbanks, next to the Fort Wainwright Army base, and

I see the spooky dude across the street like he's waiting for someone, and who rolls up in a cab but old Acardi himself. Then they commence to walk down an alley where the spooky guy gives something to Frankovich, and Frankovich gives something to the spooky guy. I'm telling you Richard; something is going on here."

Again, Callaway heard nothing but dead air on the phone line. Finally, Todd took a breath and exhaled, asking Callaway, "And what exactly do you want me to do with this information?"

Sighing, Callaway replied, "All I want you to do is run him through the DEA computer and maybe you can make a call to one of your FBI pals to get me some background on him before I go aboard his ship. This way, when I do the inspection, maybe there is something I'll find to either confirm or calm down my concern about the guy."

Todd grumbled. "You're not really going to go aboard his ship, are you?!" he asked loudly. When Callaway didn't answer, Todd continued, "Are you crazy? He could pull up the gangplank, sail out of port, and dump your sorry ass into the Bering Sea."

"Relax," Callaway answered. I'll tell him that Eldridge is in the car waiting for me. Look, Abby and I are coming down to Fort Lauderdale so she can experience the sun and an actual beach for the first time, so can you help me out when we get there?" Callaway was counting on the fact that they weren't enemies anymore, and that Todd would remember that he had never steered him wrong with a bogus hunch.

"Okay, Callaway," he finally answered. "I'll see what I can find out. Do you want me to give you a call while you're down here when I'm done checking this out?"

113

"Yes, please," Callaway answered, "give me a call. But why don't we get together for lunch and bring the ladies with us."

Through Todd's silence, Callaway could hear Donna insisting loudly, "Yes, let's do it."

"OK. Call me when you get here," Todd told him.

*****

"You're not going on that ship, Mike!" Commander David Eldridge insisted. "You don't know what this guy is up to. Hell, he might just pull anchor and toss your sorry ass in the Bering Sea for all we know."

"Wow," Callaway's said, wide-eyed. "Richard Todd said the same thing in almost those exact words," he responded.

Squinting at Callaway, Eldridge asked, "You talked to Todd about this, did you?" His volume grew as his anger mounted. "When did you talk to Todd, and why did you talk to Todd? I thought you hated the guy."

Callaway didn't want to let on that Todd had rescued him from certain death or imprisonment. "Well, we've kinda made up with each other," he said. "He's the permanent Special Agent in Charge of DEA Miami now."

Eldridge just shook his head. "Well good for him. So, why did you talk to him about the Russian?" he asked, sounding angrier by the second.

"Well, I asked him to run Frankovich's name through the DEA computer to see what comes up," Callaway answered.

Frowning, Eldridge asked, "And what else did you ask him?"

Looking away from this friend, Callaway answered, "Umm… I think I may have asked him to ask some of his friends with the FBI if they knew anything about Frankovich."

Eldridge walked over to the window and screamed, "Aaaaaaa! Do you understand that if he runs Frankovich through the DEA computer, it will probably send an alert to their offices in Anchorage and Fairbanks and the FBI up here will do the same thing? Then they will want to know why a DEA Agent in Charge in sunny Miami is asking about a former Russian spy in Alaska. And if he tells them that a guy who used to be a Customs Enforcement Agent, who he tried to fire, is looking hard at Frankovich based on a hunch that he's up to something bad, they will be looking for you, and probably me, too."

Callaway looked at his angry friend and noticed that his red hair seemed to get even redder when he was mad. Looking down, Callaway asked him, "Don't you want to know what's happening on that ship, David?"

Eldridge let out a big sigh and then turned around. "Of course, I want to know," he answered. "But like I said before, what if he kills you and stuffs your body in a garbage can? How are you going to keep that from happening?"

Callaway smiled and answered, "It's very simple. You're going to take me there, and you will wait in the car while I go nosing around on the ship. You'll be kind of like my insurance policy."

Turning toward Callaway, Eldridge rolled his eyes at him. "You know Mike, I've saved your ass from being killed by drug smugglers and in the process lost my sea command, and I've lied for you to keep you from going to prison and that's what got me sent up here to this shit hole, and now you want me to do this?" he asked. "You want me to mess with this asshole Frankovich?" He walked over to his desk and sat down. "Have you already scheduled when you're going to do your 'inspection'?" he asked in a frosty tone. "I mean, other than looking for contraband, which I'm sure they will hide well before you're aboard, what are you going to look for?"

Callaway stood and went to the window. "Well, I've been through the Coast Guard Vessel Safety Course, so I know the basics of what to look for to make the inspection look good," he replied. "You know, checking the pressure of their fire hoses and making sure their free-fall lifeboat at the stern is operational."

Eldridge's mouth dropped open slightly. "You went through the Coast Guard Safety Course?" he asked. "Why and how did you manage to do that?"

Callaway lowered his head and was silent for a few seconds before answering. "My partner George Hidalgo and I went through the course," he said, his voice cracking a bit. Thinking about his late partner in the Customs Service, he tried hard to suppress the tears that were welling up in his eyes. "We took the course because it gave us a reason to stop freighters that were smuggling into South Florida," he continued.

He turned and looked at Eldridge and continued, "That's one of the reasons that George and I had the best capture record out of all the boats working in Florida. Ya gotta be innovative to win."

As Callaway continued with the story of his previous contacts with Frankovich, Eldridge seemed to grow a little more curious about what was going on. He agreed to be Callaway's chauffeur and bodyguard for the inspection that was to take place the following day.

Eldridge picked Callaway up at 7 a.m. the next morning. When Callaway got into the old government Chevrolet, he was a bit surprised to see Eldridge wearing fatigues, along with an old canvas duty belt and holster containing an M-9 Beretta pistol. Callaway's eyes went from the Beretta to Eldridge's smiling face.

"Just in case, Mike," Eldridge said. "Just in case. And these might prove handy, too," he added, pointing to a pair of binoculars nestled in the seat behind him. Their first order of business was to get some breakfast and go over their plans for Callaway's inspection of Frankovich's ship. When they finished their steak and eggs, they drove up the peninsula, past Anchorage, until they reached the wharf in a small harbor where the *Put' Stalina* was docked next to a large cargo crane. Eldridge stopped the car some distance from the ship, and they both scanned the vessel from bow to stern.

"Big sonofabitch," Callaway muttered.

"Yeah," Eldridge responded. He pointed at an area midway between the bridge and the bow of the ship. "This tub must have been a Soviet Navy ship or a spy vessel during the Cold War," he continued. "See the raised area behind the bow that kinda looks like the roof of a house? Make sure you take a good look at what's under there. Besides that, look at all of the antennas on the roof of the control room."

Callaway smiled at Eldridge and asked, "Getting into this a little more now, David?"

Eldridge looked at Callaway and squinted. "Maybe?" he said, grinning and raising his eyebrows. He put the car in drive and cruised slowly to the ship, stopping about ten feet from the gangplank that rolled out from a closed large double-door hatch. There were two

117

crewmen standing on the gangplank outside of the hatchway. Both of them were wearing holstered pistols. One of them stepped up to the side of the hatch and punched a code into a large keyboard lock. Callaway raised the binoculars to his eyes and watched the crewman as he touched the keys. *102762,* he thought, He replaced the binoculars on the back seat and wrote the numbers down on his note pad as the hatch electronically swung inward.

As Callaway stepped out of the car, he immediately heard the voice of Acardi Frankovich from above. He looked up and saw the man two decks up waving at him with a smile.

"Welcome, my friend," Frankovich yelled. He stopped waving and smiling when he saw the driver's door of the car open and Commander Eldridge climbing out. Eldridge leaned his left side against the car, smiled, and put on his mirrored sunglasses. He turned so Frankovich could get a good look at the pistol on his side and gave him a two-fingered salute off the brim of his ball cap.

Frankovich just turned and walked away when Callaway came aboard and then came down a stairwell to greet his guest. "Welcome Callaway," he said "It's good to see you. Would you like something to drink?"

Callaway had already decided not to eat or drink anything aboard the ship for obvious reasons. "No… No thank you, Acardi," he replied. "I just had a big breakfast with Commander Eldridge and drank three cups of coffee, so I'm pretty full. We may as well get started, though. Stern first?"

Frankovich shrugged and answered, "Why not?" he replied. "Let's go." The captain and two of his crewmen lead him to the back of the ship. They climbed four stories to reach the upper rear deck. When they got there,

Callaway could see a large group of men standing by the rails staring at him. All of them were big, strong looking men. Callaway noticed how clean everything in his path looked. As they walked to the center of the vessel, he saw the ship's freefall lifeboat hanging above them. Callaway looked at the extremely large, bright orange boat. He knew that it would detach from its mounting and slide down a rail at thirty-five miles per hour before crashing into the water with the captain and the entire crew on board. That is, if they had to abandon ship.

"How many members in your crew, Acardi," Callaway asked.

"Twenty-one including me," he replied. "Almost all of them are here before you." He then said something in Russian, and the crew dispersed.

Looking back up at the boat again, Callaway remarked, "That's a hell of a big lifeboat for twenty-one crewmembers. You could have a heck of a party onboard that thing if you ever had to go into the water." Callaway turned and saw something familiar bolted to the stern rail of the ship. "Is that a skeet thrower," he asked. He walked over to the device and moved the arm that launched the clay discs.

"You like to shoot skeet, Callaway?" Frankovich sounded amazed that Callaway recognized the device.

"I like to shoot anything," Callaway replied. "Uh, I should rephrase that. I mean I like to shoot any kind of weapon. My dad and I used to go out in the woods with a thrower and bust some clays when we could afford it. He was a lifer in the United States Navy, and we didn't have a lot of money, so we had to load our own shotgun shells. I had to scrounge old broken lead wheel weights so we could melt them down to make birdshot out of them."

Frankovich laughed. "Later during the inspection, I will have to show you how we make our own shotgun shells, too. We can be at sea for long periods of time, and we run out of shells, so we make our own.

Callaway smiled and nodded. He was then led inside the ship and into the galley. "Are you hungry, Callaway?" Frankovich asked, pointing at the three large refrigerators in the kitchen. "When I asked you to inspect my ship back when we met at the restaurant you asked if I would feed you when you came for the inspection."

Callaway smiled again, shaking his head as he inspected the refrigerators and freezers, along with the cleanliness of the kitchen. "No, Captain, I told you Eldridge and I went to breakfast before we came here." he said. "I'm really stuffed."

Frankovich narrowed his eyes after hearing Eldridge's name. "Ah yes, your friend from the imperialist United States Navy," he said. "What does he think he's doing showing up here armed with a pistol? Does he think he could fight my crew if something went wrong for you aboard my ship?"

Callaway was writing on his pad while he responded. "Nope," he answered absently. "No need to storm the ship. I left him my cell phone. If anything went wrong, he would just call the "Imperialist" United States Coast guard, and you would have a swarm of orange and white "41 boats" parked around your ship with .50 caliber Browning machine guns aimed at you." This seemed to calm Frankovich down and get him back to business. *For some reason*, Callaway thought, *he seems afraid that I'll walk off his ship without completing the inspection.*

"Yes... Well, why don't we move along?" Frankovich suggested. "If you are finished here, I'll show you the ship's living quarters," he said, gesturing towards the door to a hallway. They climbed up another flight of stairs and walked along the deck to the sleeping quarters. Most of the crew cabins were pretty small, containing two, two-person bunk beds with no porthole to see outside. There was a communal bathroom, with a couple of showers farther down the hallway. Callaway looked them over and then they proceeded to the captain's quarters.

Frankovich's room was on the other side of the hallway. Callaway walked into a spacious room with two portholes to the outside world. "Nice place you got here, Captain," Callaway said, inspecting the rest of the cabin. He stopped short when he saw a tall glass cabinet containing five semi-automatic shotguns and one old military-type bolt-action rifle with a small telescopic sight. The shotguns were long-barreled Browning Auto 5's that looked older than dirt. Callaway looked the shotguns over. "Are these antiques what you shoot skeet with?" he asked.

Smiling, Frankovich answered. "They may be old, but they still do their job. You know the first semi-automatic shotguns like these were made almost a hundred years ago."

Sticking it to Frankovich again, he answered, "I get that, since these look like ol' John Browning laid hands on them himself back then," he said shaking his head.

Again, Frankovich kept his cool, although Callaway could see a red blush of anger growing on the man's face. Callaway turned to look at the guns again. "And what's this one?" he asked pointing at the long-barreled military rifle.

Frankovich stood up straighter with a proud smile. "That is an M-1891 Mosin-Nagant sniper rifle, complete with a genuine Soviet-made PU scope sight," he replied. "They were used by Soviet snipers during the Great Patriotic War. The conflict that you Americans call World War Two. Our snipers killed many, many Germans. Mostly officers."

Callaway nodded slowly. "So, let me guess," he said. "Your father was a Soviet sniper and he killed lots of Nazi officers, right?"

Giving Callaway a smug look, Frankovich replied, "No, it was my mother who was the sniper. My father was a Soviet army officer. My mother was what your army would call a Private First Class, and she became a sniper. She made 21 confirmed kills. It is well known that the female Soviet snipers killed many more Germans than the males did." In an obvious attempt to put Callaway in his place, Frankovich asked him, "So, what was your mother doing during the war, was she a good little American housewife waiting for your father to come home when it was over?

Callaway's eyes were still fixated on the rifle. "Um… Actually, in 1942 she was sixteen. She lied about her age, and she went to work in a Curtis-Wright aircraft factory in New Jersey, working seven days a week, welding propellers together for the P-40 fighter planes that my country gave to your country under Lend Lease." He could see Frankovich's frown reflected in the glass of the gun cabinet. *Time to change the topic*, he thought, shifting his eyes to the sliding-door closet to the right. He noticed sunshine from the porthole pouring through the slightly open door. The light shining through the portholes acted like a flashlight glinting off something that caught his eye. "Do you have any other firearms onboard the ship?" he asked, casually.

Frankovich hesitated for a couple of seconds, before replying, "No... Other than a couple of old Makarov pistols in my safe. We keep them for protection at sea and at the dock, as you've seen, but no other guns," he replied.

Callaway had cause to not believe him, since he could see in the closet what looked like the sealed metal cans that Easter hams came in, only these cans were painted dark olive-drab green, and though he couldn't translate the Cyrillic writing on them, he could make out the yellow numbers "7.62 X 39 mm." He could count ten of what he knew were rectangular 640-round cans stacked together in the small area of the closet that he could see. "Okay," Callaway said. "Let's see how the ship looks below deck."

They moved forward so Callaway could check out the cargo holds deep in the hull of the ship. The rear cargo hold was an unimpressive place. They walked forward through a passageway to the vast forward cargo hold containing a machine shop. It also contained what looked like a repair facility for the machines and vehicles that Frankovich and his crew bought in American and Canadian ports to sell in Russia. There were four long work benches with a tall standing toolbox behind each of them. Callaway could smell something very acrid burning somewhere nearby. He looked at the last bench and saw a small flame burning under a large, deep iron pan. He walked over and around the unoccupied bench with Frankovich and a couple of crewmen behind him.

He noted that the pan contained what looked like gray goo boiling in it. About the time that Callaway saw the flame, he heard a toilet flush down another nearby hallway. The door to what was obviously a bathroom opened, and a very thin man with glasses and a beard exited. Staring at all the men staring back at him, he stopped in his tracks gritting his teeth.

Callaway thought something wasn't right. *He doesn't look like someone who would be part of this crew. All the other crewmen look like former Spestnaz Soviet Special Forces soldiers, and this guy looks like a totally emaciated geek,* he thought. Frankovich let out a deep sigh as Callaway pointed at the fire in the hold.

"This is a problem, Acardi," he said. "You've got an unattended gas burner cooking God knows what within five feet of an acetylene torch tank. This doesn't seem the kind of mistake a member of your crew would make," he continued, gesturing toward the scrawny man. Callaway hoped to elicit a response as to the identity of this man.

Frankovich just shrugged, not saying a word.

Callaway continued. "And what is this gray crap in the gigantic frying pan?"

Stumbling for words, Frankovich started with, "Uh… Well, this is where we make our shotgun shells," he said, visibly starting to sweat. "You, see," he said, pointing at the frying pan that looked like it could easily hold two gallons of molten lead. "We boil down the lead, and then pour it through a steel strainer that lets it drip into a vat of ice water. The tiny drops turn into shot to refill the cartridges." He turned and appeared to repeat it in Russian to his crewmen.

Callaway could see the men look at each other. One of them looked at Callaway and put his arms in front of him like he was holding a shotgun. "Da… Da, boom boom!" he said smiling, like he was trying to get his point across. Frankovich smiled and looked at Callaway for a couple of seconds while shaking his head. Then the smile went away as he turned and gave an evil look to the scrawny man in the hallway. He went into a tirade in Russian, calling him several things that Callaway didn't understand, along with his usual favorite, *sukin sin,* just for good measure. Callaway could see that the man was scared as he shut off the flame. He removed the handle from the on/off valve and walked to the bench, shaking as he opened the top drawer. Callaway looked down into the drawer and could see several handles for turning different machinery in the hold on and off, but then he saw something else just for a moment before the scrawny man slammed the drawer shut.

What he saw was a large sheet of paper with a diagram of the hold they were in, and what looked like a long narrow rectangular box on the floor in the middle. There was a dashed line coming out of the box and out of the open hatch at the top of the hold, stopping above the ship. There were orange markings on the floor of the hold in the diagram. Callaway looked over at that area of the floor indicated by the diagram's markings and saw almost washed-out orange chalk marks. He made a quick diagram of the marks he saw on the floor. Looking down past the paper, he could see about fifty large ingots of what appeared to be lead under the workbench.

Walking toward the other side of the machine shop, Callaway couldn't help but notice that there were even more than ingots under the next workbench. When he got to the other side, he saw a small engine hanging on the chains of a four-wheeled, moveable engine hoist. The tractor from which the engine came was parked behind it.

Looking at the engine and then at Francovich, Callaway asked "Broken?"

"No," Frankovich responded. "Just rebuilt. My men are excellent mechanics."

Callaway looked behind the tractor at a square sheet-steel box that was about twenty feet wide and sixty feet long sitting on a movable stand. Since the partially completed box was open, he could see that it had double walls. Right next to it was another, completed, box.

Frankovich seemed very prepared and eager to explain this one. "That is a refrigeration box, that is why it is double walled," he said quickly, as if reading from a script.

Callaway became more suspicious when he saw what looked like fresh metal drippings on the frame of the stand. He turned around and leaned against the frame that was holding the box a few feet from the deck. "So, you're getting into the refrigerator business?" he asked, scratching one of the greyish drops on the frame with his fingernail. The sludge was soft compared to other metals. *Gotta be lead*, he thought.

"Yes" Frankovich continued. "There is great demand for refrigerators in Siberia."

On the other side of the hold, Callaway saw what appeared to be rock boring and mining equipment. The machinery looked kind of old and appeared to be recently used. "So, what's the deal with these?" Callaway asked. "They don't look too presentable if you're planning to sell them."

Sounding perturbed, Frankovich answered, "We bought the machines from a company working out on the Island of Korovin, in the Aleutian Islands. We are preparing to ship them north when the weather is a little warmer to sell them to an oil company up near the Brooks Range."

Callaway smiled at Frankovich. The last stop in the inspection would be the engine room. Callaway followed

Frankovich and some of his crewmen down stairwells into the bowels of the old ship. They came to the room where the actual engine was, and Callaway met Frankovich's chief engineer, the man brought to the hospital as Callaway was leaving after his near-death when he first met Acardi Frankovich.

"This is Igor," Frankovich said. "You may remember him from the situation at the hospital." Callaway could see the nasty scars on the man's face from burns he'd suffered that day. "Nice to see you again," Callaway said, staring at the man's face. The scars were a very bright reddish color, even after all the time that had passed. Callaway inspected the engines and fuel system, even going so far as to draw out a sample of fuel oil. He then checked the exhaust system to make sure that the smoke from the oil-powered furnace was going where it was supposed to. From there, he went up to the bow's top deck to check the anchoring system. Having inspected pretty much everything aboard that he could, Callaway concluded, "Well Acardi, I've checked your ship from stern to bow, and with a couple of small hiccups I can give the old girl a clean bill of health." That brought a smile to the captain's face. "I'll write up my report and send it over to you in about a week."

Frankovich appeared happy to hear the news. "Thank you so much, Michael."

Callaway walked down a couple of flights of stairs to the gangplank and left the ship. He walked to where Commander Eldridge was leaning against his car with his arms crossed, waiting. Eldridge smiled up at Frankovich again, looking at him through mirrored glasses. When Callaway got close, he looked at Eldridge, and shook his head, trying not to laugh.

"What are you doing David, trying to start a war?" he asked smiling, as he rounded the front passenger side of the car.

Eldridge kept staring at the Russian. "Anything that will piss that man off I will do," he replied. He again gave Frankovich another two-fingered salute and got into the car. "Well?" he asked, starting the car. "What did you find?" He drove toward the harbor's exit gate.

"I'll tell you what, I would kill for a cup of coffee, and some food," Callaway replied. "Let's go get some chow, and I'll let you know what I saw.

Eldridge looked at Callaway and instantly pulled off the road next to a beat-up corrugated metal building, like so many that Callaway had seen in Alaska. Callaway was surprised that they were stopping only one block from the harbor where the *Put' Stalina* was berthed. The car rolled to a stop in front of the building, and Callaway saw a sign reading "Diner."

"I'm guessing you knew this was here?" Callaway asked sarcastically.

Eldridge stopped the car, turned off the engine, and was stepping out of the vehicle at the same time. "Yep, and I'm hungry, too, Mike," was all he said. They went inside and sat at one of five small tables. The waitress, who looked like she was in her mid-seventies, walked over with two large cups of coffee and placed them on the table. She looked at Eldridge. "I never met a Navy man who didn't need coffee to survive" she said, pausing to turn and look at Callaway, who was already drinking the brew black, "And the same goes for cops, too."

The men looked at each other and laughed. "You got us down, Ma'am," Callaway said. They ordered their food, and Callaway got out his notepad and thumbed through the pages. "The biggest concerns I have with Frankovich, and his band of *Spetsnaz* retirees is what I found in the forward hold," he said. "First of all, he has a guy melting a whole lot of lead. He told me that they melt it to make shot to reload shotgun shells so they can shoot skeet when they are offshore and have nothing to do. They must do a hell of a lot of shooting, right?"

Eldridge closed his eyes and cocked his head for a second. "I don't know, Mike," he replied. When I was captain of a destroyer and we had to make the trans-Atlantic crossing, I told my armorer to bring out a couple of M-16's occasionally so every member of my crew could get in a little trigger time. We took an old sheet and tied the four corners to make it into a sea anchor. We dragged it behind the ship just below the waterline so you could just barely see it, and I had everyone shoot from the stern. It improved their gunnery and prepared them for the possibility of being boarded by an enemy. They also considered it to be a fun thing to do when you're bored from crossing the ocean. They got a kick out of it.

Look Mike, I don't like Frankovich one damn bit, and I'm not trying to defend him in any way, but... maybe that's why he's got them shooting clay birds off the stern of his ship. You know, there are still pirates out and about in different parts of the world, and maybe he's worried about something happening up here?"

Feeling as if his concerns were being brushed aside, Callaway gave his friend a stern look and asked, "So what? Now you think he's on the level?"

Now it was Eldridge on the verge of exploding. "God Dammit, Mike! I'm just trying to keep you from going too far with one of your hunches!" he said, slamming his coffee cup down on the table.

Shaking his head, Callaway insisted, "Something's going on, David! And my hunches usually, pretty much, all turn out to be right. Frankovich and his men are up to something near Fairbanks, and his ship is part of it, along with the strange man he keeps meeting up with."

The old waitress interrupted the two arguing friends. "Are you two fighting about those Russian guys from that big freighter docked down the road?" she asked.

Callaway and Eldridge looked at each other and then at the waitress. "Yes ma'am," Callaway said. "Actually, we were talking about them. Why do you ask?"

She smiled at them both. "Because they come in here once in a while and argue a hell of a lot more, and a hell of a lot louder than you two do," she replied. They go at it in Russian, and they get **really** loud."

Callaway looked back at Eldridge and again at the woman. "Do you remember anything that they've said in here?" he asked.

"Oh, hell no," she replied. "Most of what they say is in Russian. I don't understand Russian. The one thing I heard them say seven or eight times that sounded like English was 'Mex,' or something like that." Callaway and Eldridge looked at each other. Eldridge mouthed the word "Mex" and Callaway shrugged.

"Mex as in Mexico?" Eldridge asked the waitress. She shook her head and turned toward the kitchen. "How the hell would I know," she replied. "I told you I don't understand Russian." Callaway and Eldridge ate their lunch, not saying any more about what Callaway saw aboard the *Put' Stalina* and then Eldridge drove Callaway back to his hotel. On the way, they calmed down from their screaming session at the diner.

Still, Eldridge glared at Callaway as he was about to

exit the car. "Listen Mike, when you go down to Miami, be really careful about what you say to Todd," he said. "He's kind of sneaky in my opinion, and regardless of what you told me about your new-found friendship, don't think for a second that he wouldn't throw your ass under a bus. All I'm asking is for you to just present your concerns to him. Don't go overboard and make it sound like Frankovich is trying to destroy the world. For all we know, he might just be smuggling stuff in and out of Alaska. If that's what he's doing, then the Coast Guard and Customs Service can deal with it. Otherwise, I hope that you and the doctor have a great time and enjoy the warm weather." He extended his hand. Callaway shook it.

"I'll behave myself," he said. Then he smiled as he shut the door. He motioned for Eldridge to open the passenger door window. "Do you want me to tell Admiral Slingo that you miss her if I run into her?" he asked.

Eldridge's glowered at him just hearing the name of the former boss. She's the one who'd gotten him exiled to his current assignment in Alaska, never to be assigned to sea duty again. He gave Callaway a smile that looked somewhat like a sneer as he extended his middle finger and drove away.

Chapter 12

Three days later Callaway and Abby were standing in a terminal at Ted Stevens International Airport in Anchorage waiting to board a flight to Fort Lauderdale. Abby looked ecstatic. She had previously been to several states, most of which were in the northwest and once to Maine in the middle of winter. "So, how are the beaches in Fort Lauderdale?" she asked snuggling up to Callaway.

"The beaches are wonderful," he answered. "The sand is light brown, and at this time of the year, it's not too hot to walk on it barefoot. We can walk out of the back of our hotel and right onto the beach."

She gave him an inquisitive look. "Do you have a house down there, or do you just live on your boat?" she asked.

He had a tough time answering. "Umm… I had a condominium in Ft. Lauderdale for a while, but I sold it." It was too hard to talk about it. "Too many bad memories," he continued.

She tilted her head a little, giving him a comforting look. "You and your wife to be?" she asked. "I'm sure you had lots of memories in that condo."

Callaway nodded and looked away. He did not want her to see the sorrow on his face when he thought about the murder of his friend, DEA Special Agent in Charge

Alberto Cruz that happened in his former condominium. Suppressing his grief, he gave her a big smile while changing the subject. "Were you able to find a couple of bathing suits?"

She chuckled. "You've got to be kidding, right?" she answered. "Alaska is not known for its warm, placid waters. Bathing suits up here, especially in the winter, are more functional than they are stylish. I mean I could get a cold-water survival suit in bright prison orange at five different stores within a mile of the hospital, but a decent bikini... not so much. And you did say that you wanted tan lines to explore, right?"

Now Callaway chuckled. "Travel on," he corrected. "When we meet up with my friends tomorrow maybe his girlfriend Donna can take you to a good store so you can get something that is stylish and provide the appropriate travel map for me, of course."

"Of course," Abby replied.

They boarded a Delta 767 and found their seats in the first-class section of the aircraft. Callaway insisted that Abby sit by the window, since he wanted her to see Florida from the air when they reached the Sunshine State. They took off at eight o'clock in the morning, enjoyed a nice breakfast, considering that it was airplane food, and slept for most of the flight taking them diagonally across North America. Along the way, they saw the ground change from white in some places to brown, and then green when they reached the central part of the Florida Peninsula.

"So can you tell me a little about the people we're meeting?" Abby asked.

Callaway smiled. "I think you and Donna, that's Donna Kendall, will get along just fine," he replied.

"She's really nice." He stopped there, hoping that she would not continue the inquiry. It didn't work.

"That's it?" she asked. "Well, where do you know them from? What about him? I prefer meeting new people knowing something about them, Mike."

He looked away, clenching his teeth for a couple of seconds. He didn't want to give her any more information than he had to, for fear that she would find out how he, Todd, and Kendall conspired to kill the drug kingpin who ordered the death of his fiancée. He feared that if she knew of all the killing he'd done that she would leave him, and possibly even give that information to authorities who would gladly throw him in jail. He turned and smiled at her. "Richard Todd was the Special Agent in Charge of the Miami Office of the United States Customs Service," he said.

She nodded and replied, "So he was your boss. So, you were good friends with your boss. That's cool."

He licked his lips. "Well… not quite," he replied. "Todd was a self-serving, egotistical asshole who didn't care one bit about his agents. He put us in harm's way many times just to glorify himself so his superiors would be happy with him. He sent my partner Jorge and me out on a mission to intercept a drug boat that was bringing a big load of cocaine into Fort Lauderdale.

We found the boat and chased it, and we ended up in a gunfight with the people in the drug boat. I must have hit something important when I shot at them, because the boat… blew up. Todd was very upset because he wanted us to capture the boat so he could show off the load of coke to the press. He didn't get to do that since all the cocaine went into the ocean. He called me on the radio and told me he was going to have me fired, since, well, he had ordered me not to fire on that boat. I went home and found out I won $82 million that morning.

When I arrived to be fired, I turned it all around on him. First, I resigned. Then I gave him a copy of a file that I put together showing all the boneheaded things he had done to put his agents in jeopardy and then told him I had sent another copy to the Commissioner of the Customs Service in Washington. The Commissioner called him as I was leaving, and I found out later that Todd was busted down to writing grants for the Customs Service in Florida."

Eyes wide, she stared at him smiling. "And you are friends with this guy, now? How did that happen?" she asked. "And what's Donna's connection?"

Now Callaway had to do some serious side-step dancing to keep Abby out of the loop. "She was his secretary when he ran Customs." he answered. "She absolutely hated him. She transferred over to the DEA South Florida office just before Todd got kicked down to grant writing. As it turned out, some things occurred down there because there was a mole in the DEA office, who happened to be their Agent in Charge." Callaway swallowed hard. He was the person who found the hitman for the drug kingpin that ordered the murder of some of my friends. He even tried to kill David Eldridge, but he was shot and killed in the process."

He took a deep breath and continued. "The mole was killed, too. They needed someone to take over as Agent in Charge in a hurry, so they threw Todd in, and guess who ended up as his secretary again? Todd had experienced a real come-to-Jesus moment and was a changed man after that, and he did well, so they kept him in that capacity. And for some unknown reason, he and Donna ended up together."

Abby shook her head. "Wow," she said. "Sounds like a whole lot of killing goes on down south. I'm glad you weren't too involved in all that."

Callaway forced himself to smile. "Yeah," was all he could say. They landed in Atlanta and changed airplanes. He was glad when they crossed over the Georgia/Florida line and banked south over the east coast; it gave him a reason to change the subject. He began pointing out different cities as they got closer to their destination.

"Wow," she said more than once. "Just look at those beaches."

The plane slowed down and began its descent as it crossed into Palm Beach County. They could see boats offshore and eventually people on the beaches. They landed at Fort Lauderdale International Airport at 8:00 pm east coast time, got their bags, and headed outside to get a cab.

The minute Abby stepped outside, she tilted her head back and let out a sigh. "Ahhh, warmth," she said as she turned and hugged Callaway.

"Um, it's only in the high fifties," Callaway said. "This is cold for South Florida. I will bet there are fireplaces lit all over this town tonight because of the temperature."

Twenty minutes later, they arrived at the Marriott Harbor Beach Hotel and checked in.

"Look at this room," Abby exclaimed. "This so huge and so luxurious." She examined the spacious separate living room and bedroom.

"I'm friggin tired," he said. "Let's drop off our bags and get something to eat." She opened the sliding glass door to the terrace and went outside.

"What's up?" he asked. "What are you doing out there?"

"Just looking at the ocean and just listening to the waves rolling up on the beach, she answered. He joined her outside. "This is so beautiful, Mike," she said, hugging him.

He kissed her on the neck and told her, "It'll look a hell of a lot better in the sunlight tomorrow morning, and it will be warmer once this cold, easterly wind stops."

She giggled. "Can you survive without food for another hour… or so?" she asked.

"Oh yeah," he said, unbuttoning her blouse. "I can do that."

They went back inside, and he closed the door to keep the cold wind out. "Don't worry, like I said, it's supposed to warm up tomorrow," he said, taking off his clothes. They made love for quite a while, and then both fell asleep. Callaway's mind was totally calm when he dozed off.

The next morning, they woke up to sunny skies and temperatures heading up into the low seventies. They were able to get in a walk on the beach before the arrival of their guests, DEA Special Agent in Charge Richard Todd, and his girlfriend Donna Kendall. Callaway reserved a table so they could have lunch in a secluded place near the pool. When Todd and Kendall arrived, Callaway was still puzzled about how they'd gotten together. He stared at them as they walked across the pool deck holding hands. When they reached the table, Todd extended his hand.

"Callaway. How are you?" was all Todd said as they shook hands.

Donna gave Callaway a long hug. "Hi Mike," she

said, as she stepped to his left and gave Abby a hug, too. "I'm Donna," she said. "It's good to meet you, Abby." She backed up next to Todd and elbowed his side. "Say hello to Abby, Richard," she said.

Todd's smile seemed forced as he said hello. They all sat down and settled into their chairs. Donna spoke first. "Is this your first time in Florida, Abby?"

Abby smiled. "Yes," she answered. "Mike wanted me to see what life is like in another corner of the country. He wanted me to see what April feels like warm."

Donna laughed. "So have you been in the ocean yet?" she asked.

"No," Abby replied. "I need to find a bathing suit. Most of what we have in Alaska is made of neoprene."

Donna's eyes widened and she turned toward Callaway. "Hey Mike," she said, "give the young lady your credit card. We need to visit the swimsuit store in the hotel. This way we can find her a nice bikini and you two boys can talk business."

Callaway looked at Todd and smiled. He pulled out his wallet and handed his American Express card to Abby. The two women jumped up and headed into the hotel smiling. Todd followed them with his eyes until they reached the door to the hotel.

"So how did you meet her?" her he asked Callaway who was getting his notepad out from a satchel.

"Oh, it was no fancy meeting. She just saved my life a couple of times, literally."

Pulling paperwork out of a folder, Todd asked, "Really? What kind of trouble did she get you out of? Or did you catch some kind of sexually transmitted disease or something that she cured you of?"

Callaway shook his head. "No, not that kind of

saving my life. I mean I was dead, as in... dead, not living, twice in one night, and she brought me back both times. She's a phenomenal doctor." Callaway explained the circumstances about that wretched night but left out his visit with Carrie.

"So, how did you meet **Comrade** Frankovich?" Todd asked.

Callaway smiled, and asked, "Comrade?"

Todd handed him a manila envelope containing part of a dossier about Callaway's new "best pal" Acardi Frankovich. "Oh yeah," Todd continued. "Oh, this guy is still a total Commie. He wants nothing to do with Russia's new Free Market Economy. He wants to go back to work for the old KGB, since he was one of their star players for quite a while, and he wants Russia to go back to Communism. He caused such a fuss that he is currently and permanently banned from entering Moscow by his own government. I don't know who he hates more, the new Russian government or ours.

Callaway was reading the dossier from the beginning when something made his mouth drop wide open. "Oh... my... God," he said. "This business during the Cuban Missile Crisis. I've heard this story before. He turned the paper around so Todd could see it.

"Oh yes," Todd replied. "I guess he wanted to end the world. Where did you read about this?"

Callaway put the paper down and answered, "I didn't read it. Eldridge told me about it. It happened on October 27th, 1962," he said, pointing to the date marked on the page. Wait," he said and then fished out his notepad to show Todd the numbers he'd copied from the crewman. "10-27-62," see?" he said. "That's the code to open the gangplank door on his ship. I'll bet everything that's locked on that ship uses that code. And Eldridge was the young ensign in the screaming match from the bridge of his destroyer, with, as I now know, young Lieutenant Acardi Frankovich, on the Soviet submarine bridge. That submarine was about to fire a nuclear-tipped torpedo at the American fleet which would have started a nuclear war. Eldridge told me that Frankovich got so pissed off that the submarine Captain had to send some sailors up to the bridge, and they had to physically restrain him and drag him down the hatch from the conning tower."

Todd sat back in his chair. "Yes, that was the end of Frankovich's naval career," he said. "The captain of the submarine charged him with attempted mutiny, which was punishable by death under the Soviet Military Code. He spent the cruise back to Mother Russia in handcuffs. They put him in prison to await trial, but then someone high up in the KGB got him released. I guess the spy network liked the mindset of someone willing to end the world just to win a confrontation. He was recruited into that agency. So far, our State Department knows that they used him to kill dissidents all over Europe. If you escaped from the Soviet Union and talked bad about their system of government to the news agencies, Acardi would pay you a visit, and he would be your last visitor, ever."

Callaway shook his head. "So, why is an ex-hitter from the KGB driving an old piece of shit freighter from Russia to Alaska buying and selling drilling equipment and making refrigerators?" he asked.

"Well, when the Soviet Union fell apart," Todd began, "there was a huge shakeup in a lot of their government's agencies. The KGB became what they want the world to believe is the much more polite Federal

Securities Bureau. And yes, in the fine tradition of Stalin having Leon Trotsky killed in Mexico in 1940, they still kill dissidents both inside and outside of their country today. The difference is that they need killers with finesse since Russia wants to distance itself from the Soviet days. They wanted people who would slip you some poison and walk away, not someone who would slit your throat and watch you bleed to death just for fun. So, how did you get hooked up with this guy?"

Now Callaway sat back in his chair. "When I got out of the hospital, I was still in pretty bad shape after being in a coma for three months," he said. "When I was discharged, Abby pushed me out to the front door of the hospital in a wheelchair so David could pick me up. There was a commotion outside because Frankovich showed up with a couple of his goons, trying to get his engine room guy into the ER to get treated for some bad burns. Abby got me out of the wheelchair and put the burned guy in it. Frankovich's second in command, being the women's rights advocate that he is, told her that he wanted a male doctor, and the goon grabbed her by the wrist. I grabbed his arm and pulled him away. They were getting ready to kick my ass in a big way when Eldridge threatened Frankovich with having his ship inspected by the Coast Guard. That shut Frankovich right down.

Todd's eyes widened. "So, you think he's hiding something?" he asked.

"Well, the fact that he froze when David used the word 'inspection' was the first thing, but then there were a couple of other things that got me interested," Callaway answered. "When Abby and I flew to a small town outside of Fairbanks, I saw him at the airfield talking to some guy, and then three days later I saw him meeting in an alley in Fairbanks with the same guy, and they exchanged some items."

Todd turned his head and closed his eyes for a second. "So this is why you had me dig all this stuff up?" he asked. "It sounds like you may have stumbled upon a small-time smuggling ring, not someone who wants to end the world."

Callaway shook his head and answered, "Oh, there's more. So, I did a bow-to-stern inspection of his ship, the *Put' Stalina...*"

"Yeah, you mentioned your intention during that 5 a.m. phone call," he interrupted. He started sounding disgusted all over again. "But," he continued, "I didn't expect you to actually go through with it. So now I have to ask, what on earth do you mean you did an inspection? How would you have the knowledge or authority to inspect a ship, and how would you even know what to look for?"

Callaway grinned and answered, "Well, he showed up, on purpose at a restaurant where Abby and I were having dinner," he answered. "It was a setup. He obviously had someone following me around that afternoon. He came over to our table with a bottle of vodka and made himself at home. He obviously did the same thing I'm doing here with you, because he knew practically everything about me. In the middle of the conversation, he tells me that he knows that I'm certified to do vessel inspections, and he wanted me to inspect the *Put' Stalin...*"

Todd interrupted him again, to ask, "Well why would he do that? Why would he think that you could inspect a ship with any authority? You're not certified to inspect a vessel that large."

Callaway looked down at the table, biting his lower lip. "Uh… yes, I am," he replied. "Don't you remember? You sent Jorge Hidalgo and me to the Coast Guard Inspection Course for the training?"

Todd looked at him quizzically, and answered, "I don't recall authorizing you and Hidalgo to get that certification. And let's face it, given our relationship back then, there is no way in hell I would have authorized it."

Callaway smiled and turned his head to look at the ocean. "Well, maybe I told you to sign off on it under the heading of Pursuit Training or some other training opportunity like that."

Todd's eyes narrowed; apparently, he realized he had been duped. "And just how many other bullshit 'training opportunities' did you have me sign off on when I was your boss?"

Callaway grinned at the man and told him, "Mmmm… you probably don't want to know that. Hey, it got us a lot of really good drug busts. But back to this. When I went aboard, I figured, correctly, that he would have the ship as clean as an admiral's dinner table, and I was right. But I did see a few things that bothered me. He has some weapons on board, shotguns that he claimed are used for skeet shooting off the stern of the ship when they are at sea to keep down boredom, which could be the case, and he said they had some pistols aboard used to deal with pirates if they ran across any, but I just happened to get a look in a closet of the captain's stateroom. In it I saw a lot of cases of ammunition of the caliber for AK-47's."

Nodding, Todd told him, "Go on."

"Well, then we left his room and went to the holds in the front of the ship. There was some strange stuff going on there, for sure. There was a crew member down there that didn't match the rest of the crew. Everybody else in the crew was your typical muscled up, buzzed-haircut, former-Soviet-Special-Forces type guys. But the man I met in the hold was short, skinny and had hair that went almost down to his ass, and he was wearing glasses… and…"

"So, he has a geek on board," Todd interrupted to say. "Maybe they use him to keep the ship's computers running right."

Callaway laughed. "That ship is so old that I'm surprised that they don't have to shovel coal to keep the boilers going," he said. "If he's doing something with a computer, it has nothing to do with running the ship. The way he was acting, I actually think he wasn't supposed to be seen by anyone other than the crew."

Looking confused, Todd asked, "So, what was he doing down in the hold?"

Shaking his head, Callaway answered, "Well, the first time I saw him he had just come out of the head. Then he caught hell for leaving a propane burner going, unattended. He was melting lead. A whole lot of lead. When I asked what all the melted lead was for, Frankovich said it was to make shot so they could reload shotgun shells for skeet shooting."

Smiling, Todd answered, "Well maybe that's what he was doing. Maybe he's the ship's shotgun shell reloader."

"No… I don't think so," Callaway replied. "I saw some gigantic sheet-steel crate frames they'd been building. They said it was for transporting frozen food on their voyages to Siberia."

Todd grinned and said, "I thought all food in Siberia is frozen, along with everything else."

Callaway smiled and answered, "But that's not all. The boxes were double walled, which I know uses trapped air as insulation, but I found smudges of some gray substance that I'll bet is lead. Is lead a good heat insulator, too?" he asked as he continued to consult his notes.

"Well, yes," Todd answered. "I know I'm older than you but growing up we used to have an old Frigidaire that had a lead liner in between the sheet steel walls of the box. That was before it was discovered that lead is toxic. I mean, that fridge kept everything very cold." He chuckled. "We used to joke that the first member of the family who got in the refrigerator would survive a nuclear attack if the Russians launched on us, because radiation cannot penetrate..." He stopped and narrowed his eyes before ending with the word, "lead."

Callaway looked up from his reading. "You don't think he's messing around with something radioactive, do you?" Callaway asked. "I mean the guy seems to have a hard on for the United States, but... I mean how would he get his hands on any radioactive material? Unless he's bringing it in from Russia, I guess. There's no way he could get a hold of a nuclear bomb from Russia. Is there?"

Todd closed his eyes and shook his head. "Highly doubtful," he replied.

"Maybe someone from the Kremlin who thinks like Frankovich and didn't want to leave his Communist ways?" Callaway replied.

"Nope," Todd answered. "Highly doubtful. Extremely highly doubtful for that matter. The Kremlin locked all their nuclear weapons down with a vengeance well before the changeover to a market economy. They needed us to be friends with them for the time being to get through the change." Todd sat back in his chair and sighed. "He's probably making the coolers to haul reindeer meat to the Siberians. Did you see anything else aboard the ship that was interesting?"

Callaway looked at the floor, clenching his jaw for a couple of seconds as he remembered Abby's famous recipe for reindeer before he answered. "Uh, yeah." he said. "While Frankovich was chewing out the geek guy for leaving that propane burner burning, I was standing by the work bench where the lead was being melted. After Frankovich was done yelling at him in Russian, the guy shut off the propane valve, and removed the lever from the shut off valve. He opened the top drawer of the workbench to secure the lever, and I couldn't help but notice this." He handed Todd the drawing he'd made of the diagram he saw in the drawer.

Looking it over, Todd gave Callaway a puzzled look. "What… exactly am I supposed to be seeing here, Callaway?" he asked.

Callaway put his finger on the paper and began pointing things out. "These four spots on the deck were barely still there when I saw the original diagram," he said. "I can't help but wonder what this line of dash marks is doing. Is it something coming into the hold, or going out?"

Todd stared at it for a few seconds. "It could be a diagram of a conveyor belt that they use to load and unload wheat, for all we know," he said. "Have you got anything else?"

Callaway began shaking his head, but then stopped. "There was one other thing," he said. "After I finished the inspection, Eldridge and I went to a little breakfast place by the harbor where the ship was moored. We got into a screaming match about what I saw. The old lady waiting on us asked us if we were talking about the crew of that Russian ship, because they came in there to eat a lot. She said they always talked in Russian, but the one word they kept bringing up was 'Mex.'

Todd's mouth opened a little. "I'm guessing neither you, nor Eldridge know what Mex might mean"? he asked.

Callaway shook his head. Todd glared at him for a moment. "Well neither do I," he finally said. I'll run it through the computer to see if it means anything sinister. Who knows, maybe they run digging equipment down to the Pacific side of Mexico.

Callaway looked up and saw Abby and Donna walking back to their table. He couldn't take his eyes off Abby when he saw the incredibly tiny red and green bikini she was wearing. He put Todd's papers back into their manila envelope and gazed at his lovely lady.

"Well, what do you think, Mike?" Donna Kendall asked.

"Wow," was all he could say.

"This should take care of your tan line requirements," Donna said with a big grin.

Callaway looked down at the table, slightly embarrassed. *Damn,* he thought, *I forgot that women tell each other everything.* And then he shook his head and smiled. "Well, I guess it's time to check the temperature of the Atlantic Ocean," he said, as he stood up and gave Abby a kiss. "You two are welcome to join us," he told Todd and Donna.

Giving him a blank look, Todd answered, "No, I think we're going to head back home. I'll let you know if I find anything new about your Russian friend. I've got work to do at the house.

Donna, standing a couple of steps behind Todd rolled her eyes and silently mouthed, "Bullshit." Todd turned around and took Abby's hand. "It was a pleasure meeting you, Abby," he said. "Callaway," he continued, staring at his old nemesis, and then he and Donna walked toward the hotel.

Abby told Callaway, "She's very nice. But I can't figure him out at all. She is very warm and friendly, and he's so damn cold. I guess opposites do attract."

Callaway laughed. "Yeah, he's kind of a strange one," he replied. "So, you want to see what a real ocean feels like," he asked, holding his hand out. She nodded. "Let me go back to the room, and put my paperwork away first," he said, leaving her by the table.

He returned, and as they approached the shore, he suddenly stopped and just stood there looking at the water. He was suddenly a little afraid of diving in.

Abby grabbed his hand, asking, "What's the matter, you afraid of swimming into an iceberg here?"

He raised his head and looked at the sun. "No, my one-time swimming in ice water was enough for me," he answered quietly. "You seem to have forgotten that I literally died a couple of times after I fell off my boat."

"Oh yeah," she said, squeezing his hand. "Sorry."

He looked at her as they walked across the warm sand of the beach. "It was worth it," he said. "Even though the State of Alaska only has a population twice the size of Fort Lauderdale, I wouldn't have met you unless I fell off the boat and you came to my rescue." He kissed her and gave her a long hug.

"Ocean, Callaway. Concentrate," she said softly. "If you don't get in the water soon, we'll end up back in the room, and in bed. Focus on the beautiful water."

He took a deep breath and let it out. "You're killing me, you know," he said as he broke loose and ran for the water. "Come on, slow poke," he said as he took off.

She gave him a dirty look and took off after him. He ran into the small waves and dove into the water. Abby splashed into the water and stopped when she was waist deep.

"Oh my God!" she yelled.

Callaway shouted, "Are you okay? He half-ran, half-swam toward her."

Seeing the concerned look on his face, she smiled and glided her arms smoothly through the water. "This is amazing," she answered. "It's so warm. What did you think that I hurt myself?"

Callaway smiled. "I thought maybe you stepped on something," he answered.

She looked down at the water toward the sandy bottom. "Why? Is there something down there I should be worried about?" she asked.

He answered, trying to keep from alarming her. "The first rule a child born in Florida learns when he goes to the ocean is to shuffle his feet in the sand underwater so you scare away any sting rays that might have buried themselves on the bottom."

Her eyes widening, she answered, "Callaway, if you're screwing with me now, you won't be screwing me anytime soon," she said.

"No... No, it's the truth," he replied. "It's not something that occurs often, but it can happen. It's kinda like a courtesy for the sting rays so they don't get stepped on and you don't get stung. I mean it's not like they want to sting the unfortunate human that steps on them by accident or anything. They bury themselves to hide from the sharks." When he saw her smile turn into a frown, he realized that he shouldn't have said that. She turned her head rapidly peering through the water around her.

"Don't worry about the sharks," he said calmly, trying to settle her down. They seldom come in close to the beaches, and if they do it's usually at night." He saw her relax a little, knowing he had just told her a lie almost as big as when he said her cooking was great. "Hey, come here," he said, pulling her towards him. "Just take a deep breath and relax. I mean look around. There have been hundreds of Yankee tourists in this water since sunup. Anything living underwater would have left the area a long time ago." He hugged her for a long time, turning both slowly around through the water.

She calmed down and closed her eyes. "Now I know why you like living here," she said. "It never gets too cold, and you never have snow."

He tilted his head to one side. "Well actually," he said. "We did have snow back in 1986. I mean it was just little flakes coming down, and it didn't stick, but it was genuine snow. We were coming in on the boat after a patrol at daybreak, and I saw little white spots on my dark blue windbreaker. I thought I had dandruff for a minute, but when I brushed it off, it was cold and wet. So yeah, it can happen. Hey. Do you like Cajun food?

She nodded as he continued to pull her around. "I know a place in town that has great Jambalaya and a pretty good band."

She gave him a dreamy look. "That sounds great," she replied. "I'd really like to try Cuban food, too, if we can. I'd like to get as much South Florida in as I can, and all that garlic and onions sounds amazing. Maybe I can pick up some new recipes to take back home."

He kissed her on the neck, and asked, "Do you want the Cuban food as an early lunch or a late lunch?"

"Why, what's in between?" she asked, coyly.

He gave her a look.

"Oh," she said. "So, before or after we go to the room?"

He nodded.

"Okay, after," she said. "The sex wouldn't be much fun after we eat all that spicy stuff, anyway."

Chapter 13

While Abby had to come all the way to Fort Lauderdale to find a bathing suit that was made in the second half of the twentieth century, she did own some stylish clothes. Callaway was amazed when she came out of the bathroom at their hotel wearing a short, sleeveless, red dress with high heels, and, for the first time with Callaway, she was wearing makeup. Callaway looked her up and down and whistled. "Wow," he said. Did you buy that dress for this trip?"

She whirled around. "No," she replied. "I do have some nice clothes for going to clubs back home."

"Clubs… really?" Callaway asked. "Where do you have clubs up there?"

Shaking her head, she answered, "We have clubs in Alaska, silly man. They're in the cities, like Anchorage and Fairbanks."

He laughed, and asked, "So, I'm guessing that you get to wear that dress, and the heels, what, a week or two in July?"

She smiled and narrowed her eyes. "Very funny, smartass," she replied. "We are a hardy people, ya know. We don't wear an overcoat to go out when it's sixty-nine degrees outside, like you do here. Do you have any more wise remarks, or are we going to dinner?"

Callaway smiled and then hugged her. "You know, if we didn't just finish screwing our brains out, I would peel that dress right off you," he said

"Well, you could try," she answered, smiling, "but I would punch you because I'm really hungry."

He took her hand and led her out into the hallway. As they approached a corner in the hallway, Callaway said, "Really, food before sex with me. I'm shattered." Just then two elderly ladies rounded the corner and walked by them. When they were about ten feet past Callaway and Abby, they heard one of them say. "I hope the food is good."

Their cab pulled up in front of the Cajun restaurant. Callaway and Abby walked into the place, and Abby sniffed the air. "Oh my God that smells good," she said, squeezing Callaway's arm.

"Have you ever had Cajun food, before?" he asked her as they stood in line for the maître d'.

She looked around the place. "Yes, but no," she answered. "I mean we have a couple of places that serve what are supposed to be real Cajun meals, but from what I'm smelling here, they're not even close. They made their way to the lectern, and when the maître d' looked up, he smiled and stuck out his hand.

"Mr. Callaway! It's so good to see you," he said as they shook hands. "It's good to see you, too, Lucas," he replied. "I'm glad you made a reservation, bon ami," the maître d' said. "Cause we are packed tonight. C'mon, I got you a great table near the stage." Lucas seated them and their waiter took their drink orders.

Looking confused, Abby asked, "When did you make the reservation for this place?"

Callaway took a sip of his Crown Royal. "When we

got back from the camping trip," he answered. "I love the food and the jazz music here. I wanted you to enjoy the way I used to live down here."

She looked at the menu and coughed slightly. "Based on the prices, she said, "I'm guessing that you started coming here after you won all that Lotto money."

"No, actually," he replied. "I brought my partner Jorge Hidalgo here late one night for his fortieth birthday. It was in September when there weren't a lot of tourists in town. We docked our patrol boat behind the buildings across the street and walked over. There were only five or six people here. And we ended up having a very interesting night. We wore jackets to cover our U.S. Customs shirts. We had a great meal and were enjoying the music, when two idiots walked in and tried to rob the place.

We were at a table by the maître d' station, and Lucas, who happens to be the owner, had a gun to his head. The other scumbag went into the kitchen to take the chef's wallet. The guy with the gun to Lucas' head yelled at a patron who started crying, and he pointed the gun in the air, yelling at her to shut up. I was close enough to kick the bad guy in the side of the knee, hard enough to hear it go crack, and then I took him down. Jorge drew his weapon and ran into the kitchen, where he arrested the other bad guy.

From then on, Lucas became our best friend. He fed Jorge and me for free whenever we came in here. It was great that he did that, but we got to the point where we stopped coming here because we were embarrassed about not paying. I mean it's not like getting a free cup of coffee at McDonalds. This place ain't cheap.

When I won the Lotto money, I brought in a copy of the newspaper article from Tallahassee about me winning and made him read it. He congratulated me, but still wanted to give me free food. I had to threaten him with never coming back here to get him to stop."

Abby smiled at him, and then looked behind him. "I see the band members are here," she said.

"Well let's see who we have tonight," he replied. He looked over the three men and one woman and turned back to Abby. "Oh, you're gonna love these people," he continued. "She's a great singer, and the saxophone guy really tears it up."

Abby watched them tune up. The band started playing a couple of New Orleans jazz songs just as their food arrived.

"You're right about this group," Abby said. "But the sax guy is just kind of loafing."

Callaway replied. "Just wait a little bit." The sax man suddenly put his instrument down in the middle of a long instrumental and walked by their table. As he reached them, he looked down at Callaway and smiled. Callaway gave him a slight wave, and watched the man walk into the men's room. Two minutes later he walked past them again and back to the stage.

Callaway touched Abby's shoulder. "Wait for it," was all he said.

She watched the man pick up the sax, and right on cue, he started playing a solo as if was on fire. He was sweating profusely as he ripped through the music like a rocket launching from Cape Canaveral.

"Holy shit!" Abby said, glancing back at Callaway. He just smiled. When the sax player finished the solo, everyone in the restaurant stood and applauded and then Abby sat back down, staring at Callaway.

"What got into him?" she asked.

Callaway looked down at the table and replied, "A couple of lines of cocaine."

Her mouth dropped open. "Seriously?!" she asked. "How do you know that?"

He leaned forward and motioned for her to do the same. "I always questioned his musical "transformation," too," he answered. Then one night when Jorge and I were here eating free food, I got up to use the bathroom right after he went in. I walked in and heard him snorting it up in one of the stalls. He came out, saw me, and just froze. He knew I was a federal agent because he was here the night Jorge and I broke up the robbery."

"So, did you arrest him?" she asked.

Callaway chuckled and answered, "No. After all, he'd already snorted up all the evidence. I smiled and said, 'Have a great set,' then I winked at him and went over to the urinal. He walked out and played like a son-of-a-bitch."

Abby turned and looked at the sax man, who then looked at Callaway. Callaway held his index finger in front of his chest, and waved it side to side, like a mother scolding her child. The sax man lowered his head and stuck out his lower lip like he was ashamed and then laughed.

Abby looked at Callaway for a couple of seconds. "Damn, Callaway, you do have a conscience," she said.

They returned to the hotel too tired to do anything but sleep. Callaway opened the sliding glass doors and took an extra blanket from the closet. "I want you to experience the full-on Florida wave effect since it's a little warmer tonight," he said. He spread the blanket over the bed. Abby stripped off her clothes and got under the covers. He did the same, and they held each other listening to the soothing sound of the waves. She was asleep instantly, and he wasn't far behind.

He was resting peacefully, but then something happened. The sound of the waves triggered something. He was suddenly dreaming that he was looking at the waves washing serenely ashore in the darkness when he suddenly saw Carrie's body lying on the sand. He could see her lifeless eyes staring at him. His breathing accelerated to the point where he couldn't take another breath. "Carrie, no!" he screamed, sitting up straight in the bed.

Startled by his cry, Abby woke and grabbed him, trying to calm him down. He was soaked with sweat. "Mike!" She yelled, turning on the light next to the bed and trying to make him understand where he was and who he was with. He blinked several times and then stared at Abby. His breathing began to calm down.

Hugging him, she put two fingers on the side of his throat to check his pulse. "Calm down, Mike," she said softly. "Your heart is going a mile a minute. Shhh. It's me, Abby. Relax, lover."

Callaway began to settle down and then hugged her tight and began to cry. "I... I'm sorry," he whispered. He felt both embarrassed and upset.

She got up from the bed and walked to the mini-bar and took out a small bottle of Jack Daniels, twisting the top off and walking back to the bed. "Drink this," she said.

He looked up at her and said, "I'm okay."

She shook her head. "Doctor's orders, Callaway," she said, holding the bottle out to him. "Every last drop." He downed the little bottle in two gulps. His breathing was getting down to normal. The bourbon hit the mark and he lay back down.

"You want to talk about this?" she asked. "I'm guessing that your late fiancée's name was Carrie?"

He wanted to say no, but he was already falling in love with this woman, and he wanted to tell her about his past. Still, he was afraid she would leave running like hell if he did. "Yes, that was her name," he answered.

Abby stroked her fingers through his wet hair. "I love you Michael Callaway, I hope you realize that, and I hope you feel the same way, but I'm going to need to know what's going on in your little brain before our relationship goes any further," she said. She spoke in the same stern tone that she would use to tell a lung cancer patient to quit smoking.

"Okay," he said. "Let me start by telling you that I am madly in love with you," he stopped to take a deep breath. "Although this isn't quite the way that I wanted to tell you that."

Abby smiled. "Go on," she said.

"I told you that Carrie was a DEA agent, and that she was murdered," he said. Abby nodded. He started breathing heavy again. "They found her, washed up on the shore in Miami Beach with the waves splashing over her." He began to shake. "She had been drowned, I told you that before. But what I didn't tell you... was her throat was cut... and they pulled her tongue out through the wound."

Abby stared at him, and then jumped up and walked back to the mini bar. She grabbed two more bottles of Jack and a bottle of vodka, too. She stood by the bed and opened one of the Jacks and handed it to Callaway and then she opened the vodka and drank that one herself. "Jesus Christ," she said. Her voice was barely audible.

Callaway gulped down one of the bottles of Jack and fell back against the headboard, feeling like a devil had just been exorcised from his body. "I guess the sound of the waves triggered the dream," he said.

Abby looked deep into his eyes. "Okay, I've got to know this," she said. You told me that the guy who ordered her murder was killed." There was a long pause, and Callaway was sweating again because he knew what the next question would be. "Did you kill him?" she asked.

He looked at her and then looked down. "Yes," was all he could say.

Abby took a deep breath and let it out slowly. "I mean, was it up close and personal and it was him or you?" she asked.

Callaway clenched his teeth for a couple of seconds. "Uh, no," he replied. Actually, he was about 500 yards away."

Now she was breathing heavy. "So, how did all of this happen?" she asked. "I want to know what went on from when Carrie died to when you set out for Alaska."

Callaway took a deep breath and began spewing out most of the details of what went on between him and the Drakes, both father and son. He also told her about the murders of his friends, Jorge Hidalgo, and Al Cruz.

"So did you kill the man that murdered your friends, too?" she asked.

He closed his eyes and nodded without saying a word. "I'm sorry I didn't tell you about this," he said, leaving out all the others he killed in the process. "But in all three cases, I had to do what I did."

She stood there, looking very uncomfortable. "Does anyone else know about this," she asked.

He sighed and looked at her. "Yes, there are a couple of people," he answered.

"I'm not going to ask who, because I don't think you would tell me," she said. "Were all of the killings, what's the word I'm looking for, legal, or sanctioned, or are you hiding them."

"You mean justified?" he asked. "No, they're not. And yes, I'm hiding them," he answered. "Because if this information ever got to the wrong people, I would most likely end up in prison for a long time, and some people I know would end up in jail, too, for some things I did wrong."

She started looking around at the glass doors and then to the hallway door.

He started to panic because he thought she was looking for an exit. "Please don't leave me, Abby," he said.

She looked down, avoiding eye contact. "I've got a lot to think about, Callaway," she said. "I think I'll sleep in the living room tonight, and we can get a fresh start in the morning." She handed him the other bottle of Jack Daniels and picked up her suitcase and the blanket off the bed. She walked into the living room and shut the bedroom door, leaving him alone. He opened the bottle and drank the bourbon quickly. The mental exhaustion he was suffering from made him drop off into a deep sleep not long after his head hit the pillow.

*****

He was awakened hours later by sunrise blazing through the glass terrace doors. He rolled over on his side trying to figure out what time it was. He could see into the bathroom and out to the terrace, and Abby was nowhere to be found. *She must be sleeping*, he thought, as he slid out of bed. He put his pants on and opened the door to the living room. He was shocked to see that she wasn't there. He thought she might have gone downstairs to get some food, or maybe to the beach, when he noticed that her suitcase was gone. He went into panic mode. He grabbed his shirt and shoes and was about to put them on when he saw a note on the table He sat down on the couch and began reading.

"Mike,

I'm sorry, but I had to leave. I am too stressed to be around you right now. Honestly, I don't know if I'll ever be able to be around you again. I'm taking a cab to the airport and catching a flight north at 7 am. Please don't be upset. I promise I won't tell anyone what you told me last night. I just don't know what to think about all of it. Please don't contact me if you come back up here.

Abby."

He fell back on the couch breathing hard. "I've got to get her back," he whispered.

*****

Late that Sunday evening, Commander David Eldridge was sitting on the couch in his on-base apartment. He had finished dinner and was sipping a cold beer, waiting for the ABC Sunday movie *Midway* to start. It was one of his favorites. His relaxation was disturbed by the telephone ringing in his kitchen. *What the hell is this about,* he wondered, figuring that another bear had broken into the supposedly bear-proof dumpster behind the mess hall, as this had been getting to be a normal occurrence.

"Commander Eldridge?" He answered, "Yes," sounding disgusted. "Oh, hi Commander," a male voice said. "I'm Sergeant Post, Anchorage Police." Eldridge closed his eyes and shook his head. "Okay, Sergeant, let me guess," he responded. "Somebody from my base got caught pissing in the street in front of one of the nicer hotels again, right? Let me give you the number to Base Security and they'll send someone over to pick him or her up."

There was silence for a couple of seconds. "Uh, Sir," the Sergeant began. "I'm at the Ted Stevens Airport with a gentleman who told me to call you. He says his name is Mr. Callaway."

Eldridge took a big swig of beer. "What does he want from me?" he asked.

"Sir, he needs a ride, said the Sergeant.

Eldridge sighed. "Look Sarge, the guy's my friend, but he's got plenty of money for a cab," he said.

"Uh, Sir," the Sergeant said, sounding a little less friendly this time. "He's really drunk, and he kinda picked a fight with one of the airport security guards, and it took three of us to settle him down. I have him sitting in my office, handcuffed, and as I said, he wanted me to call you."

Eldridge heard Callaway's voice in the background. "Hi David," he slurred the words out.

"Asshole," Eldridge whispered.

"Sorry, Sir?" the Sergeant answered.

"Not you Sergeant," Eldridge said. "Him. What did his girlfriend have to say about the way he was acting?" Eldridge could hear muffled talking between the sergeant and someone else.

"What girlfriend, Commander?" he answered. "Mr. Callaway is here alone, Sir. I just checked with my officers, and he came off the plane blitzed drunk and alone. He told me he's ex law enforcement, which is the only reason he's not sitting in jail. If you won't come for him, then that's where he'll be going."

"Now I know it's serious," Eldridge muttered under his breath. "Abby's gone; why?" I'll be up there in an hour, Sergeant," he said aloud. "Take good care of him till I get there… Please."

After he hung up, Eldridge asked himself aloud, "What the fuck did you do to drive her away? I will sure as hell find out." He got there fast and parked across the access road from the airport's police and fire station. The front desk officer directed to him to the Sergeant's office. When he walked in, Sergeant Post stood up from his desk. Eldridge looked right and saw Callaway sound asleep in a chair. The Sergeant started walking toward Callaway when Eldridge cut him off.

"I got this Sarge," he said. He can be a little testy when he's drunk.

"What branch of law enforcement was Callaway involved in, Commander?" Sergeant Post asked.

Eldridge grabbed Callaway by the arm and pulled him to his feet. "He was a Customs Enforcement chase-boat driver," Eldridge replied. "And a damn good one." He half-dragged Callaway towards the door.

Callaway turned his head towards the Sergeant. "Sorry Sergeant… Thanks," he said as he and Eldridge walked to the baggage area and picked up Callaway's suitcase and his carry bag. They crossed the street and got into Eldridge's car.

Eldridge didn't say anything until they were away from the airport and on the highway south. "So, what happened, Mike?" he asked. "Where's Abby?"

Staring out the window into the darkness, Callaway

answered, "Home, I'm guessing, or camping in the middle of nowhere for all I know."

"So, what happened?" he asked, hesitantly, looking straight ahead at the empty road.

Callaway shook his head. "I told her, David," he replied. I told her almost everything. We went to sleep last night, and I had this God-awful dream where I saw Carrie washed up on shore with her throat cut. I guess I was screaming in my sleep. She woke me up, cleaned out the mini-bar and fed me bourbon until I calmed down enough to talk."

Eldridge glanced sideways at him. "and what happened after that?" he asked. "So, you got diarrhea of the mouth or something and told her everything?" Callaway tilted his head back against the headrest.

"I told her that I killed Derrick Drake and the hit man. She was not pleased. She went to sleep in the living room of our suite, and when I woke up in the morning she was gone. She snuck out and got a flight home. I tried to call her from the hotel before I left for the airport, but she didn't answer at her house. I called the hospital, and nobody's seen her there either. I've got to make this right, David. I didn't think I could ever fall in love like this again, but..."

Eldridge glanced at him again and told him, "You look like you're hurting. When did you start drinking?" he asked.

Grinning, Callaway answered, "This morning. Then at the airport, and all the way across the North American continent."

Changing the conversation, Eldridge asked, "So, did you find out anything interesting about our Russian friends from Agent in Charge Todd?"

Callaway rubbed his forehead trying to calm the earthquake tremor of a headache that was building in his brain. "Oh yeah," he replied, smiling. "You remember the story you told me about that rather tense moment you had during the Cuban Missile Crisis?"

Eldridge narrowed his eyes and asked, "What, you mean with the guy on the submarine?"

"Yeah," Callaway replied. Guess who that asshole on the conning tower of the sub calling you a son-of-a bitch was?"

Eldridge slammed on the brakes, sliding the car to a stop, straining Callaway against his seatbelt. "Are you fucking kidding me?" he yelled. "That was Frankovich?"

Callaway pushed himself back from the dashboard and slid back on to the seat. Then he smiled and said, "Yes sir; that would be him."

Eldridge got the car moving again and was quiet for a few minutes. "Mike, I know I thought you were full of crap about Frankovich doing something hinky, but given his background, I'm in on trying to figure out what he's up to."

Callaway picked his carry bag up from the floor of the car and patted it. "I've got a copy of the dossier that Todd put together," he said. "Old Acardi has killed a **lot** of Russian dissidents, and God knows who else." He shifted in his seat. "He's even persona non grata to the Russian government. They banned him from coming into Moscow. I've never heard of that happening to anyone before. Oh, and Todd has no idea what "mex" is all about, but he said he would run it through the Fed computers to see if anything comes up."

Again, it got quiet. "So… are you gonna try to find her?" Eldridge asked.

Callaway again shifted uncomfortably in his seat. "I want to, but I'm afraid I might spook her even more," he said. "I'll give it a little time so she can calm down. In the meantime, I will devote myself to seeing what Mr. Frankovich is up to."

Eldridge pulled the car into the parking lot of Callaway's hotel. "Well, just be real damned careful how you do that," Eldridge said. "I'm sure Todd's information about all the people Frankovich has killed is correct, so watch your ass."

Callaway closed his eyes and shook his head. "There's a little greasy spoon down the street that stays open all night for breakfast," he said. "You want to go and get some eggs and bacon?"

Eldridge gave him an exasperated look. "It's a little past three am, Mike," he replied. "I'd really like to go over there to watch you eat, but I have an hour ride back to the base, and I have to be at work at eight, so, thank you but no."

Callaway smiled at his friend. "Thanks, David," he replied. "Once again, you pulled my nuts out of the fire." He opened the door and got out.

"Yeah, well, don't get those nuts too deep in the meat grinder, pal," Eldridge replied sternly. "Otherwise, I might not be able to help you get them out.

Nodding, Callaway, walked through the lobby and into his room. He collapsed onto his bed and fell instantly to sleep. The next morning, Callaway woke up with what felt like a jackhammer pounding away between his ears. He managed to drag himself to the bathroom, took a shower, and then he ate four Tums to kill the burn in his stomach. He got dressed and went to the greasy spoon for some eggs and toast. He wanted to be able to look for

Abby and to start his snooping on Frankovich right after breakfast.

The first stop he made was the marina where his boat had been secured by Abby's brothers while he was in a coma. The water, while still extremely cold, had warmed up to where the waterways were mostly clear of sheet ice. He could see large chunks of ice, some a couple of stories tall, floating by, but the channel was still navigable for slow moving ships. The people who owned the marina had put the *Orinoco Flow* in the water and had her tied front first into a slip. Callaway went aboard and checked the boat from bow to stern. The marina people did a spectacular job of winter prepping both the old shrimp boat and his 17-foot *Hewes* fishing skiff that was hanging on davits across the stern. Both vessels had their fuel tanks filled to 90 percent to allow expansion. The batteries had been reinstalled after spending their winter in a shed charging.

Callaway went below deck to check the interior and make sure his guns and other equipment were where they should be. He opened a locker and grabbed a pair of binoculars and his Pentax K1000 Camera. He replaced the short distance lens with one with considerably more range. After loading a roll of film, he put the camera in a carry bag and brought both items with him to his car. He drove south to Abby's house, not to make contact, but just to see if she was home. When he saw she wasn't there, he headed for the hospital, but she wasn't there either. He knew she might be down at the reservation hospital, where they had taken him after he fell off his boat, but he felt the need to go watch the Russians instead of driving all the way down the Kenai Peninsula. He drove up to the small port where the *Put' Stalina* was docked, but the ship was gone. Since there was no one around to ask about the ship's departure, he drove out of the port and stopped at the restaurant he and Eldridge had gone to after Callaway did the inspection on the ship. He badly needed coffee. He sat down at a table and the old waitress who'd taken care of him last time brought him a cup.

"You remember me," he asked.

She looked at him and smiled. "Yep," she replied. "You were here a while back with that Navy officer, right?"

Callaway nodded. "So where are our friends from Mother Russia today?" he asked.

She placed a cup in front of him and poured his coffee. "How should I know," she answered. "They left port a couple of days ago."

Callaway took a sip of coffee. "Did they come in here and say where they were going?" he asked.

"I told you guys. I don't speak Russian," she replied, tartly.

He took another sip. "Well did you see which way the ship went?" he asked, thinking they might have left for Siberia.

Sounding a little touchy, she answered, "All I know is the ship went north."

Callaway almost spit the coffee out. "North?" he asked, confused, since the freighter was too large to go much farther north. "Where would they go north from here? Are there any other ports north of here other than Anchorage?"

She had her back to him as she wiped down another table. "The only place I can think of where they could dock that big of a ship is Point MacKenzie, up the coast," she replied.

Finishing his coffee in one gulp, Callaway put five dollars on the table headed out to his car. He pulled the road map from the car rental out of the glove compartment and started looking for Point MacKenzie. He saw where it was and was unhappy to find that it was on the **other** side of the Knik Arm, a waterway extending out of the top of Cook Inlet north of Anchorage. He looked for a bridge over the waterway but found none on the map. He headed north, driving for hours to at least get a look at what the *Put' Stalina* and her crew were doing so far up the coast. North of Anchorage, he started down road after small road to get to the south side of the waterway across from Point MacKenzie.

He used his binoculars to find the ship over the wide expanse of water and found the *Put' Stalina* docked with the bow of the ship facing him. He also saw a large semi-tractor trailer rig parked on the dock next to the ship. Callaway watched one of the large dock cranes, used for loading and unloading items from ships, lifting the trailer part of the rig. He switched to his camera and started taking pictures. He could see two men standing on the bridge of the ship, pointing at the trailer and gesturing. Callaway assumed that one of the men was Frankovich, since he could make out that the person had a beard, but the other guy appeared to be clean shaven.

He snapped pictures of the men and the nondescript trailer. The giant crane slung the trailer over the front deck of the *Put' Stalina*, and then lowered it until it disappeared into the ship. "That went into the forward hold," he said to himself. He continued taking pictures for about five minutes. He reloaded the camera and pointed it at the ship just in time to see the crane cable moving upward from the hold, where it had dropped off the trailer. It appeared to be the same trailer.

"What the hell?" he whispered. "They unloaded whatever was in that trailer pretty damn quick." The trailer was lowered down to the dock and reattached to the semi-tractor, after which the driver started the truck and headed towards the harbor's main road. Callaway snapped pictures of the truck and hoped that when he enlarged the prints, he would be able to make out the writing on the side of the tractor cab and the tag on the trailer. He watched a little longer, and then it was time to go have a talk with David about what he saw and give his friend another big thank you for driving him home the night before.

He drove for two hours until he arrived at the base. He noticed that the Military Police Officer at the gate looked really glum when he waved Callaway through. *Wow, who died?* Callaway wondered as he pulled up and parked next to Eldridge's office.

He started talking as he walked down to the Commander's office. "David, I've got some interesting shit to talk…" He shut up quickly when he got to the door and saw that Eldridge wasn't alone. Another Navy Commander was sitting across the desk from Eldridge. Neither man was smiling, and Callaway was shocked to see a bottle of Dewar's scotch and two empty glasses on the desk.

Not knowing what else to do, he said, "Oh, I'm so sorry, Commander Eldridge," trying his hardest to sound formal. "I can come back later."

Eldridge gave Callaway a somber smile. "Come in, Mike," he said, taking another glass out of an open desk drawer. "Pull up a chair." Eldridge put the glass on the desk in front of Callaway. "Mike, this is Commander Ronnie Burns. I call him 'Rowdy.'" Callaway extended his hand, and Commander Burns stood up to shake it.

"Pleasure to meet you, Mr. Callaway," Burns said.

"Please call me Mike, Commander, uh, Rowdy."

Callaway replied. They all sat down, and Eldridge filled the glasses. "Rowdy and I graduated from Annapolis together," Eldridge said, sounding a bit like he had been drinking all afternoon. "He's one of the few African American submarine commanders in the Navy. He's the skipper of the attack submarine *USS Atlanta*, currently docked at the harbor in Anchorage. He came by to say hello, and to celebrate the good news."

Callaway saw Commander Burns lower his head and close his eyes for a few seconds. "David, what's going on?" Callaway asked, almost afraid to hear the answer.

Eldridge downed the contents of his glass. "This base will shut down in a couple of days... and my career as a United States Naval officer will come to a rather unexciting end when that happens." Callaway could see the sadness in his friend's eyes. Eldridge sat back in his chair. Callaway looked at Commander Burns, who looked back and shook his head slightly.

Eldridge looked at the ceiling. "But the good news is that the Commanding Officer of the base got transferred to a new command, so I get to be the Acting CO," he said with a laugh. "At last, I get to command again. And what I will be commanding is a sinking ship." He looked out of his office window toward the setting sun. "Well gentlemen, I hate to cut this party short, but I'm going to my room, and I'm gonna hit the rack early," he said. "How long are you in town, Rowdy?" he continued, shaking his friend's hand.

"We sail in a week, brother," Burns replied.

Eldridge smiled. "I'd like to come down and see your boat, if you have some time," Eldridge said.

"Sure, David," he replied. "Come down toward the end of the week. I've got a really good cook aboard, so we'll have a great lunch."

Eldridge looked at Callaway, who was practically speechless. "Mike, why don't you come by tomorrow, not too early, so we can talk," he said.

At a loss, Callaway answered, "Uh... Okay, David. I'm just gonna go by the cafeteria and get a cup of coffee for the ride home, and I'll come by at about 10 am." Callaway shook Eldridge's hand. "If you need to talk, David, I'll be at the hotel."

Eldridge slowly shook his head and sat back down in his chair.

Callaway walked out of the building and headed to the cafeteria. As he entered, he saw Flanders, Markham and Cheshire sitting at a table in the NCO section, each with three empty bottles of beer in front of him. They were all sitting in the same position, leaning way back in their chairs, with their legs straight out and their chins almost touching their chests. They were just staring at the empty bottles.

Callaway grabbed a chair from the next table and sat with them. It was totally quiet for a couple of minutes. "Any chance you'll get transferred to another base?" Callaway asked, already knowing the answer.

"We're done, Mr. Callaway," Cheshire said. "Totally and completely screwed. When they shut the doors to this place, our hitches will end, and we will be civilians."

Flanders tilted his head and looked at Callaway. "And of the three of us, Cheshire's the only one who has a decent shot at finding a good job," he said. Then he looked at Markham. "I don't know, Mark. Maybe we can open a shooting range someplace. We can teach people how to shoot."

Markham looked at him and, forcing a smile, told him, "All I really wanted was to go on one more combat mission. Just one more. That would have been nice."

Searching for something to cheer the men up, all Callaway could come up with was, "I'm sorry this is happening. You guys are great at what you do." He excused himself and then got up and walked out the door and to his car.

On the way to his hotel, he stopped at a camera shop that developed film. He gave the man at the counter fifty dollars to develop the film right away. While he waited, he bought a magnifying glass so he could see what was going on aboard the *Put' Stalina* while she was docked at Point MacKenzie. He went through a drive-in on the way to the hotel and picked up a couple of burgers and a Pepsi. As he pulled into the parking lot, he couldn't help but notice a familiar looking pick-up truck in the lot. He wondered if it was Abby's brother Matthew's truck, and why he was at his hotel. He shook his head. *Gotta be hundreds of dually trucks like that in Alaska*, he thought. He got into his room and started eating a burger while looking at the pictures. He got out the magnifying glass and looked at the picture of the two men on the bridge wing of the *Put' Stalina.* "Holy shit," he said. "It's that tall guy again. The same son-of-a-bitch that Frankovich met with twice before. Who the hell is this guy?"

A knock at the door broke his concentration abruptly. He walked to the door and looked through the peep hole. All he saw was a person's neck. A rather thick neck. He opened the door, and there stood Matthew Tika'a, with a frown on his face. Callaway thought quickly about throwing the first punch or trying to slam the door shut before Matthew could destroy him where he stood.

"Callaway," Matthew asked calmly. "Can I talk to you?"

Dumbfounded, Callaway answered, "Uh… Matthew, sure, come on in." He still felt like he was about to be mauled by a big, angry bear.

Matthew sat down on the chair where Callaway had been eating and looking at the pictures. Matthew looked down at the one empty hamburger wrapper and the burger sitting next to it. "Uh, are you gonna eat this?" he asked. "I haven't eaten since lunch, and I'm starved."

Still hungry, but figuring that food might keep the man calm, he answered, "Sure, Matthew. Have at it."

Matthew wolfed down the burger in two bites. "Oh, that makes me feel much better," he said. "So, listen, Callaway. I don't know what went on with you and my little sister, but she is a mess. She hasn't been the same since she got back from Florida. Now I don't know what happened down there, because she won't talk about it, and I'm not sure I really want to know, so I'm asking you, man to man. Did you hurt her in any way? And I'm not talking physical hurt, because she could probably kick your ass. And God only knows how bad I would fuck you up if she had come home with a bruise on her. But I've just got to know because she really loves you. Still."

Callaway took a deep breath and let it out. He didn't want to tell him about the things he had done. "Look, Matthew, I had a little bit of a flashback from my days in law enforcement. I freaked out, and when she asked me about details, I gave them to her. Then she freaked out. And then she took off in the middle of the night without telling me she was leaving. I'm not blaming her for doing that, but it hit me hard, cause I do love her."

Matthew leaned back in the chair. "And I'm guessing you're not going to tell me any of the details that set her off?" he asked. Callaway was shaking his head midway through his sentence. Matthew picked up Callaway's soda and started drinking it.

"Alright then, here's the deal," he said. "You two need to talk this out."

Callaway told him, "I've been trying to find her, but she hasn't been at her house or the hospital."

Matthew smiled. "That's because she's up at the campground," he replied. "She always goes there when her life turns to crap. She goes there to rest her mind. So, you need to go up there. Paul will be at the airfield tomorrow morning at nine o'clock. It's not as bad as the last time we were there, but it's still cold, and there's still a lot of snow on the ground up that way. So, get up there, get things straight between the both of you, screw your brains out, and head back home."

Okay." Callaway answered, he was stunned.

"Okay?" Matthew said a bit louder.

"Uh… yeah, yeah, I'll be at the airfield in the morning," Callaway said.

Matthew got up and opened the door. "Oh, Callaway," he said. "Don't forget to bring that pea shooter pistol of yours. Bears are starting to wake up."

Callaway just nodded. He closed the door and stood there. After about ten seconds, he let out a yell. Suddenly, he stopped, realizing that Matthew probably heard him and went laughing all the way home. Callaway quickly got his gear together, including his "pea shooter" pistol, and packed it in his duffle bag. *Tomorrow will be a wonderful day,* he thought.

Chapter 14

A little before 8 a.m., Callaway parked his rental car next to Paul's hanger. He was surprised that the de Havilland wasn't outside and ready to go. He slung his duffle bag over his shoulder and grabbed two cups of coffee that he brought from a donut shop along the way to the airfield. When he walked around to the doors, he could see Paul sitting on the floor at the bottom of the right landing gear wearing overalls, working on what looked like the brake on that wheel.

"This old wreck gonna get me north?" he asked, purposely trying to get a rise out of Paul. "It will," Paul replied. "Even if I decide to throw you out halfway there."

Callaway squatted down and handed Paul one of the cups. "I didn't know what you took in your coffee, sooo I just put in everything they had."

Paul sat up and wiped his hands with a shop rag. "Coffee is coffee to me," he said. "As long as it keeps me awake at eight thousand feet, I'm good with it."

Callaway looked at the brake assembly in pieces on the floor. "I'm guessing this isn't routine maintenance?" he asked.

Paul swallowed a gulp of coffee and looked down at the parts. "Nope, this side started sticking a little when I landed last night," he replied. "So, I came in at 5 a.m. to rebuild both of them. I don't want to ground loop this thing before you can square things away with Abby."

Callaway shook his head. "News does travel fast around here, doesn't it?" he said. "So, can I help?"

Paul smiled and answered, "Sure, you can make yourself useful passing tools and parts to me. That'll speed up the process."

They finished the rebuild and used an old farm tractor to pull the airplane out of the hanger. Within minutes, they were airborne. At cruising altitude, Paul let Callaway take the controls again. Once they reached Nenana, Paul took control back and prepared for landing.

"One day, you need to teach me how to land this thing," Callaway said.

Glancing at him, Paul answered, "I'll tell you what, I'll do the next best thing. Put your hands on your wheel, but don't do anything. I'll make the moves on my wheel, and you'll be able to feel what I'm doing before we touch down. That's how the man who taught me to fly did it."

Callaway did as Paul told him. He could feel all the movements of the wheel and see how the aircraft reacted to them. The de Havilland touched down and Paul began taxiing. As they neared his Quonset hut, they felt a slight snag in the right brake that acted like something pulling them backwards for a second.

"Dammit all!" Paul said. "I thought I got those brakes right. I guess I'll fix them again while you're trying to fix your situation with my cousin."

Callaway smiled at him. "You have such a way with words, Paul," he said, pouring on the sarcasm.

Paul pulled the plane up to the hut and shut the engine off. Callaway looked at the other Quonset hut and saw Lapinski's Cessna Caravan parked there. "I see your buddy is back up here again," he told Paul.

Looking over at the other plane, Paul answered, "Yeah, I've been seeing him up here a lot lately. Seems like he's been flying the same bunch of people back and forth."

Callaway took off his coat and retrieved his duffel bag. He pulled the holstered pistol out of the bag and strapped it on. He put his coat back on and helped Paul push the wheeled pallet that carried one of the supercharged snowmobiles outside. Abby had taken the other one. "Those guys that Lapinski flew up here, was one of them kind of tall, with short blond hair and round wire-rimmed glasses by any chance?" he asked.

Paul was filling the fuel tank on the snowmobile when he stopped and looked at Callaway. "Yeah, he was with them yesterday," he replied. They got in here at about 7 p.m. when I was getting ready to take off."

"How many men were with him?" Callaway asked.

"Uh… there were four if you include the tall guy," Paul answered. "One must have been the boss, 'cause he was barking orders at the other two guys, and at Lapinski, too. He talked nice to the tall guy wearing the glasses, though."

"Did you hear what those two were saying?" he asked.

"Well, that's a strange question, but, in fact, no, I don't know what they were talking about, Callaway," he replied. "I don't speak Russian."

Callaway turned suddenly toward Paul. "Wait, are you telling me that the tall guy spoke Russian, too?"

Paul nodded, piquing Callaway's interest further. "Did he sound like an American speaking Russian, or did he sound fluent?"

Giving Callaway a surprised look, he answered, "He

sounded just like the other three guys," he answered. "Why does that matter so much? Do you know who these guys are?" Paul asked. "What the hell is going on?"

Callaway leaned against the back of the snowmobile looking at Lapinski's airplane, and then back at Paul. "Something's strange with this bunch," Callaway responded. "The guy you thought is the leader is the captain of a cargo ship and the two that he was yelling at are part of his crew," he said, then continued, "They supposedly buy used heavy construction equipment and transport the stuff to Russia for sale. I keep running into the captain in different places, and every time I see him, I am more and more convinced that this guy and his crew are up to something very bad. Something way worse than maybe smuggling. And whoever the tall guy with the glasses is, he's in on it, too. I just haven't been able to pin down what they're doing."

Paul interrupted, "Fascinating, Callaway, really. But first…"

"Yeah, you're right, first I get things settled down with Abby. Then, I'll be on these guys like fleas on a dog."

Suddenly sounding genuinely interested, Paul asked, "Do you want me to see if I can get anything out of Lapinski, if I see him? I mean I'll be staying over here tonight, so he might show up. He usually does when he has a layover. It depends on how many of the strip joints he hits in town. When he runs out of money, he wanders back here to sack out."

Callaway smiled at him. "These guys could be pretty dangerous, Paul," he said. "I don't want you to get hurt, so you should Lapinski alone, okay? If he's involved in whatever these Russian guys are doing, he might send them after you."

Grinning at Callaway, Paul answered, "I can take care of myself, ya know." He screwed on the gas cap and then handed Callaway a road map, telling him, "You might need this." The map included some hand-drawn routes through the woods to get him to the camp. "There's a compass in the storage compartment. If all else fails and you get lost, head east until you hit the main road and turn left. It's a much longer ride that way, but it will get you to the camp."

Callaway nodded at him, climbed onto the machine, said his good-bye, and pushed the start button. The engine came to life with a howl, and Callaway went speeding away out of the airport and into the woods. He followed the paths that he remembered, and when it got confusing, he looked at Paul's homemade map drawings. After a couple of hours of zooming along through the snow, he couldn't help but notice that the day was getting lighter earlier than usual. He was also getting cold since the temperature was beginning to drop. He turned a corner and finally saw the camp up ahead. He slowed down, coasting into the campsite and came to a stop as snow was beginning to fall hard.

He saw the other snowmobile parked by one of the igloos, but he saw no sign of Abby. He shut off the motor and climbed off the machine, stretching his legs that were stiff from the ride. All was quiet until he took off his helmet.

"Dammit Callaway!" he heard Abby yell. "What are you doing here?" She stepped out from behind a tree by the edge of the woods with her rifle at the ready.

Callaway looked at the gun. "Is that meant for me?" he asked, not knowing if she was angry enough to take a shot at him.

"No, it's for the idiot who just came tearing into my camp without blowing the horn first." she said, slinging the rifle over her shoulder.

"I didn't know I was supposed to honk the horn," he said, not moving a step.

"Well, that's what we do," she replied. "That's the way we know if the person coming here is a friend or foe."

"So, if bad guys show up, you gonna pick 'em off from the woods?" he asked in a thicker version of his Florida drawl. He could see that she was trying her best not smile but failing miserably.

"No, I would hide unless they found me, and then I'd come out guns-a-blazin'!" she replied loudly with an even worse imitation of a southern accent and then continued with, "You gonna stand there until the snow covers you up or are you gonna come over here and give me a hug?" she asked. Her tone had softened considerably.

Callaway smiled and strutted over to her, giving her a big warm hug.

"I've been hearing other snowmobiles running around in the woods, so I got concerned when you pulled up. Are you hungry?" she asked.

Callaway leered down at her.

"No… no, Callaway, I meant food," she said. "We need to talk some before anything else happens."

He had to think quickly. He was hungry, but he really didn't want to eat her cooking.

"I went into town yesterday and got a barrel of chicken at Kentucky Fried," she said. "There's still plenty left."

Letting out a breath, he answered, "Yes, I am hungry."

They entered her igloo and sat down on the floor.

There was silence for a while until Callaway couldn't take it anymore. "I'm sorry about what happened in Fort Lauderdale, Abby," he said. "But I'm upset over the fact that you left me down there. I mean I was totally honest with you, and I totally freaked out when I woke up and you were gone. I flew home that night so drunk that I almost got arrested at the airport."

Her eyes widened. "What did you do that almost got you arrested, Mike?"

Sensing that she was worried that he had gone crazy and hurt someone,

he knew he had to reassure her that nothing bad had happened. "I mean, I was clearly, **really**, drunk," he told her, "And the airport cops tried to get me out of the airport, and I guess I got a little argumentative with them. I mentioned that I was ex law enforcement, and their sergeant was kind enough to call David Eldridge, and he was kind enough to come and get me."

She looked at him and shook her head. "You know, Commander Eldridge was right about one thing," she said. "You are one total pain in the ass. What would you do without him?"

He tilted his head up and sighed. "If it wasn't for David, I would be either dead or in prison," he answered. "Anyway, he drove me home, and here I am, just trying to find out where we stand."

She sat there quietly for about ten seconds, and then hugged him. "How did you know I was up here?" she asked.

"Well, Matthew showed up at my hotel room. I thought he came to kick my ass, but he was really nice. He told me to come up here and see you and set it up with Paul to fly me up here this morning."

She started to cry, and for a second, he thought their relationship was over. "I've missed you so much," she said, and then she kissed him.

Confused as he was, he held her tight.

"I thought about all of the things you told me that you did to those people," she said quietly. "The thing is, even though they were the wrong things to do, I can understand why you did them. I know there's more that you can tell me about what you did, but… I really don't want to know. I just can't imagine being in a situation like the one you were in and doing what you did. I don't think I would be able to react like you, no matter how horrible the situation was."

He rocked her back and forth, soothingly. "Never say you never will do something." he said. "I hope it never happens, but you never know how you will react in a bad situation, Abby. I will tell you this, though, unless your life is in danger, I promise I won't kill anyone anymore." She gave him a doubting look.

He looked deep into her eyes. "So where are we?" he asked.

She sighed. "We're not where we were before, and I don't think we will ever be able to get to that point again, Mike," she replied, gently pulling away from him.

Callaway didn't want to let go of her, but he knew he had to. He looked down, trying his best to keep from crying. Abby opened a cooler and pulled out the barrel of fried chicken. She pulled a pocketknife out of her coat pocket.

Callaway was surprised when she pushed a button on the handle and the blade shot out like a bullet. "A switch-blade?" he asked.

She started cutting the chicken and explained, "Paul

gave it to me. They're good to have in a bad situation. It's getting dark. Too late for you to ride back to the airport. You can sleep here with me, if you want, or sleep in one of the other igloos after you're done eating."

Callaway wasn't mad at her because he knew why she was so upset. He just couldn't see lying down next to her and just sleeping. "I've lost my appetite, Abby," was all he could say, as he crawled out of her igloo and headed for the one he had slept in during their previous camping trip. He took off his coat and shoulder holster, found a blanket, and lay down without undressing.

It took him a while to calm down, as he kept wondering if Abby was able to sleep. "God, please keep me from having another one of those dreams, so I don't scare her off again," he whispered, before pulling the blanket over himself and falling asleep—a sleep that only lasted about a half of an hour. Some noise startled him awake. Then he heard Abby screaming. A bear was the first thing he envisioned. He grabbed his holster and put it and his coat on as he crawled through the door. He pulled the pistol from the holster and ran toward Abby's igloo, when an extremely bright light blinded him. He shielded his eyes and pointed the pistol at the light, when he heard a burst of automatic weapons fire and saw snow go flying in front of him. He stopped and lowered his weapon, finding himself hopelessly outgunned. Someone walked up behind him and pulled the pistol from his hand. The bright light was still glaring at him, restricting his vision to a few feet in front of him.

"Put your hands above your head!" he heard from a man with a strong Russian accent. Callaway had no choice but to obey the command. The light was lowered to his feet. It took his eyes a few seconds to see everyone around him. He saw men armed with AK 47 rifles moving around. Then he heard the voice that he knew would come next.

"Mr. Callaway!" Acardi Frankovich bellowed, as he walked up and stood in front of his captive. "I wasn't expecting to ever see you again, but I found it necessary to find you since I heard that you've been nosing around about my business up here." Frankovich pointed at Callaway. "Take his holster and make sure he has no other weapons," he said to the man who took Callaway's pistol from him. "That big pistol will be a nice memento for me to remember you by."

Callaway was looking everywhere in front of him, trying to find Abby when he was grabbed from behind. The person searching him pulled the holster from his left hand and then patted him down from his head to his feet. He then turned him around. Callaway was startled to see it was the tall mystery man with the round wire-rimmed glasses. "You!" he yelled. "Who the hell are you?"

The man, who was wearing a long overcoat, just smiled at him, said something in Russian and then spun him around to face Frankovich again. "Where's Abby?" Callaway asked.

Frankovich waved to someone over his shoulder. He could hear Abby yelling, "Let me go, asshole!" as she was pushed up in front of Callaway. She gave Callaway a look that was more anger than fear.

"As I said, Mr. Callaway, I had no reason to ever see you again, but a little bird told me that your pilot friend was asking questions about me," he said. "He has been silenced, which actually came in handy, but I need to know who else you have talked to about me, and what you have told them."

Abby's mouth dropped open. "What did you do to him?" she screamed staring a Frankovich.

Frankovich chuckled. "I guess the pilot was someone close to you, my dear?" he asked. "Let's just say that there will be one less stupid aborigine flying around Alaska, now. But we actually found a good use for him." She began to weep. Frankovich chuckled again. "I'm guessing that your friend the navy commander knows what you've been up to. So, I will send some of my men to silence him, too. Now, you will be coming with us, Doctor, while Mr. Callaway will be going somewhere else with my men," he said.

"No!" Abby yelled, as she ran to Callaway and hugged him. Callaway felt her sliding something into his coat pocket. All of Frankovich's men laughed. One of them pulled Abby from Callaway and half-walked and half-dragged her away. Callaway lunged at the men who were pulling her away and was knocked to the snow-covered ground by the buttstock of an AK 47. He was lying there holding his bruised ribs when he heard a couple of snowmobiles start up.

"Get up, Chicken!" the man who'd hit him with the rifle demanded. Callaway rolled up onto his knees and pushed himself up to a standing position. He put his hands in his coat pockets and found that the object Abby had slipped into one of them was her switchblade.

"I must say goodbye to you now, Mr. Callaway," Frankovich said. "I have many, many things to do."

Callaway smiled at him, which made Frankovich frown. "So, just what are you up to, Acardi?" Callaway asked.

Frankovich laughed. "I'm not going to tell you anything just in case you manage to somehow escape. At least you won't be told at this place and time," and then he said something to the mystery man in Russian. "Perhaps my colleague will be willing to enlighten you about what I have planned when you get to where you are going. Suffice it to say, it will be both monumental and catastrophic. *Dasvidaniya*, my friend. I would wish you a long life, but... I don't see that happening." He smiled and walked away leaving the mystery man and three of his other men behind. One of them, the one who'd hit Calloway with the rifle butt, was the man he'd tussled with at the hospital. Now he punched Calloway in the stomach, dropping him to his knees again.

"Get up, American asshole, we must go to where you will die," he said, grabbing Calloway by the shoulder and pulling him to his feet. He slung his AK 47 onto his shoulder and walked Calloway to his snowmobile. "You will drive," he continued, as he unloaded Calloway's pistol and threw it and the holster into the snowmobile's storage container. The mystery man and the other four walked into the woods where they had left their snowmobiles. The Russian directed Calloway southeast, heading towards Fairbanks.

They rode for close to an hour and then veered away from the main path, heading towards Fort Wainwright. They were near the base when Calloway was told to stop near a nondescript building outside the perimeter of the base. It looked like an extremely overbuilt airplane hangar. They stopped to wait for the other four. The mystery man arrived and removed his overcoat. To Calloway's complete surprise, he was wearing a United States Army uniform with captain's bars on the jacket's epaulettes, and an identification card clipped to his front pocket. He was also wearing a belt and holster carrying a Colt 1911 pistol.

"What the hell?" was all Callaway got to say before he was yanked off his snowmobile by his captor.

The Army officer walked to the door of the hanger and stood in front of a very robust security station built into the wall. He pulled the identification card off his jacket and slid it into a slot in the security station panel. He then stood at attention in front of a camera lens in the panel and said, "John Agnew," without a hint of a Russian accent. A green light lit up on the panel, and Callaway heard two loud clicks coming from the door. The captain pulled open the door and then motioned for Callaway to come with him.

The man Callaway had ridden with hit him in the back with the barrel of his AK 47. "Move," he said. "And goodbye, Callaway."

Callaway walked to the open door and the captain motioned for him to go in. As he passed through the door, he noticed that the outer wall of the hangar was about six inches thick and looked like it was made of solid steel. He entered a large room with a kitchen and tables. He could see bunk beds lined up in an adjoining room. The captain left the first door open and walked to a second one about thirty feet away. He pulled open the second door and motioned for Callaway to go ahead. Callaway walked through the second door, with an equally thick wall, and into darkness, until the captain flipped a light switch that lit the interior like an operating room.

Callaway was stunned by what he saw. There were five ballistic missiles, some of them out in the open, and a couple in train cars, parked in the hangar. Callaway looked at one of the missiles protruding from inside two open doors in the roof of the train car. He saw four steel legs, one attached to each corner of the railroad car and bolted to the floor with orange lines around the feet of the steel legs. His mouth opened slightly, as he remembered the sketch he made in the hold of the *Put' Stalina*. "Oohh shit," he mumbled.

"Do you know what this is, Mr. Callaway?" the captain asked. Callaway let out a breath. "Yeah, it's a hell of a lot of trouble." he answered.

The captain smiled. "Fort Wainwright's primary mission is the testing and research of new ballistic missiles," he said. "I just happen to oversee the security detail that guards these particular missiles. Most of them have actually been around here for a while. They are derivatives of what was called the MX Missile, or "Missile X." The original MX carried multiple nuclear warheads; this smaller version is called The Midgetman. It only carries one warhead, but it can be transported around the country by train or truck without anyone knowing where it is. This way those pesky Russians, or Chinese, can't zero in and blow it up if they decide to launch a first-strike attack.

Callaway closed his eyes. "MX is the MEX." he whispered. Then Callaway looked the man in the eyes. "And you, you son-of -a-bitch are betraying your country to steal one of these?"

The captain cocked his head to one side and smiled, telling him, "Oh, you have me so wrong, sir. I'm not really an American. Oh, I am registered as an American citizen, but I was born in Russia. Near Murmansk, to be exact. But I was trained to be a Russian agent since I was five years old. You see, my parents were dissidents. They despised our excellent Communist system, so I was taken from them, and they were... eliminated. Somewhere in Siberia, I'm guessing. I was raised by the state, and I was trained to be, oh what is that cute name that your security analysts like call us… oh yes, a sleeper agent, since I was seven. In my early teens, I was added to a family that immigrated to the United States. I went to an American high school and college, and when the time came, I entered your military service. The United State Army to be exact.

My assignment was to infiltrate and get as close to your nuclear missile stockpiles as possible, and to supply the Kremlin with information about your weapons systems. All was well, but then… Glasnost—and whatever other garbage Mr. Gorbachev came up with—ended the Soviet Union. Fortunately, the person in charge of sleeper agents in the KGB was our mutual friend Acardi Frankovich. He came up with this idea to damage the recent good will between the U.S. and Russia. And that put me back in action."

Callaway was stunned listening to what he thought only happened in spy movies. "And just what is Mr. Frankovich's plan, if you don't mind me asking?" Callaway inquired.

The captain leaned back against the frame of one of the missile launchers. "Well, I guess it doesn't matter if I tell you now, since you'll never see the exterior of this facility again," he answered. "You see, there are still people in my homeland who want to go back to the system Comrade Lenin started and Comrade Stalin perfected. We want to change things back to the way they were, so, the goal is to launch a Midgetman missile from the waters of the Bering Sea and have it strike somewhere in Russia, say at any small city close to the coast—so it can get there too fast to be stopped—and blow it up. It will start an uprising, if you will, its main goal being to prove that the current Russian government can't protect its people from those horrible Americans. This will allow us Communists to regain control of our country. Don't you think it's pure irony that such an act of war will be triggered by an American missile?" he asked smiling.

"God almighty," Callaway whispered.

"Oh, but wait, there's more," the captain continued. We already moved the missile inside one of the train cars a couple of days ago and loaded it into the hold of the *Put' Stalina*. I told my security people that it was being transferred to the maintenance building on base for an upgrade. What we did yesterday was remove the radioactive material from the warhead of the missile that is sticking out of the train car here, and that radioactive material is being loaded on another single train car that will be taken by rail and driven by some of Comrade Frankovich's men. The spheres of uranium and plutonium are housed in these ingenious boxes that Comrade Frankovich's men made. They are lined with lead."

Callaway grasped Abby's switchblade with his right hand inside his coat pocket. "And what are you planning to do with the uranium and plutonium?" he asked, trying to buy time and move a little closer to the man.

The captain shook his head. "I'm not sure, Mr. Callaway," he replied. Comrade Frankovich did mention the possibility of spreading the material around down in the Port of Valdez."

Callaway was getting sick of the man's condescending attitude. "So, he's using it to make a dirty bomb?" he asked. "And how does that help your cause to make Russia Communist again?"

Grinning at Callaway, the Captain answered, "Valdez is where Alaskan oil leaves the U.S. bound for other countries. He wants those countries to buy Russian oil."

"And he's going accomplish that with a dirty bomb?" Callaway asked. "That will make the port unusable for years. He doesn't care how many people he kills, does he? So, how do you expect to get away with this? I mean people are going to notice when you don't show up for work, and then you're screwed."

"Comrade Frankovich has his men monitoring Fort Wainwright and all the other bases in Alaska, along with all police agencies," the captain replied. "The *Put' Stalina* was a spy ship years ago. They have equipment on board that can monitor everything that goes on in this state. If the authorities come for him, he will launch the missile at Washington D.C. and blow up his ship, himself, and your girlfriend in the nearest port.

Callaway needed to get closer if he was going to take down this big man. "And your security officers," Callaway added, inching closer. "Wait, where are your security officers?"

The captain walked to the rear of one of the trailers and motioned for Callaway to follow him. The captain watched his every move. Callaway followed him past the trailer and stopped when he saw two members of the security team lying on the floor dead. He could see that they had both been shot. He saw numerous bullet holes and marks throughout the hanger looking like there had been one hell of a gun battle. Both of them had pistols in their hands and there were shell casings on the floor next to them. "My two-man teams go on duty for three days at a time, Mr. Callaway, that's why we have a kitchen and a bunk room," the captain replied. "These men just got here last night when this 'tragedy' occurred, so I will have plenty of time to get away.

Callaway was stunned by how cold the man was.

"So, you killed them," he said, "and then you shot the place up and put the pistols in their hands to make it look legit. So, who do you plan to blame this on?"

Staring at Callaway, the captain answered, "The prime suspects, of course, will be you, and your accomplice will be that aborigine over there," he said, pointing behind him with his left hand. Callaway turned to look and froze. "Paul," he whispered. He walked over to him and crouched down. Paul's eyes were open and there were two bullet holes in his chest. There was an old revolver in his hand. Callaway was seething with anger. He had warned Paul not to talk to Lapinski at the airport to avoid something like this happening.

The captain walked up behind him. "Don't bother going for his gun, Mr. Callaway. We used all of his bullets to kill my men. We also used a couple of others from the gun that will be found next to you. And now, you must join your friend as one of the criminals that helped steal the missile and the future dirty bomb."

Callaway heard the man unsnap his holster on his right side. He sprang up and grabbed the man's right arm with one hand, keeping him from drawing the weapon. With his other hand, he rammed the tip of the switchblade grip into the right lens of the man's glasses and pushed the release button. The four-inch blade sprang through the glass and into the man's brain, killing him instantly. Callaway watched him crumble to the floor. He bent down and took his Colt 1911 pistol out of his hand. He also retrieved the switchblade, wiping the blood off the blade on the man's uniform. He retracted the blade and put the knife back in his pocket. He had to figure out how he would escape the four men outside and somehow get help to save Abby, all while keeping Acardi Frankovich from launching a suicide shot.

193

Chapter 15

Callaway stood by the inner door to the missile hanger. He listened through the open outer door to the four men outside, trying to determine where they were by the sound of their voices. He needed to get to Matthew's turbocharged snowmobile if he had any chance of getting away and stopping the hideous events that Frankovich had planned. He went back into the missile hanger to see if the dead guards had any live rounds in their pistols. He checked the chambers and removed the magazines from both of their pistols and found a total of four .45 ACP rounds. He loaded them into one of the magazines to augment the seven rounds in the captain's pistol. Quietly he walked back to the outer door of the building and peaked around to see where the men were. He could see one man sitting on one of their snowmobiles, while the other three were leaning against the other machine. Their rifles were propped up against a nearby tree.

He wondered how he could lure them into a position where he'd have the element of surprise. *They're waiting for a gunshot, expecting me to be killed,* he thought. *I'll just give them what they're waiting for.* He cocked the hammer on the Colt and fired a shot into the hanger. He heard an exclamation in Russian from one of the men and then footsteps advancing in the snow. He turned around and steadied his pistol against the door frame. *Let me introduce you to something known in police work as the 'fatal funnel,'* he thought, hoping to catch them bunched together coming through the door. He hoped that all four of them would want to see him dead, but only one of the men came through the door. Callaway opened fire, expending all six rounds that were still in the pistol. The man went down, soon to be dead. He ran toward the open door, while ejecting the empty magazine and reloading with the spare magazine holding only four rounds. He hit the slide release getting the pistol ready to fire as he exited the door.

While the other three ran towards the tree to get their rifles, Callaway put the .45 into his left coat pocket and jumped onto the turbocharged snowmobile. He started it and left, fishtailing down the path he took. He saw puffs of snow jumping into the air next to him from gunfire. He kept his right thumb on the throttle lever and pulled the pistol from his pocket firing blindly behind him with his left hand, dropping the pistol when it went empty. He headed south to find help, looking behind him over and over to see if Frankovich's men were still chasing him.

He relaxed a little as he zoomed through the woods, forgetting that he wasn't out on the ocean and that all they'd have to do to find him was follow the snowmobile's tracks. He came to a paved road and began following it, continuing to move south. He looked to his left and saw a small amount of smoke rising above a line of trees. As he raced down the road, he saw a break in the trees and a single diesel train engine pulling one boxcar behind it. He stopped the snowmobile and checked the rear storage compartment for a pair of binoculars.

He found them, but more important, he found his

Encore pistol. He put on his shoulder holster and loaded one of the five remaining .458 Magnum cartridges into the pistol. He looked through the binoculars to check out the train engine and boxcar. Sure enough, he could see *Put' Stalina* stenciled on the door of the boxcar. He pulled Paul's map out of his pocket and determined what road he was on. He also noticed that the map showed the railroad tracks on which the train was traveling and that his road would allow him to get ahead of the train since the tracks took a longer route before they approached the road again. He was preparing to give chase to the train with the intent of somehow stopping it, when he heard the sound of a snowmobiles approaching from behind. He got off the machine and ran to a couple of large trees for cover. He pulled the pistol from the holster, cocked the hammer, and aimed it at the path where the sound was coming from. *Their friends fell for an ambush once, let's see if it works again*, he thought. He saw movement through the trees, as a snowmobile turned onto the path behind him. The driver of the snowmobile tried to turn, but was too late, Callaway touched the trigger and the big pistol recoiled straight up. The thick bullet hit his attacker squarely in the chest throwing the man straight back off his saddle and into the snow. He opened the breech of the pistol to reload, pulling the empty shell casing out and plucking another round from the cartridge loop on the holster strap. He was trying to get the cartridge into the chamber when bullets hit the ground behind him. He ran for the cover of a rockpile, dropping the live round into the snow. He peeked over the rocks and saw the other two men standing on a ridge, near the top of a hill a few hundred yards away firing their rifles at him. He reloaded his pistol with another round, which left him with only two more. He aimed high above the two

196

men, since the .458 Magnum was built for taking down dangerous game at close range and fired. The bullet crashed into the mountainside above the men and caused a miniature avalanche.

Both shooters dove to the ground to shield themselves from the snow and rocks that were dropping on them. One of the men on the ridge recovered quickly enough to get off a few more shots at Callaway, making a run for the snowmobile impossible. Callaway saw only one way out and took off down a path through the woods on foot. He ran for about a half a mile when he heard gunfire again from a distance behind him. He continued to run between some low mountains that looked familiar. He stopped by some trees to reload. *One in the gun and only one more left*, he thought. He saw a cave opening ahead and ran toward it as fast as he could. When he got within twenty yards of the opening, he slid to a halt. He realized why the area looked familiar when he saw the warning signs stating that this was the cave where *Big Ivan* the bear was slumbering. *I hope these guys can't read English*; he thought as he walked slowly toward the other end of the clearing when he heard yelling behind him. The two Russians were catching up with him.

He dove behind some small trees hoping they hadn't seen him. Peering around a tree, he saw one of the men pointing at Callaway's footprints in the snow. The men split up and started walking around the clearing in opposite directions with their guns at the ready. He realized that if they came all the way around, he'd have to shoot it out with them on both sides… with two bullets for a pistol that takes some time to reload. He only had one choice. *I hope Ivan's home*, he thought. He aimed his pistol towards the closest man coming around to his left.

He couldn't see him too well as he was behind some small trees, too. He saw the man's legs from the knees down and tried to aim where his chest would be. He fired the pistol and heard a loud crack, from the area where the man was walking.

Callaway saw the man's legs fly out from under him as he fell to the snow-covered ground surrounded by large rocks, one of which must have hit him in the head. Callaway reloaded with his last round as the other man dove for cover behind a boulder by the entrance to Ivan's cave.

"Callaway, you need to give up this fight," the man yelled. "I can keep you pinned down until dark and then I will sneak over there and cut your throat. That will be very painful. Come out now, and I'll put a bullet in your head, and it will be over quickly. I'll make sure that your woman is released unharmed. Don't make me wait!"

Callaway recognized the man's voice; he was the man from the hospital. He kept looking at the entrance to the cave, figuring that the bear would have heard the commotion and come outside to see what was going on. "What the hell, Ivan?" he whispered. "Why did I get a goddamn bear that's hard of hearing?" Wondering where his second pursuer was, he decided to use his last round to try and wake the bear up, since the previous one hadn't done the job. *Time to deliver your mail, Ivan.* He aimed the Encore at the inside wall on the other side of the cave. *If I can ricochet the bullet into the cave, maybe it'll piss the friggin bear off,* he thought, squeezing the trigger.

The bullet whizzed past the Russian's hiding place and struck the inside wall of the cave. He could hear the bullet bouncing off the walls inside. Then things got quiet.

"You are a stupid man, Callaway," the Russian yelled. Callaway heard him pull the magazine out, drop it to the ground, and reach into his magazine pouch to pull out a full one to reload. He was laughing until a low moaning sound came from the inside of the cave. Something moved toward him until Ivan's huge head blocked the light. Callaway heard him fumbling with the magazine, trying to lock it into the weapon. By the time he did, Ivan charged him at tremendous speed.

Now, he had broken cover and Callaway saw him pull the bolt back and swing the barrel around as the bear swung one of his massive claws at him, striking him in the chest and knocking him through the air for a good ten feet. Watching him try to crawl away, Callaway noticed the man was bleeding from the claw marks in his chest. Callaway watched as Ivan lumbered to the Russian and crushed his skull with one bite. The bear bit into his prey's right leg, turned around and dragged his kill into the cave.

Shocked by the spectacle, Callaway whispered, "Enjoy your lunch, Ivan."

He walked quietly around the clearing and saw the Russian that he had almost buried with a round from his pistol. The man was still breathing but appeared to be unconscious. Callaway took his AK 47 and ran back toward his snowmobile. When he reached the machine, he double checked his map and took off, running parallel to the road again. After about forty-five minutes of traveling at high speed and seeing no cars on the road, he slowed down. Looking ahead, he saw a couple of trucks parked across the road. He looked to his left through the trees and saw railroad tracks some distance away. He looked at his map to make sure it was the rail spur he was looking for.

Approaching the trucks, he heard a loud generator running. Callaway rode up and stopped across from the trucks and saw that one of them was hooked up to a recoilless rifle which was aimed at a mountain farther up the road. He saw George, the operator of the cannon whom he'd met before, get out of the truck. Callaway walked quickly toward him.

George smiled at Callaway and asked, "Haven't we met before?"

Callaway walked up to him, trying to act calm. "Yeah, George, I met you a couple of weeks ago farther north," he answered. "What are you shooting at today?"

George pointed behind himself at a snow-covered mountain to the right of them. It was between the road and the railroad tracks. "I'm waiting for my crew to get back with lunch and the state troopers to get here and close the road before we take down that snow. We've got one more train coming by and then we start shooting. I wish they'd get here; I've got the gun all loaded and ready to fire."

Callaway looked north when he heard a train whistle.

"What's up?" George asked.

Callaway gave him an apologetic look and then punched him in the side of his head, knocking him unconscious. "Sorry George, but I need to borrow your gun," Callaway said. He put his arms under George's shoulders and dragged him to the truck. He opened the door and pushed the unconscious man onto the front seat. He ran to the cannon, as he could now hear the sound of the train engine approaching. He climbed into the gunner's seat and looked at the controls.

George had the gun sighted to hit a mountain that

would drop snow down to the road for cleanup. Callaway needed to stop a train without blowing radioactive stuff all over the landscape. He started turning the windage hand crank to aim the gun at the railroad tracks. He turned the elevation crank raising the barrel well above the tracks, aiming at a mountain just beyond the tracks. There wasn't a tremendous amount of snow on the mountain, but he hoped it would be enough to stop the train from getting through.

Callaway imagined the train's engineer looking his way as they headed towards Valdez, and shouting "There is a cannon aimed at us!"

Just as Callaway put his right foot on the trigger pedal, he heard a heavily Russian-accented voice behind him command, "Do not move, Callaway. Take your weapon out of the holster with your left hand and throw it into the snow."

Callaway's thought was that this had to be the guy he left alive but unconscious by the bear cave. The man had a pistol aimed at Callaway but couldn't fire. The back of the gunner's chair for the cannon was clearly made of rusting steel plate that went all the way up to Callaway's ears.

"Stand up, Callaway!" he said. Callaway looked down at his foot resting on the firing pedal before he replied. "Whatever you say, boss," he said, standing while pushing down the pedal firing the cannon. He leaped off the deck of the trailer and landed in the snow. He looked behind the trailer and saw only half of his assailant. Every part of the man's body from the waist up was gone. His torso and legs stood in the snow for a couple of seconds, then his legs folded at the knees. Then they fell over. Callaway stood up and saw a triangle shaped area, about ten feet wide behind where the man was standing. The triangle was covered with blood, body parts and guts.

Hearing an explosion behind him, he spun around to see smoke close to the top of the mountain next to the train tracks. He knew that he could not have been the only one who'd heard the explosion.

The train engine's crewman probably looked high and forward to the shell impact on the mountainside. He might have laughed and thought that whoever shot that cannon had terrible aim. Callaway could hear the squeal of the engine's wheels locking up on the tracks when the occupants of the engine saw a massive avalanche rolling down the hill at them. He watched the engine and boxcar slide into the middle of the avalanche. They must have hit some large boulders mixed in with the snow, as both the engine and the boxcar toppled sideways into a ditch below the mountain. The boulders rolled onto the train as the snow buried the engine and boxcar.

After the crash, there was absolute silence, other than the noise from the generator, after the crash. Callaway looked at the mess he'd caused and decided it was time to move along, quickly. He opened the door to the truck and checked on George just to make sure he was resting comfortably and then hopped on his snowmobile and continued heading south toward the airport. He had to get down to Cook Inlet in a hurry to save Abby and stop the carnage that Acardi Francovich had planned.

At the same time, he worried about the late captain's claim that Frankovich could monitor all communications from American bases in Alaska. If the surveillance equipment on the *Put' Stalina* could detect any U.S. military or police organization coming for him, he would launch the missile at Washington D. C. As scary as that was, Callaway was even more concerned about what he would do to Abby, who was now a hostage. He had to figure out how to get on board the *Put' Stalina* without Frankovich knowing and get her off the ship. *The government could deal with the ship, its cargo and Frankovich after that,* he thought.

Now the biggest problem that clicked into his mind was how he could get south in a hurry to even find the ship. He rode the snowmobile up to Paul's hanger at the airport in Nenana and shut the machine down. He walked around the Quonset hut trying to find an open door or window to get in. As he approached the front of the building, he heard someone talking.

The conversation seemed to be coming from the front of the next Quonset hut. Callaway walked to the snowmobile and grabbed the AK 47 he'd taken from the crewman he'd blown to bits with the recoilless rifle backfire. He could see that the door to the other hut was open. He could hear only one side of the conversation, indicating that the man was on a telephone call. Callaway snuck up to the front door just in time to hear the man say goodbye. He peeked around the door frame and saw that it was Lapinski, the guy who'd had been flying Acardi Frankovich back and forth- the man who, as Paul told Callaway, hated his country.

Apparently catching a glimpse of Callaway, Lapinski stood up. As Callaway charged into the building, he saw Lapinski drop the telephone and reach behind him for a pistol. Callaway pointed the AK at the man and ran the muzzle into Lapinski's throat. It knocked him backwards and caused him to drop his pistol. Lapinski fell hard to the floor. He was trying to breathe when Callaway straddled the man's chest with his knees and sat down hard, knocking even more air out of his lungs.

Looking deep into Lapinski's eyes, he said, "All right, asshole." He continued in a menacing voice, "You're gonna answer my questions now, or I **will** kill you without giving it a second's thought."

Lapinski coughed and tried to catch his breath. "I… I don't know what you're talking about," he gasped.

Callaway reached into his pocket and pulled out Abby's switchblade. He held the handle over Lapinski's face. "Tell me where Frankovich is, and where his ship is going?" Callaway commanded. Lapinski shook his head. Callaway pushed the button, extending the blade instantly. He touched the tip of the blade against the man's throat and pushed it ever so lightly into his skin. "I am halfway to putting a hole in your carotid artery," he said. "Answer me or you'll be bleeding out on the floor very quickly."

The pilot's eyes were wide open. "I can't tell you!" he said. Frankovich will kill me if I do."

Callaway pushed the tip of the blade in a tiny bit more. "Tell me where he's going or **I'll** kill you, you piece of shit!" Callaway yelled.

Lapinski was breathing even more heavily. "If you kill me the cops will put you in jail!" he hissed.

Smiling, Callaway told him, "I will bleed you and then drag your body into the woods with my snowmobile for the bears or the wolves to eat. The only evidence of you the police will find will be bear or wolf crap. Now tell me what he's doing!"

Lapinski nodded. "He's already left Point MacKenzie. He's probably near Anchorage already and he'll be heading down the peninsula to the sea." Then he sneered at Callaway. "So, you see, you're too late to do anything. It will take too long for you to get to him, and if you call the military, he'll know about it and kill your girlfriend and do whatever else he's got planned. You'll need an assault team to stop him, and I don't think you have one of those handy.

Callaway dropped the knife and pulled Lapinski's head and shoulders up off the floor and smirked at him. "Maybe I do," he said and then he smashed the back of the man's head into the concrete floor, knocking him out. He tied Lapinski's hands, legs and feet and then lashed his body to a pipe attached to the floor and the roof. He got up and was about to go outside when he noticed the telephone Lapinski had been using. "A satellite phone," he whispered. He grabbed the phone and ran out of the hut to Paul's airplane; he found the left side door open. He climbed inside and stared at all of the dials, levers, and buttons.

"What the hell am I doing, here?" he asked himself. He tried to remember the sequence that he'd watched Paul follow when he started the airplane on their last flight together. He looked down at a round device on the bottom lower left of the instrument panel.

"Okay, I think he used this to make the priming thing work. He pushed the soft circular device a few times and then started pumping a lever next to him on his left. He could feel the lever getting harder to pump as he did so. He looked at a switch. "I think he said this is the master switch, or something," he whispered. Now he got confused. "Which lever do I push first?" he asked himself. "I don't want to get this backwards."

He grabbed the one on the left and moved it forward and then he moved the one on the right up and back. *I sure do hope that's the throttle!* he thought, moving the levers around. He looked down at the start switch and began to sweat, "I don't know if this thing's gonna start or blow up," he said, taking a second to pray. He pushed the start switch, and the engine began to turn over. Then he gritted his teeth and pushed the magneto switch higher up on the dash.

"C'mon baby, run!" The engine coughed a few times and then started to run smoothly. He let the engine run for a few minutes trying to think through exactly what he was going to do. He had flown this plane twice, straight, and level at altitude—he had flown a couple of Customs Service planes the same way with a trained pilot—but he did not have a pilot's license and had never taken off or landed an aircraft in his life. He blessed himself and then recited Alan Shepard's "Astronaut's Prayer"—the one he'd recited before he lifted off to become the first American in space: "Lord, please don't let me fuck up." Callaway disengaged the brakes and pushed the throttle forward slightly.

The plane began to roll. He turned the steering wheel, and nothing happened. "Oh crap!" he said. "Steer with your feet, dummy." He stepped on the right pedal and the airplane turned right, a little more than he wanted. Correcting with the left pedal, he continued down a taxiway towards the runway. Checking the airsock farther down the taxiway, he saw that he was taxiing the wrong way to take off into the wind. So, he pushed both pedals forward and the plane stopped. He heard the voice of an approaching pilot crackle through the radio. "Hey Paul, what are you doing?" he asked.

"Dammit," Callaway said. He turned the plane on to a parallel taxiway and kicked the throttle up a little higher.

"Paul, is that you?" the voice asked again. Callaway continued along until he got to the end of the runway. Then he heard the pilot's voice again. "Mayday, mayday, mayday, airport police, this is Cessna Whiskey Poppa 333, and I think we have an aircraft theft in progress!" he said. "There's an old white de Havilland Otter down at the north end of the Nenana runway. See if you can get over there before he lifts off."

Suddenly he saw the red and blue lights flashing from the other end of the field. Shocked that law enforcement had arrived so quickly, Callaway took a deep breath. He said, "Okay Abby, here I come," pushed the throttle forward and released the brakes. The plane lurched forward. He could see the police truck trying to cross the field to get in front of him. He remembered watching the speedometer the last time he flew with Paul. He pushed the throttle farther forward and felt the tailwheel leave the ground. "C'mon baby, I need 182 knots for you to lift off." he said.

The police truck was right next to him now. "Stop the aircraft now!" he heard the officer say over the truck's loudspeaker.

He pulled away from the truck as his speed increased. Seeing he was at takeoff speed, he pulled back on the wheel. Nothing happened. "Oh shit! Flaps!" he yelled, pushing the lever to lower them, and suddenly giving the plane lift. Lots of lift. Callaway found himself climbing at a very high angle of attack. He heard an alarm beeping as the plane began to stall. He lowered the nose and the plane settled down. He was soaking wet with sweat as he cautiously began to gain altitude.

"Okay. Okay," he said. "Now where the hell am I going?" He put the plane on the opposite course that Paul had him follow when he flew with him the first time. He found one of Paul's charts and looked it over to find where the airport down south was. "Then all I have to do is keep from getting arrested when I land, cause I'm sure my 'theft' of this aircraft has been broadcast to every airport within this plane's range. Then all I have to do is find some transportation to get aboard the *Put' Stalina*."

He was trying to figure out a game plan for when he got farther south. *If Frankovich is heading south,* he thought, *I need to get down where my boat is. Then I can chase him down with my skiff. Then all I have to do is find a way to get on board, find Abby and get her off that ship.* He decided to call the only person he could trust when he landed. David Eldridge had helped him before, and Callaway hoped he would do it again.

Chapter 16

Callaway cruised south at 6,000 feet. He flew over the port at Point MacKenzie just to verify that the *Put' Stalina* had sailed. The ship was gone as Lapinski had told him it would be. From there he went low, down to 500 feet over the water on the western side of Knik Arm and then flew along the coast of Cook Inlet. He wanted to stay low and as far away as he could to avoid detection by Ted Stevens Airport radar in Anchorage. *Thank you to a pilot I can't even remember,* he thought, *for that small nugget of flying wisdom.* South of Anchorage, he banked left to fly diagonally across the inlet to get to Paul's home airport. He stayed below some thick clouds that appeared to be rolling in from the Gulf of Alaska.

Passing over Fire Island, he noticed a large ship up ahead. He flew behind the ship and saw that it was the *Put' Stalina.* He was close enough to see that there were men stationed on the deck. "I'm sure you boys are armed to the teeth," he said. As he flew over the airport that Paul normally flew from, Callaway saw four police cars parked out near the runway. *Okay, so much for landing there,* he thought.

Checking this airport's windsock, and seeing the wind was blowing from the peninsula into Cook Inlet. He circled back towards where his boats were docked.

Coming in low, he could see the *Orinoco Flow* tied to the dock, with his skiff still hanging from cables on the stern. He climbed to 2,000 feet and circled back towards land. From this altitude, he could see the channel's numerous icebergs which had broken loose from ice flowing along the river. Some were small, but some were the size of a two-story house. Callaway thought they might prove handy. He figured, based on the speed of the *Put 'Stalina* moving south through the channel, that he would have time to intercept the ship.

Close to the inlet, he spotted a long clearing up ahead with some large patches of snow. "Okay, that clearing looks pretty smooth," he told himself. "Let's see if I can land this thing without killing myself." He lined up the airplane with the clearing and this time remembered to lower the flaps. He broke into a cold sweat as he started pulling back on the throttle to lower his air speed.

All he could think of was, *too little, I stall, crash and die, or too much and I fly into the trees on the other side of the clearing, crash and die.* He was also jumping out of his skin every time he got the nose of the plane too high, causing the stall alarm to ring. He was up and down on altitude as he got below the tree line. He thought of how the wheel felt when Paul was lowering the nose gradually to land the plane smoothly. *No turning back now,* he thought as he was flying ten feet off the ground. He cut the power and held his breath. The airplane slowly dropped to the ground, bounced a couple of times, and settled into a smooth roll.

"Thank you, Canadian Air Force!" he said, praising the original owner of the plane. He put both feet on the pedals and slowly pressed down. The plane began to slow. "Hot damn I'm good!" he said smiling, when suddenly the brake on the right wheel seized, causing the aircraft to slowly roll over at an angle, breaking off the left wing and landing the aircraft upside down. Callaway found himself hanging from his seatbelt.

He was breathing heavily, but other than being a little bruised up, he was not badly hurt. He was looking at the field upside down. "I guess Paul never got around to fixing the bad brake," he said, as he unlatched his seatbelt and fell to the cockpit's ceiling. He grabbed the AK 47 and the satellite telephone and managed to open the door. Crawling out, he stood up, aching from the crash landing, and walked toward his boats at the marina.

*****

In the meantime, Navy Chief Petty Officer Flanders was sitting in his quarters packing to leave the now almost-deserted base. His friends, Gunnery Sergeant Markham and Technical Sergeant Cheshire were in their rooms across the hall from him doing the same. He stood up to take a break and look out the window of his room. "I think I'm gonna actually miss this place," he said out loud.

Markham, across the hall, laughed. "Yeah, I feel the same way," he said. "As bad as this place might be, it beats the hell out of unemployment."

Flanders was about to continue his packing when he saw movement across the compound. "Hey Mark, come here quick," he said. Markham came over to Flanders' room. Flanders pointed at a building near the sound. They could see a person peeking around the corner of the building.

"What the hell is this crap," Markham asked.

Hearing their excitement, Cheshire joined them. "What's up?" he asked.

"We've got an uninvited guest in the compound," Flanders said. Then they saw three men, wearing white camouflage survival suits and carrying pistols, sprint to the cafeteria building.

Flanders reached into his pants pocket and pulled out his keys. He handed them to Cheshire. "Go to the weapons building and get us some MP 5's," he said. "Be careful. There may be more of them out there."

Cheshire took off through the back door. Flanders grabbed his knife and then he and Markham went out the door, hunting for the three strangers. When they got to the cafeteria building, they saw one of the men run around to the rear of the Administration Building where Commander Eldridge's office was located.

*****

The phone rang twice before David Eldridge picked it up. "David!" Callaway said. Eldridge was sitting at his desk sharing some more whiskey with his pal "Rowdy" Burns.

"Hiya, Mike," he said. "Why don't you come over to the base for a drink. Rowdy and I are toasting my last day as commander of this wonderful base."

Callaway took a deep breath. "David, listen to me closely," he said.

Eldridge scribbled information on the note pad, his eyes widening as Callaway gave him the low-down.

"Mike, this is a matter of national security. We have to notify Washington, the Pentagon, and the local author-ities." Callaway was breathing heavily, as he continued with, "David, you have to understand: if Frankovich sees the Navy, Coast Guard or even a State Trooper boat, he'll kill Abby and launch that missile at Washington. You've got to give me some time," he said, sprinting toward the marina as he talked. "I'm going after Abby, and if I have the opportunity, I'll kill Frankovich, but I'm not going to sit around and do nothing. He's probably going to send people to try and kill you, too, because he knows that you helped find out what he's doing. Keep your pistol with you."

Just then, Burns and Eldridge heard a commotion from a room down the hall. "Hold on, Mike," Eldridge whispered, I think they may be here now!" He opened a desk drawer and pulled out his Beretta. He racked a round into the chamber, looked at Rowdy and put his left index finger to his lips. He motioned to Rowdy to follow him. They walked quietly down the hall to an office when they heard someone gasping. Eldridge opened the door and he and Burns ran in.

They saw Markham on the floor holding one of the strangers in a choke hold. He let go of the dead man, picked up his pistol and whispered, "There's two more," pointing at the front of the building. They started walking towards the secretary's office when they heard a scream. Markham ran to the office first, pistol at the ready. When he got there, he lowered the pistol. Eldridge and Burns ran in and saw Flanders standing with his bloody knife in his right hand, one of the strangers dead on the floor and the other bleeding profusely from knife wounds in his side and abdomen. His pistol was on the floor. The man was wobbling from blood loss, trying to pull a knife from its scabbard.

He muttered "*Dedushka*," and fell to the floor dead.

"I wonder what he called me," Flanders asked as he picked up the dead man's pistol.

Eldridge chuckled. "He called you Grandfather."

Burns shook his head, looked down at the dead man, and answered, "Well, Grandfather just kicked his young ass."

Just then the front door swung open, and all pistols in the room were instantly pointed at Sergeant Cheshire, who'd burst in carrying three submachine guns. Eldridge and the others lowered their guns.

"Did you forget how to knock, Cheshire." Eldridge turned and looked down the hall. "Callaway," he said, as he ran toward his office. "Mike!" he yelled into the phone, but there was no answer.

Callaway had apparently hung up the phone. Eldridge stood there stunned. Rowdy looked at his friend's face, which signaled that something very bad was going on.

"What the hell is happening, David?" he asked. Flanders, Markham, and Cheshire joined them, and Eldridge told them all about the situation and then shook his head. "Jesus, Rowdy!" he said. "If I call this in, which I'm supposed to do, D.C. gets nuked, and Callaway's girlfriend gets killed. I want to help him but how am I going to get on that ship?

Rowdy answered, "If we had a SEAL team, and orders, I could run 'em out there submerged and maybe they could assault the ship, but we don't have either, right?"

Eldridge raised his head and narrowed his eyes. Looking at the three men who'd just saved his life, he answered. "Maybe we do have a team, Rowdy. We just won't have any orders. But I don't want you getting jacked up for breaking the rules like I did."

After a few second, Burns said, "I see this as a

situation requiring an instant response, David." Burns continued, "If you've got the troops, I'm in."

Eldridge smiled at Flanders, Markham, and Cheshire. "You guys interested in sneaking aboard a freighter off the coast to rescue Mike Callaway and his girlfriend, kill a bunch of former *Spetsnaz* commandos and disarm a nuclear missile?" he asked. "Keep in mind that this is totally unsanctioned and with no orders. Can you do that?"

The three looked at each other and then back at Eldridge. "Yeah, we can do that," Markham replied. "But how ya gonna get us there."

Nodding toward his friend, Eldridge answered, "This is Commander Ronald Burns, Skipper of the *USS Atlanta*. He has volunteered to put you alongside that ship, submerged, in his Los Angeles Class submarine. Do you have a way to covertly enter the vessel?"

Cheshire bit his lower lip and then smiled. "Oh yes we do, Commander," he replied. "Yes, we do. We have to go get our gear. We should be ready to go in twenty minutes." Eldridge said something to Burns and followed them all out the door.

In the hall, Flanders asked, "Are you going to get us a truck for our gear, Commander?"

"No, I asked Commander Burns to do that," he replied. "I'm coming with you to the gear shack because I'm going with you on this mission."

Flanders stopped dead in his tracks. "Wait, no you're not, Commander," he said.

Eldridge turned and confronted Flanders face to face. "Listen to me, Chief," he commanded. "You're gonna need all the help you can get. My friend may be aboard that ship, and I'm going to help him. And besides that, I may only be your commanding officer for another twelve hours, but during that time I call the shots. You got that, mister?"

Flanders grinned at him. "Aye, Sir. Let's go," he replied.

They grabbed black drysuits to keep the icy water from killing them, along with small scuba tanks, full-face dive masks with radios, and everything else they would need to get on board a moving ship. They also grabbed Markham's parachute, rope, and pulleys. Then they headed for the armory. They loaded magazines for the Beretta pistols, MP-5 submachine guns and an M16 to take with them.

"We don't have any fragmentation grenades, but we might be able to do something with these flash bang stun grenades that we use for training," Markham said.

Eldridge turned and stared at Cheshire for a couple of seconds. "Technical Sergeant, with training in engineering," he said. Cheshire turned and stared back at him. "Can you deactivate a nuclear bomb, Cheshire?" Eldridge asked.

Cheshire's mouth dropped open. "Um… I don't know, Sir." he replied. "My expertise is mostly in computers, but I can take apart almost anything. I mean, I'll give it my best shot."

Putting his hand on Cheshire's shoulder, Eldridge answered, "I know you will, son." He looked at Flanders and Markham. "We ready to rock and roll?" They nodded. They heard Commander Burns pull up in the truck. "Let's load up," Eldridge said.

*****

Callaway took his jacket off and wrapped it around the AK 47 to avoid some observant bystanders in the marina calling the police. Crossing the marina, he saw a brown survival suit draped across a chair. Seeing no owner nearby, he grabbed the suit and continued sprinting through the marina where he boarded his boat, the *Orinoco Flow*. Once aboard, he donned the survival suit and then jumped off the stern into his 17-foot *Hewes Redfisher* flats boat hanging a foot above the water. The skiff was built to chase fish in the shallow water of the Bahamas and South Florida, but today he would use her fifty mile per hour speed to somehow get aboard the *Put' Stalina*.

Looking northward, Callaway saw the ship emerging from the heavy mist engulfing the channel. He started the outboard motor with the boat out of the water so it would warm up quickly. He hit the switch to lower the skiff on the stern of the *Orinoco Flow*, but nothing happened. "Come on, goddammit!" he yelled. He punched the switch over and over, but the boat continued to sit, hanging in the air. The people in the marina were looking at him now because of the yelling. Then they ran for cover when Callaway pulled the AK out from the jacket. He put the muzzle against the coated steel cable and fired, cutting it, and dropping the bow of the boat into the water. He pushed the throttle forward and then shot the rear cable.

The boat took off as soon as the propeller hit the water. He grabbed the steering wheel trying his best to keep from sideswiping any of the other boats docked nearby. He slung the AK over his shoulder, steered the skiff into the channel and turned north towards the *Put' Stalina*.

Approaching it, he stayed about two hundred yards off her port side. He saw the lookouts at the bow and stern of the vessel, just as he had seen them from the air, only now he could see that they had rifles slung across their chests. He navigated into the mist ahead of the ship and then turned across her bow. As he emerged from the mist, he saw an iceberg ahead. He turned and got behind it for cover, peeking around it to see the starboard side of the ship.

He could clearly see the gangplank door about six feet above the waterline. The ship began to disappear into some low fog and Callaway saw his chance to get aboard. He shoved the throttle forward and ran out a couple of hundred yards on the starboard side of the ship this time. He pulled the throttle back and matched speed with the ship, approaching it slow and quiet. He could see the ship through the mist and coasted up to the hull with the gangplank door.

He kept watching up above for Frankovich's men who were on the middle deck. Callaway maneuvered his boat's port side up against the hull of the ship and then stood up on the helm seat with one foot on the steering wheel, trying to reach the lever for the gangway door. There were enough small waves to make his attempt difficult, as the flat-bottomed skiff was bouncing from right to left. A wave picked the hull up just enough for him to grab the lever. Now he had to press the keys correctly on the lock next to the handle to open the door.

Callaway tried to swing his arm up and in the process the sling for the AK slipped down his arm and the rifle fell into the water. "Son-of-a-bitch," he whispered, as he punched the code 10-27-62 into the lock. The door unlocked and he pushed the steering wheel to the right to direct the skiff out away from the ship. Callaway was able to pull open the door and go aboard. He closed the door behind him and walked quietly down one of the dark corridors. *I need a weapon*, he thought. *I can't do much of anything to save Abby with just a knife.*

He knew of only one place on the ship where there were guns, and, hopefully, where he would find his girlfriend. That would be Captain Frankovich's cabin. He followed the hallway to a staircase and tiptoed up to the level of the captain's cabin. *Hopefully, Frankovich is being a good Captain and guiding his ship from the bridge and hopefully all his men are at their stations,* he thought as he made his way to the room and listened at the door. *Silence.* Callaway pulled the switchblade from his pocket, opened the door quickly, and ran in.

The room was empty. He went to the gun cabinet and used the knife to pry the flimsy lock open. As he lifted one of the ancient Browning A5 shotguns out, he noticed something. The Mosin Nagant sniper rifle was missing. He pulled open the drawer at the base of the cabinet and found a box of bird shot, the kind that could be used for skeet shooting but not much of anything else unless he had to fight a flock of quail. *Wonderful. This stuff won't stop anyone unless I'm right on top of them, especially with the heavy clothing they're wearing.* He checked the closet where he saw the AK 47 ammunition and found nothing else for the shotgun. *Well… any port in a storm, I guess,* he thought, as he loaded the shotgun with four rounds in the magazine and one in the chamber. He then loaded his pockets with the remaining twenty rounds. He opened the cabin door and peered quickly in both directions. *Now where would he keep Abby?* he asked himself, as he got to another set of stairs. His first thought was the galley.

*****

"Sonar-Conn," the Sonar Operator of the USS *Atlanta* announced, "I have a ship at 1,000 yards dead ahead."

Commander Burns replied, "Understood Sonar. Up periscope." The Type 18 search periscope went up to a level just breaking the surface of the water. Burns put his eye to the scope and zoomed in on the stern of the ship in front of him. "I've got the *Put'Stalina* in sight," he said out loud. The submarine was crawling along at the same slow five knots as the ship. "Down scope," he ordered. Burns picked up the microphone by the chart table and switched communication to the area outside of the escape trunk, near the middle of the boat. "You guys ready to go?" he asked.

Commander Eldridge answered, "Yeah, Rowdy. Take her to all-stop and we'll let you know when we're up on the conning tower."

Burns cupped the microphone in his hands, making sure his crew members couldn't hear him. "I'm calling this in as soon as you're aboard the ship," he whispered. "I've got a torpedo ready to go in a forward tube just in case. Stay away from the stern as much as you can in case I have to fire. You told me that the nuke was in the front hold of the vessel, so if I shoot the ship in the ass, it should be safe, right?"

Eldridge took a deep breath before he answered. "You're guessing that you'll get orders to shoot, right?"

Now Eldridge heard Rowdy take a deep breath. "Yeah, man," he replied. "I'm guessing that's exactly what my orders will be to keep them from launching the missile."

Eldridge bowed his head. "You do what you have to

do, brother," he said. "Just give us as much time as you can, please."

Rowdy replied, "I will. I hope your friend and his lady are alright, too. Stay safe."

Eldridge joined his men in the escape trunk. They donned their head covers and full-face masks and checked their communication system so they could coordinate with each other and with the submarine. The submarine slowed to a full stop. Flanders had the most expertise in this type of operation. Even though he'd trained Markham and Cheshire in the egress and ingress from a submarine, all he'd had time to do was to explain the process to Commander Eldridge on the ride down to the submarine. While Eldridge was a certified scuba diver, this was a big change from looking at fish and reefs in the Bahamas.

Flanders secured the hatch from the interior of the sub. They all put on swim fins to help them move from the deck to the top of the conning tower. Flanders then gave them an OK signal with his hand, and they responded with the same. He turned the wheel, opening the valves that poured ice cold water from Cook Inlet into the chamber. He watched Eldridge for signs of panic, as many men he'd trained had shown in the past. Eldridge winked at him through his mask. A green light lit up to let them know that water pressure in the trunk had equalized with the water pressure outside. Flanders turned the wheel to unseal the deck hatch and then slowly opened it. He climbed the ladder and pulled himself up onto the deck followed by Markham, who was carrying his equipment; Cheshire, who had a bag of tools scavenged from the submarine's crew to hopefully deactivate the nuke; and Eldridge, who was carrying a bag full of flash bang grenades.

They worked their way forward, using their fins to

kick their way up to the bridge compartment at the top of the conning tower. Flanders keyed his microphone. "On top," he said. Markham unpacked his parachute and strapped it on. Cheshire attached a carabiner clip and heavy-duty rope to the front of Markham's harness. Eldridge tied the other end to the hatch handle atop the conning tower. Markham racked a round of 9mm ammunition into the chamber of his H&K MP-5 and set the switch to semi-automatic He checked the sound suppressor to ensure it was attached tightly to the barrel, after which he turned on a red-dot holographic gun sight. While it had been sent out to training units for evaluation, it had not yet been approved for warfare. He put on his short skis and signaled that he was ready.

Flanders keyed his mike again. "Let's move," he said.

Down below them, Commander Burns was plotting the sub's movements. "Helm, all ahead, make six knots. Up scope." The sub moved forward slowly as Commander Burns looked through the periscope. It was a pretty good chance that the mist on the water would keep the two lookouts on the back of the ship from seeing it.

When they got within one hundred yards, he ordered down scope, as the *Atlanta* pulled up alongside and submerged next to the ship. Eldridge and the others could see the hull of the *Put' Stalina* underwater from fifty feet away. They had to watch for any movement towards the submarine and warn the crew so they could move the sub out of the way. At the conning tower, Flanders looked at Markham and nodded his head. Markham stepped back a few feet on the conning tower bridge and jumped up, pushing his ski-covered feed toward the bow of the boat. Water pressure against the short skis pushed him behind and up from the conning tower. He continued emerging until his head broke the surface. He looked at the starboard rear of the ship and saw the back of a lookout at the rear corner. He stuck his right hand down and gave an OK signal to the team.

Flanders keyed his microphone and said, "Speed 10 knots."

Commander Burns turned to the chief of the boat. "Make ten knots, Chief and bring her up ten feet!" he said.

The chief relayed that order to one of the two helmsmen. One dialed the speed in, while the other just slightly changed the ballast to push the bridge of the conning tower slightly above the water. The sub moved forward, beginning to rise out of the water.

Markham flipped his gun's safety off and pulled the ripcord. The parachute deployed, and he ascended to the level of the lower deck while Flanders and Eldridge held the rope tightly. They slowly let the rope out to position Markham near the lookout without losing any altitude. He passed over the man and said "Stop" over his Vox microphone. The lookout was lighting a cigarette as the Marine materialized out of thin air off the side of the ship. He dropped his cigarette lighter to go for his rifle. Markham held the red-dot sight on the man's chest. *Say goodnight,* he thought, as he squeezed the trigger twice.

The man fell to the deck and did not move. Markham pointed toward the front of the ship, and he was pulled forward by Flanders and Eldridge. He pulled on the static lines of the parachute to move left toward the ship. It was a bumpy ride because of the wind coming off the hull, but he managed to make a hard landing hitting the deck and a bulkhead at the same time. He said "Slow," over the microphone, and the sub matched speed with the ship again. He pulled the parachute in and rolled it up.

Then he unsnapped the carabiner from his chest harness and clipped it to the deck railing. He pulled the rope toward him, until he reached a section with a large pulley with two ropes attached to it. He unhooked the pulley and clamped it to the railing below the other rope.

Now Cheshire clipped a carabiner to his chest harness, grabbed the upper rope, and began pulling himself up to the deck. Flanders watched to make sure Eldridge, who was the next one to go up, was able to pull himself up to the deck. *Son-of-a-bitch, he's doing it*, he thought as the older man shimmied up to the ship. Flanders then hooked up and pulled himself to the deck. They unclamped the ropes and threw them into the water.

"We're in, Rowdy," Eldridg said. Burns clicked his microphone twice to acknowledge. "Be safe," his men heard him whisper. The four men had already discussed their duties prior to boarding the Russian ship. First and foremost, they had to avoid contact with the seventeen members of the crew who had them outnumbered and outgunned.

Eldridge gave them their last order as he handed out flash bang grenades to his men. "Do the best you can, and we'll all meet up at that big lifeboat on the stern," he said, giving them a proud look.

Flanders and Markham left to assault the bridge and try to take control of the ship. They would try to run the *Put' Stalina* aground on the shore of Kalgin Island in the middle of the Inlet where only a few people lived. Cheshire would go to the forward hold and try to disarm or damage the Midgetman missile and/or the nuclear warhead it would carry, and Eldridge would go hunting for Michael Callaway and Abby, hoping that they hadn't already been killed.

*****

Callaway removed his borrowed survival suit and stashed it in a storage closet on his way to the galley. When he got there, he listened at the closed door to find out who was in there and how many people there were. Mostly, he wanted to know if Abby was being held there. He could hear two men speaking Russian. He didn't want to enter the room if Abby wasn't in there. *Why fight two against one if you don't have to*, he thought.

He was just turning to look for her elsewhere when he heard her voice in the galley, saying, "If you touch me again, I'll kick your balls all the way to Siberia!"

Callaway spun around and crashed through the wooden door. The two men who had her tied to a chair and were apparently getting too close to her, turned and went for their pistols. They froze when they saw the shotgun aimed at them.

"Drop the guns!" he yelled. They just stood there looking at him an then dropped their pistols. Callaway then motioned the muzzle of his weapon toward a wall. *Oh good, they learn fast,* he thought as they walked to the wall. He then spun around his left index finger a couple of times to get them to face the wall. Then he squatted down next to Abby, pulled the switchblade from his coat pocket, pushed the button, and cut the ropes binding her arms to the chair.

"I believe this is yours," he said, handing the knife to her and picking the pistols up from the floor. She cut the ropes from her ankles and stood up. Callaway expected her to give him a hug, at the very least, but she walked past him and shoved one of her captors against the wall face-first. She then stuck the tip of the blade between his thighs and against his testicles. He began breathing very hard. "I've never neutered a dog before, but I'm thinking of doing that right now."

The man didn't need a translation. "*Mne Zhal! Mne Zhal*!!" he yelled.

Callaway watched what she was doing, trying not to laugh. "Uh... Sweetie?" he asked. "I don't speak Russian, but I'm guessing that means 'I'm sorry.' Why don't we tie these two up and get ourselves off this tub?"

She squinted at Callaway, pulled the knife away, closed the blade and put it in her pocket. She took the rope that she had been tied with and bound the other man to a six-inch pipe that went from the floor to the ceiling. Then she got a filthy dishrag from the kitchen and gagged the man with it.

"So, what did the other guy do that pissed you off so much," Callaway asked. She looked at him angrily and answered, "Well let's put it this way: I didn't ask him to touch my boobs, okay. Oh, and I don't have enough rope to tie him up."

Callaway walked to the other man and tapped him on the shoulder. He turned around and looked at Callaway, who was smiling. The man smiled back, and then Callaway hit him in the face with the butt of the shotgun, hard enough to knock him unconscious. "Only I get to touch those, jackass," he said. He then went into the kitchen and found a large package of dish towels. He tied several together and secured the unconscious man to the pipe.

Abby stared at Callaway. "I'm glad to see that you escaped," she said.

He hugged her. "I couldn't have done it if you didn't slip me your knife," he said.

"Did you find out who killed my cousin, Paul?" she asked.

"Yeah, I found out," he replied.

Still pressing her face against his chest, she asked, "Did you kill him?"

Callaway didn't want to answer the question, remembering how she'd reacted in Fort Lauderdale when she asked him about the people he killed before. He couldn't lie to her. "Yes, I did," he answered. "With your knife."

After a few seconds of silence, she whispered, "Good. I wish I had done it myself."

He squeezed her. "We need to go, now," he told her, handing her one of the pistols as they left the galley.

*****

Technical Sergeant Cheshire entered the forward hold of the *Put' Stalina*. He walked around the hold with his MP-5 at the ready but found nobody in the compartment. *The captain must have everyone either driving the ship or keeping lookout*, he thought. He stopped when he saw a very long, partially completed sheet steel box with the front end and top open. He looked into the opening and froze. There was the Midgetman missile sitting on its launcher. There were more cover panels being constructed next to it. He could smell the molten lead being used as an insulator that would keep any radiation meters from detecting the missile's presence. He turned and saw more pots of lead cooking on one of the work benches. He looked at the nose of the missile and saw a couple of access hatches that the weapons operators on the submarine had given him a quick tutorial on. He went into his bag of tools and found a screwdriver that would fit the flush-fit screws on the hatches. He removed the screws, but he could only move the hatch open about an inch. He went through the tool bag, looking for something heavy duty that he could pry the hatch open with, without any luck.

"I guess the Navy is too high class to keep a crowbar around," he whispered. Looking around the hold, he saw something on the workbench next to a pan full of boiling lead. It was long and looked strong enough to pry the door open. He walked over and found a three-foot long piece of shiny polished metal that could be useful, except it was too thick to squeeze into the opening on the hatch on one side and curved too much on the other to fit the opening. He saw a large sledgehammer on another bench. *"Well, I hope nobody hears this,* he thought, figuring one or two good hits would flatten the curved edge enough to fit it into the hatch.

He laid a couple of shop rags on the bar to muffle the clanging noise he knew the impact would make. Cheshire held the large side of the piece down with his left hand and lifted the sledgehammer with his right. He swung down hard and hit the bar. Looking it over, he raised the hammer again.

"Do not move!" he heard from behind him. "I have gun," the person said with a heavy accent, his voice shaking. Cheshire could see the thin man's fuzzy reflection in the polished piece of metal. *He doesn't look special forces,* he thought.

The Russian computer technician kept the Makarov pistol aimed at him. "Put down hammer," the man said. Cheshire looked to the right and saw the large pan full of boiling lead.

"Put down hammer, now!" the man insisted.

"Sure thing, buddy," Cheshire replied, swinging the hammer down as hard as he could, hitting the panhandle and flipping a gallon of boiling lead onto the man's face and chest. The assailant screamed, fell to the floor, and lay there in shock, twitching. Cheshire took the Makarov from him and gave the metal bar another hit with the sledgehammer. He returned to the missile and easily pried open the hatch. He could see the warhead of the missile with its single nuclear payload reentry vehicle. He took a deep breath, let it out and grabbed some tools. *This should be fun,* he thought as he went to work.

*****

Callaway and Abby worked their way towards the ship's stern. They took passageways that he had seen during his inspection of the ship that would keep them away from contact with the crew. He knew that they would probably have to shoot their way to the lifeboat at the rear of the deck they were on. He tried to prepare Abby for a gunfight, making sure that the Makarov pistol that they took from her captor had the safety off. He explained quickly how she needed to use cover in a gunfight. They were about to move out onto the deck when they heard

"Mike!" behind them. Callaway spun around and crouched, pointing the shotgun behind him. He was amazed to see David Eldridge there.

"Holy shit, David," he said. "What are you doing here?"

Eldridge smiled. "Trying to save your ass as usual," Eldridge replied. "Are you heading for the lifeboat?"

"Yes," Callaway said, still astonished that his friend

229

was on board the ship. "Are you alone? How did you get onboard?" he asked.

Eldridge waived his right hand. "There's no time for that now, Mike," he responded. "We've got to get in that lifeboat and wait for the others."

Puzzled, Callaway asked, "Others? What others?"

Just as Eldridge opened his mouth to answer, they heard gunfire erupting from above. Eldridge looked up. "Is the bridge up there, Mike?" he asked.

"Yeah," Callaway responded. "What's going on, David?" he asked.

"That's got to be Flanders and Markham trying to take control of the bridge," he answered. "I've got to get up there."

Grabbing his arm, Callaway said, "I'm going with you. They are totally outnumbered."

Eldridge shook his head. "Negative, Mike. You need to get Abby on the lifeboat, and the two of you need to get the hell out of here," he responded.

"All three of us need to go!" Abby said.

Just seeing her expression, Callaway realized she would go with them whether they liked it or not.

"Okay, then, let's go," Eldridge said to them. They started up the stairs, with Callaway and Eldridge side by side, and Abby acting as tail-gunner in case any crew members snuck up behind them. At the top of the stairs, they saw several crewmen lying dead on the deck of the wheelhouse, and they could hear Markham's silenced MP-5 and Flanders M-16 blasting away at men on the outside bridge wings.

"Hey!" Abby yelled, as she fired three shots from the Makarov down the stairwell at two crewmen who came up behind them. Eldridge took cover on one side at the top of the stairs, and Callaway and Abby ran to the other side. The men at the base of the stairs took turns firing bursts up the stairs. Just then Callaway looked up and saw shadows moving towards the roof windows of the bridge. He waved at Eldridge and pointed up. Eldridge saw the same thing. Crewmen were trying to get to the windows at the top of the bridge so they could shoot Flanders and Markham from above. Callaway signaled that he would go upstairs to intervene. He kissed Abby on the cheek and ran outside. He climbed the ladder holding the heavy Browning shotgun with one hand. When he got to the top, he could see three men ahead of him preparing to shoot. He leveled the Browning and shot the one farthest away in the back of the head. The man fell to the roof of the bridge dead. The other two stood and turned their guns on Callaway. He fired two quick rounds of birdshot, hitting one of the men in the face and the other in the throat. Both fell through the glass roof windows and landed on the control room floor dying.

Flanders and Markham looked up and saw Callaway standing there. Eldridge was keeping the two men at the base of the stairs pinned down. Flanders and Markham came out of the bridge to help.

"Can we run the ship into the island?" Eldridge asked.

Flanders shook his head. "She's on autopilot, and they've got the controls locked down," he replied. We can't get the helm wheel to move."

Callaway came down the ladder to join them. He drew fire from the men below who were blocking their way to the lifeboat. Eldridge, Markham, and Flanders pulled out their flash bang grenades and Eldridge handed Callaway another one. They pulled the pins on the grenades, and on Eldridge's command, they threw the grenades down the stairs. Four explosions rang out, and the concussion knocked both crewmen out.

Callaway, Abby, Eldridge, Flanders, and Markham ran down the stairs onto the rear deck. They checked both sides and above them and saw that they were clear. They ran to the lifeboat sitting on the launching rails at a steep angle downward and pulled open the hatch to get in. Flanders was the only one who stayed outside, resting his rifle on the hatch and searching with its telescopic sight for any other crewmen who might want to take a shot at them. Callaway was looking out through the windows when he realized that someone was missing.

He asked Eldridge, "Did Cheshire come along on this excursion?"

Eldridge nodded. "Yeah, he went forward to try to disable the nuke and the missile," he replied in a worried tone. "I don't know where he is."

Hearing this, Markham keyed his microphone and called Cheshire, but didn't get a response. There wasn't even a squelch from the radio. He reached down to check his radio unit and saw that it was gone. "Shit, I lost my com!" he said. "It must have come off my belt when we were fighting in the control room."

"You guys need to get off that ship now!" they heard Commander Burns yell from the submarine. "I'm about five thousand yards off the stern and I'm watching you through the periscope. I've been ordered to fire, so you need to go now!"

Eldridge replied, "Rowdy, you need to give us a little more time. I'm still missing one of my men."

"Dammit, David, I'll give you a few more minutes, but that's it," he said. "I've got to sink that ship before

232

they launch the missile. And I need to do it soon, because we're coming up to an area that's too shallow for this boat to run in, even if I surface, and there are F-15 fighters coming down from Elmendorf Air Force Base loaded with missiles." Just then the hatch opened, and Cheshire climbed into the boat.

"Talk about perfect timing," Callaway said, as he took the helmsman's seat. Flanders climbed in and secured the hatch.

"Rowdy, we're leaving now!" Eldridge shouted. "Shoot this tub in the ass!"

*****

Burns called the torpedo room. "Conn, Torpedo! Do we have a firing solution?" he asked.

His torpedo officer came back instantly with, "Working on it, Skipper."

Burns let out a breath, and told him, "Shoot as soon as you're lined up."

*****

At the same moment, Callaway told the others on the boat, "Hold on!" as he pulled the release lever that sent the boat sliding down the rails and crashing into the water thirty feet below. Callaway started the engine and went to full throttle, which was a slow ten miles per hour, knowing that very soon the one thousand pounds of high explosive in the torpedo would detonate under the stern of the *Put' Stalina*.

Eldridge grabbed Cheshire by the arm. "Were you able to disable the missile and the warhead?"

Cheshire stared at him for a second before answering, "No, and yes. I couldn't stop him from firing the missile if he wants to. I mean I messed with the guidance system, but I couldn't keep it from being launchable."

Confused, Eldridge asked, "So he can launch the nuke and we don't know where it will explode?"

Shaking his head, Cheshire answered, "No. No, I removed every radioactive thing in that warhead," he replied. "And then I threw it into the forward bilge tank under the deck. I put the access panels back on in case anyone came nosing around after I left."

Grinning at Cheshire, Eldridge grabbed the back of his neck and kissed him on the forehead. "Well frigging done!" he said. "Looks like we're home free," Eldridge said, and then they heard a loud **crack** on the roof of the lifeboat. Markham, who had been watching the ship through the clear plexiglass roof panels, fell to the deck, holding his shoulder. There was blood everywhere.

Abby jumped down next to him, shouting, "He's been shot." She grabbed a first aid kit from under the control panel of the boat, opened it, and put pressure on the wound front and back with gauze pads.

Then they heard the voice of the man who sent the bullet. "Did you think you could get away from me?" Acardi Frankovich had found Markham's radio. "You tried to stop my ship and you failed," he continued. "You tried to sabotage my missile and you failed. Now I have started the sequence to launch a large nuclear device at your capital. That and another bomb that will go off soon as my final blow against your country!"

Two more bullets came through the rear windows of the boat and hit the engine's fiberglass cover. The bullets damaged the induction system of the diesel engine causing it to sputter and die. The lifeboat was still moving away from the *Put' Stalina*, but at a snail's pace. Flanders lifted an escape hatch on the roof of the boat and propped the fore end of his scoped M-16 on the frame, trying to search out where Frankovich was hiding in the five-story superstructure at the rear of the ship.

"I can't see him!" he yelled, when another bullet from the old Mosin-Nagant sniper rifle tore through the plexiglass and hit him in the left lower leg. Flanders dropped down into one of the seats and grabbed his bleeding calf.

"Everyone get on the floor," Callaway shouted. "David, take the helm!" Cheshire took some gauze pads and held them on both sides of Flanders' leg, while Abby was still trying to stop the bleeding from the wound in Markham's shoulder. Eldridge crawled up and kneeled in front of the helm seat, where he'd be partially hidden. Callaway picked up Flanders' rifle and crawled to the other side of the boat. He slid open one of the side windows and leaned out of the cabin aiming the rifle at the rear of the *Put' Stalina*.

Frankovich had seen movement and had Callaway in his sights. He was smiling and just beginning to squeeze the trigger when he heard Commander Eldridge's voice over the radio.

"Hey Acardi, remember that day on the bridge of your submarine in 1962?" Frankovich took his finger off the trigger. "I was the guy on the bridge-wing of the destroyer," Eldridge continued. "You remember, right? You tried to end the world with a nuclear torpedo. You called me a son-of-a-bitch in Russian, and I flipped you the bird. Good times, right?"

"You!" Frankovich yelled furiously. "Now you will see how I get my revenge!" A couple of seconds passed and then a bright orange glow came from the front of the *Put' Stalina.* The missile came out of the hold and accelerated into the misty sky. "You see! You see!" Frankovich screamed. "Washington D.C. will be a wasteland!" He raised his arm toward the missile.

Callaway placed the crosshairs of the scope where he saw movement and fired. The bullet hit Frankovich in the chest damaging his left lung. They heard him yelling. Callaway watched him through the scope sight.

"Jesus, Acardi," Callaway yelled, didn't your mother teach you anything?" A sniper never moves if he wants to stay alive."

"I don't care if I die," Frankovich shouted back, wheezing from the gunshot wound. "I will hurt your country like it has never been hurt before," he said.

"No, you won't," Callaway answered. "The warhead of your missile is empty!" he said. The missile may crash, but it won't do much damage."

Frankovich growled in rage.

"Oh yeah," Callaway continued, "You won't be nuking Valdez, either. I buried your train in the snow."

Frankovich lifted the old sniper rifle, intent on killing everyone in the lifeboat. He aimed the rifle at Callaway again. He stopped suddenly, staring at something in the water below. It looked like the wake of a torpedo. He looked up at the lifeboat and whispered "*Sukin Sin.*" The Mk 48 torpedo traveled under the stern of the ship and unleashed its payload of high explosive straight up, obliterating the entire rear of the ship along with its captain, Acardi Frankovich.

The *Put' Stalina* slowed to a stop and began to settle

into the water stern first. The *Atlanta* surfaced and headed straight for the lifeboat. Eldridge had advised Rowdy Burns that they had wounded aboard. The submarine came to a stop and dispatched an inflatable boat to take everyone aboard the sub. Commander Burns met them on the deck as Markham and Flanders were taken below to the sick bay. The surgeon on board was able to stop the bleeding enough to keep both men stable until they could be brought ashore and to a military base hospital.

They were all on deck watching the *Put'Stalina* slip below the waves, when Commander Burns and his Weapons Officer started asking Cheshire how he neutered the missile. "I couldn't get into the guts of the missile itself," Cheshire said, "So I decided to remove all of the nuclear material in case Frankovich was able to launch. I figured that the empty nose cone coming out of space and crashing into the Earth would be a better thing than a 400 plus kiloton nuclear bomb going off. And yeah, in case you're wondering, I am very worried about where it will land."

Burns' Weapons Officer looked at his captain and shrugged. "Without the weight of the payload in the nose cone, the inertial guidance system will be thrown off, and the missile will go to God knows where within 6,800 miles, Skipper," he said. They all looked up at the smoke trail left behind by the first of three solid fuel rocket boosters now pushing the empty nose section of the missile at three times the speed of sound. They all knew that, although there were no nuclear explosives in the missile's warhead, there was no telling where the now nukeless missile was going to land and what destruction it would do.

*****

"Well, what do ya think?" Rae, the one-toothed once owner of a greasy-spoon truck stop and campground in western Pembroke Pines, Florida asked. It had been a year and a half since her original truck stop was blown to bits, unintentionally, by an explosion in a dynamite bunker three miles south in the City of Miramar, courtesy of one Michael Callaway.

She was showing off her brand-new truck stop that took a little over a year to build. She wanted her two favorite patrons, Miramar Police Officers, Fred Benini and Jack Flowers, who happened to be there when the explosion occurred, to be the first to see her new place. Rae had her car parked alongside the officer's marked patrol car about one hundred yards from the building, talking about the past when they were assigned to Zone 7 right along the Everglades Levy.

"God, that was a hell of a night when the old place was blown up," Flowers said sipping coffee from a Styrofoam cup. "I'll be happy when you get this place opened up, Rae. The dump where I got this cup makes crap coffee. And you know how cops run on coffee." Flowers laughed. "And what about the plane crash we handled down the road a year before your place was blown up?' he said. "There's always interesting stuff going on in Zone 7. How are you gonna get by out here without us when we retire in six months?"

Rae turned around and put her hands on her hips. "What do you mean, retire?" she replied. "How in hell am I gonna get by out here without you two?" The officers laughed.

Benini put his arm around her. "Don't worry about

it, sweetie," he answered. We'll make a point of coming out here just to get coffee, I promise.

She smiled and took a deep breath, staring at the clear dark sky. "Look how beautiful the stars are tonight," she said.

Looking up, Benini said, "Yep. Look, there's the Big Dipper," he said, pointing at the stars… except that one of the stars seemed to be moving… quickly, and right toward them. "Holy shit," he said. "Get in the car, now!" he yelled.

In a panicked voice, Rae shouted, "What's the matter?"

Benini grabbed her by the arm and pulled her to the car. She was still looking up when she said, "Oh my God!" "What is it?"

Benini opened the rear door on the passenger side of the car and threw Rae onto the seat. He slammed the door shut and jumped into the right front seat as Flowers was starting the car.

"Get us out of here, Jack!" Benini ordered. Flowers floored the gas pedal hard enough to break the rear tires loose, causing the car to fish-tale wildly until the tires got some traction. They were moving east while Rae was looking out through the rear window. The nose section of the missile looked like a huge fireball hurtling from the sky. It hit the truck stop building at an angle, completing its 4,943-mile journey from Alaska. Once it penetrated the roof, it created a pressure wave that blew all four walls outward with enough power to shower the patrol car with cinder block fragments from almost a mile away. Rae and both officers tried to duck down when the flying pile of broken concrete hit the car, shattering all but the front windshield. Flowers floored the brake pedal, and the car spun one hundred eighty degrees facing where the truck stop had been.

Then there was quiet. Benini and Flowers stared through the cracked windshield in disbelief. They slowly drove back past Rae's car that had been pummeled to pieces by the concrete barrage and onto what was left of the building. While Benini called for help on the radio, Flowers looked around and shook his head.

"There's a floor," he said. "There's nothing left but a goddamn floor." They got out of the car and Rae started crying. "Why does this keep happening to me," she said. "It took me forever to get the damned insurance company to rebuild my place. Now I'm gonna have to do it all over again." The two officers leaned against the front of the busted-up police car, staring at the scene as they heard sirens approaching from the east. Benini looked up at the stars before he spoke to Flowers.

"What do you say we put in our retirement papers tomorrow?" he asked.

Flowers just looked at the ground. "Works for me," was all he said.

Chapter 16

One year later

"They're late," David Eldridge complained. He stood on the aft helicopter deck of the Navy Cruiser *USS Ticonderoga*.

"Skipper, the launch is pulling alongside now," his executive officer reported in a soothing voice. Eldridge was now the captain of the Aegis-equipped war ship, named after a city, where a short, but important, battle of the American Revolutionary War had been fought. Eldridge was clad in his dress white uniform. He was pacing about like a nervous cat because he had a very important job to do this cool but beautiful night in Anchorage, Alaska. He was to be the best man at the wedding of Michael Callaway and Dr. Abigail Tika'a this evening.

A lot had happened between the sinking of the *Put' Stalina* and this beautiful starry night. The Department of Defense had decided not to discipline all those involved in the unauthorized assault on the *Put' Stalina*. It would be too embarrassing to admit they had lost both a nuclear missile and fissionable material, as well. All involved were sworn to secrecy and rewarded as a way to guarantee their silence. Flanders and Markham spent a week in the hospital at Elmendorf Air Force Base after being transported by helicopter there from the deck of the *USS Atlanta*. After all the dust had settled, Flanders was promoted to master chief and was reassigned to train new candidates for the eight-week Naval Special Warfare Preparatory School in Great Lakes, Illinois.

Markham was promoted to master gunnery sergeant and reassigned as a trainer at the Marine Corps Scout Sniper School at the base in Quantico, Virginia. Cheshire was advanced to his previous higher rank of master sergeant and sent to Keesler Air Force Base in Mississippi to train enlisted personnel in something new called computer warfare.

Eldridge and Rowdy Burns were submitted to what they referred to as the *forty-five-minute ass chewing* by a four-star admiral for acting without orders, and then both were promoted to the rank of captain for keeping a madman from potentially taking millions of American lives. No charges were preferred against Mr. Michael Callaway for the numerous statutes that he broke throughout the affair. Lapinsky was arrested by the FBI and was awaiting trial. Rae finally got her business back up and running courtesy of an insurance reimbursement and a check for $100,000 dollars from a mystery donor. The envelope was postmarked from Alaska.

A Navy dive team was able to remove all the nuclear material from the forward bilge of the *Put' Stalina*. One of the divers, while inspecting the wreckage that had once been the stern of the ship, found an old Mosin-Nagant sniper rifle, complete with an original PU telescopic sight, among the shattered piles of steel on the bottom of Cook Inlet. The rifle was cleaned up and, somehow, made its way to the captain's quarters aboard the *USS*

Ticonderoga. Captain Eldridge proudly displayed the trophy on the wall of his office.

The launch pulled alongside the cruiser and a large group of people came aboard. The first to climb the ladder to the helicopter deck was Callaway. He walked over to Captain Eldridge and gave him a hug.

"So how do you like your new ride, David?" he asked, indicating the sleek cruiser. "I'm guessing the Navy pushed back your retirement?"

Smiling, Eldridge answered, "Yep, they gave me two more years. They also asked me what I would like to do for those two years and... here I am."

Callaway looked Eldridge in the eye. "I owe you a lot, my friend," he said.

Eldridge laughed and answered, "Oh yes, you do! But you know what, I wouldn't have wanted it any other way, Mike. It's been a fun ride. So, what's in the future for Mr. and Mrs. Michael Callaway?"

Looking out at Cook Inlet, Callaway answered, "Well, we will live up here during the summers so Abby can work and live in Florida during the winters, cruising the Caribbean and South America. Abby has become a real lover of sand and salt water, and I absolutely hate the winters up here, so we'll be Florida snowbirds."

They heard loud voices coming from the stairs. Abby's three brothers, Matthew, Mark, and John came up on deck, dressed in their traditional Ninilchik garb, with their mother and father. Behind them were the trio of Flanders, Markham, and Cheshire, all in their respective dress uniforms, and finally, DEA Special Agent in Charge Richard Todd accompanied by Donna Kendall.

When he saw Todd and Kendall across the helicopter deck, Callaway smiled and waved. Donna lifted her left hand to show Callaway an engagement ring. Callaway walked across the deck and gave her a hug. Todd put his hand out to shake, but Callaway grabbed him and gave him a hug, too.

"Oh… Well, okay," Todd said.

"Congratulations," Callaway said. Just then he heard a bosun's whistle sounding off, indicating that someone important was coming aboard. Callaway looked toward the stairs and saw his bride standing there, dressed in formal tribal clothing, and giving him a smile that almost made him cry.

"Ladies and gentlemen, would you please have a seat," Captain Eldridge said. Callaway walked across the deck and stood next to Eldridge as he continued addressing the guests. "Welcome aboard the *USS Ticonderoga*, ladies and gentlemen," he said. "My name is David Eldridge, and I am the commanding officer of this ship. We are here tonight to witness the marriage of Abigail Tika'a and Michael Callaway.

He introduced the Navy chaplain who would officiate the marriage. Abby's maid of honor walked up to the chaplain and stood across from Callaway and Eldridge. Callaway watched his future wife and her father walk towards him. When they reached the chaplain, Abby's father gave her a hug and kissed her on the cheek. He then turned and shook Callaway's hand. The ceremony was short and perfect. David handed the ring to Callaway, and he placed it on her finger, and she did the same with his. The chaplain pronounced them husband and wife and that resulted in a huge round of applause.

Captain Eldridge addressed the guests again. "Ladies and gentlemen, please follow the bride and groom down the stairs and board one of the launches.

They will take you to the beautiful yacht that Michael rented for the reception." As Callaway and Abby walked to the stairs, Eldridge turned to his executive officer and nodded. The executive officer then spoke into a headset microphone. "Forward mount, three round salute, fire!" The forward turret of the cruiser had its five-inch diameter barrel aimed almost straight up. Callaway, Abby, and their guests, and most likely anyone within a mile of the harbor in Anchorage ducked when the cannon fired three times in quick succession. They heard three explosions high up in the air and saw what looked like white fireworks on steroids. The white phosphorus star shells lit up the entire harbor. Callaway turned and looked at Eldridge, who just smiled and shrugged.

The reception on the yacht was a tremendous affair and everyone enjoyed themselves. Callaway told Abby that he had selected the song for their first dance as husband and wife. She seemed none too keen on not knowing what the song was, but she went along with him. They walked out onto the dance floor, and the DJ played a song that started with a flute and cellos. She laughed, as did everyone in the room who'd been involved in the situation with Acardi Frankovich when they heard "Isn't Life Strange" by the Moody Blues.

Callaway danced with his wife, and he was happy for the first time in years. Eldridge and Rowdy Burns were talking with Abby's brothers when Eldridge's Executive Officer walked up and handed him a sheet of paper. Eldridge read it, shook his head, and then passed it to Burns. Callaway saw what was happening, and he and Abby walked over.

"Everything okay, David?" he asked. Eldridge handed the paper to Callaway, who started reading it. He looked at Abby.

245

"Sorry kiddo, but we need to leave," Eldridge said. "The *Ticonderoga* is needed in the Strait of Hormuz. Some nasty stuff is starting up in Iran." He turned to his executive officer. "Spool up the turbine and get the ship ready to move, Lieutenant," he said.

"Aye, aye, sir," the exec said, and then called in the orders on his head set as he headed for the launch. Eldridge gave Abby a hug, and then did the same for Callaway. "You take good care of her, you understand, Mike." he said quietly. "And don't kill anybody, 'cause I won't be around to bail you out, okay?"

Callaway felt like he was being given advice by his late father. And that was fine by him. "I'll give it my best shot, David. No pun intended," he replied.

"I've got to go, Mike," Eldridge said. Callaway grabbed his arm.

"Give me a couple of minutes, David." he said. "I'll meet you at the launch." Callaway disappeared into another room, and Eldridge walked to the ladder for the launch. The next thing he saw was Callaway coming out on the deck with Abby. Callaway handed him a gift-wrapped box.

"I thought you'd want this to remind you of the first time we met."

Taking it as a joke, Eldridge reminded him, "We met at Greasy Dick's Bar in Nassau," he said. "What's in the box, a six pack of crummy beer?"

Callaway smiled. "No, not that time," he replied. "You'll figure it out. Just wait until you're back aboard the *Ticonderoga* before you open it."

Eldridge walked down the stairs and climbed into the launch. "Okay, now you've got me worried," he said.

*****

When Eldridge was back aboard the *Ticonderoga*, he immediately went into action. His exec followed him as Eldridge barked out orders. When he got to the bridge, he ordered the helm officer to get the ship underway as soon as the anchor was secured. He opened the box and found... another hat. This one was a black baseball cap with two gold bars embroidered on the front. It occurred to him that the last time he'd worn a hat like this was when he was commanding the hydrofoil *USS Pegasus*—a command he lost saving the life of Mike Callaway. He put the cap on and walked out to the port side bridge. He looked down at Callaway and Abby standing where he'd left them on the yacht when he suddenly remembered when he first met Michael Callaway. He was bringing the *Pegasus* out of Miami Harbor to start another boring, no-action drug interdiction patrol. He had looked down into the cockpit of a blue United States Customs Enforcement Blue Thunder boat riddled with bullets and stained with blood. It looked like the aftermath of a high seas gun battle with drug smugglers. He saw two men in the cockpit and made eye contact with one of them. Eldridge had come to attention, and saluted the man in the boat, and that man, Michael Callaway, had come to attention and saluted back. Now, once again, Callaway looked up at Eldridge, came to attention and saluted his friend. Eldridge came to attention and returned the salute as the cruiser moved away and down the inlet toward the Gulf of Alaska. Callaway hugged his wife thinking of the life awaiting them but wondered if he would ever see his good friend again.

The End

About the Author

Doug Giacobbe is a retired law enforcement officer and a retired college professor. Having worked the mean streets of South Florida for 25 years, Giacobbe achieved the rank of Major, and Commander of the Criminal Investigations Division of the Miramar Police Department. Following this distinguished career, he went on to teach American and Military History. After 21 years of teaching, he retired as Professor Emeritus and the Lead Instructor of History at Daytona State College. He now devotes all his considerable energies to crafting his Michael Callaway series of thrillers.

Other Books by Doug Giacobbe

By Unknown Means
Book 1 of the Callaway Thriller Series

A Fierce Vengeance
Book 2 of the Callaway Thriller Series